STAINED PERCEPTION

STAINED SERIES
BOOK I

JORJOR BATTLE

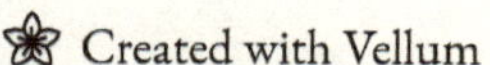 Created with Vellum

TRIGGER WARNINGS

Stalker, kidnapping, sexual content, knife and blood play/mention, death, torture, mentions of trafficking, and graphic violence.

To my obsession with vampires and werewolves

FLORA

Steam raised from the pitcher full of boiling hot water — the final stage of braiding box braids finally in sight for Flora — nine treacherous hours after she had started. Flora's cramping hands dipped the braids into the water. Finishing off with a hair mousse, her waist-length braids were complete. Dragging her gaze around what she called her "hair nook", which consisted of a huge gold antique floor-length mirror, a pillow, and an end table to hold her hair products, she glanced at the digital clock on her nightstand to confirm the time. Midnight was considered finishing early and she'd take that small win to bed with her.

Braids were a lifesaver in terms of time saved in the morning and everyday styling. They were also a pain in the ass when Flora's braider canceled on her the morning of and forced her to do them herself. Looking the part of a fashion CEO and shoe designer had become of the utmost importance now that her fashion accessory company, Dainty Rebel, had become successful in dressing Shifters all around the United States. Rainfall Avenue was her home and so it was also Dainty

Rebels'. Most fashion companies relocate to big cities like L.A, New York City, Atlanta, etc. when they reach whatever milestone they deem successful. Flora, on the other hand, preferred to remain tax-free in her Shifter "town" of Rainfall Avenue, part of a town in Michigan that had a supernatural side and a human side. Knowing what humans do while fearful, the supernaturals of the world decided to keep their "unnatural" being-asses a secret, creating areas where the supernatural could live in peace known as Shifter towns or Shifter sides.

Dainty Rebel had become extremely popular among those in the supernatural world. Shifter types especially can't say no to a pair of good shoes let alone a signature necklace that represents their animal or special ability that they have. While Flora's company focused on shoes, jewelry had been the new hot item when it came to Packs and Shifters, which she had famously tapped into. Shifter Packs, whether of bears or vampires, loved having matching jewelry signifying which Pack they were from. Though Flora was sure Shifters' animals could not care less about a moon-shaped pendant hanging from their necks by a thick silver chain, there was something appealing about wearing something that wouldn't break during shifting, that created another connection to Shifters' animals. Her own animal didn't try to rip off any of the necklaces, bracelets, or anklets that remained on her body after the shift.

Beauty is in the eye of the beholder, a reminder Flora kept printed above her wide, floor-length antique gold mirror. She kept it there to remind herself and anyone who asked her for an opinion on anything style related. Being in the Shifter fashion industry, it seemed Flora's opinion was as important as her customers opinions, something that was oddly similar between the human mindset and the Shifter mindset. The thing was, Flora didn't mind what others had to say about what she did, what she wore, or whom they thought she was with romantically. It was simply not one of her concerns. According to Flora's PR team, she should most definitely care.

"Flora, why is there a photo of you walking out of Lust Lane on 90th street, for the third time this week?" Willow Buttercup, Flora's personal assistant and best friend asked. Willow refused to reveal her last name to anyone: Flora was only privy to it after reading her résumé. She also wouldn't share her next darkest secret, what animal she shifted into, but Flora could understand the need for privacy, seeing as her ex-best friend had dropped Flora like a hot cake after finding out what animal she shifted into. She kept that shit on lockdown ever since.

"Well," Flora started, placing the pitcher of hot water on the end table, "you know my best clients work at the strip club." The one strip club in town was Lust Lane, a dub on the name Lover's Lane. Flora thought the name was clever when everyone else thought it was cheesy. Lust Lane gave her great business. No one bought her fun, exotic accessories like they did. The way Flora saw it, she got to make extravagant, eye-catching pieces and the strippers bought them for their equally extravagant and eye-catching performances. It was a win-win situation.

"Why can't you sneak in through a back door or something? You know the media goes wild every time they catch you at the strip club," Willow stressed. Being sneaky was a part of who Flora was, something she was good at, thanks to her animal. Not only were strippers and entertainers her best customers, but she envied their dancing skills. Flora definitely broke the "all Black people can dance' stereotype. She couldn't catch a beat if someone threw it at her.

"I *could* sneak through the back, but I *won't*. Everyone goes to the strip club, why lie about it?" Flora explained, sweeping her hair off the floor.

"I'm not saying lie but sneaking in would make my life easier and get the rest of the PR team off my back." Willow's auburn shoulder-length ringlets defied gravity as she plopped down in a sherpa rocking chair.

"We said go big or go home with the height of our curls today, didn't we, Willow?" Flora flirted, glancing through her eyelashes toward her friend. Willow had a hard time accepting compliments, so Flora made it her duty to change that. How could such a kind beauty get shy at compliments? Willow was a 5'6" Black woman with round hips and a soft nature; a book-loving friend who'd been Flora's rock since they met six months before.

"Yeah...do you like it?" Breaking eye contact, Willow looked anywhere but at Flora, all shy and nervous. She was as cute as a buttercup, Flora thought.

"I love it, don't worry, it's hot," Flora reassured.

Pulling an oversized t-shirt over her sport bra, and careful of her tender scalp, Flora laid down on her queen-sized bed. It was midnight — she was tired as hell and ready to become dead to the world. Her hands, arms, legs, and hips all hurt like a bitch. Being as weak as Bambi in human form and being a badass panther in Shifter form made little sense in terms of biology. Her panther was strong as hell. Climbing, no problem. Running 50 miles per hour, no problem. As long as Flora was in panther form, she was one of the strongest predators among Shifters. Flora's human form was a different story.

"Don't forget your scarf and bonnet dumbass." Willow crawled onto the bed with both in her hands, smoothly wrapping a silk scarf around Flora's head, sliding her braids into the bonnet.

"Goodnight, darling."

"Goodnight, Flora."

* * *

TOO MANY THINGS TO DO, NOT ENOUGH HOURS TO do them in and stress was at the top of Flora's to-do list. At least she didn't have to do her hair for the next month and a half.

"That design is not going to work."

"Like that neon-orange knit dress you have on isn't work-ing?" Willow joked.

"This dress is cute, but that camel toe of a shoe is not," Flora said, side-eyeing her product design assistant, Kacy. Kacy knew Willow and Flora's relationship ran deeper than a work-related one. Being best friends gave them the room to joke around more than Flora could with any of her other employees. Flora's floor-length orange dress was totally cute, especially with her complexion. Oversized at the top, it nipped in at the waist. "Flattering" was an understatement. Going back and forth with the product design assistant was unprofessional as much as it was unproductive, and Willow could tell this meeting was going nowhere hence the jab, but creativity was running low, and she only had a few weeks to design a collec-tion. Flora was supposed to drive out to meet the production team a few towns over in a month, but nothing had been confirmed for the designs of the shoes.

"Let's go back to the drawing board and meet again on Thursday," Flora stated, ending the meeting with Willow flanking her side. Frustration flowed; the energy kept other employees from talking to her. They strode back to her office. Keeping up with fashion trends was becoming more and more difficult, as trends tended to fade out as fast as it took to run out of barbecue chips. It was time to create trends, not just follow them.

"You know what we need to do," Willow lectured. This was the second meeting on this issue, and it still wasn't resolved.

"Ain't no way Shifters are going to wear camel toe-shaped boots!" Flora exclaimed, plopping into her oversized office chair.

Flora knew they were both right. Shifters were not going to wear something that looked like other animals' feet. Pride was a big deal with animals, so Shifters naturally also had an intense amount of pride, and egos the size of planets.

"Off-topic, but what is this new addition to the office?" Willow questioned, pointing towards the left wall of Flora's office. There was a jungle gym-type platform designed to look like a tree with lots of branches, with enough room for Flora's panther to climb eight feet high without destroying the office, as she'd done before.

"Just some new decoration," Flora answered shortly. The Shifter Black Market was hot in the United States. Made up of trafficking and cage fighting, the SBM was a deep-rooted fear in every Shifter. The stronger a Shifter's animal was, the more enticing the fight or bid would be. The U.S. was filled with a diverse array of Shifters, but panthers were known as some of the strongest. Flora's panther would be worth a couple hundred million dollars at least. Willing participants must not have been making enough money anymore, so kidnapping Shifters to force them to fight was the new booming illegal practice. A Shifter could work their way into the SBM by finding themselves a manager that already had an in. These 'managers', better known as Collectors, wouldn't make as much money off a willing fighter since part of their earnings would have to go back to the Shifter, hence the push for unwilling participants. Shivers ran down Flora's back and arms at the thought of it.

While she would love to say the SBM was the only reason she kept her animal's identity so close to her chest, it was not. Humans, Shifters, vamps, fairies, and everything that fit under the supernatural umbrella were terrified of panthers.

Flora thought back to her childhood to little Shifter Suzie, the first girl to break Flora's heart. Their sleepover turned into a nightmare when Flora shifted into her panther for the first time. A celebratory moment meant to be shared with friends and family, a joyous milestone into "Shifterhood" was destroyed by the terror etched in Suzie's eyes. Flora learned later that night that if she'd turned into a wolf, or a bear, or literally anything besides a panther, Suzie wouldn't have had such a reaction. A child's first shift into their animal was something to celebrate, like a birthday party. Signs would become apparent, like having a high temperature and itchy skin; family, friends or Pack members would gather around for weeks on end until the child finally shifted. Those signs for Flora came in hot and quick. Shifting in Suzie's presence wasn't the plan, but a Shifter can't control their first time. From then on, she had to protect her mental state and keep her animal identity a secret. Selfishly, she liked the connection between her and her panther and wouldn't have it any other way.

With respect to one another, Shifters didn't ask each other what their animals are but making guesses was acceptable. Flora was sure her friend had made connections and guesses as to what her animal was; this jungle gym was a big hint. Flora guessed Willow's animal was a wolf, since wolves are extremely family-oriented, and Willow had become so close to her that they were practically family with that though Willow could also be a lioness or cheetah. With Willow's caring and loving personality, Flora thought her friend would fit perfectly into a Pack.

She couldn't say the same about herself; being part of a Pack was a foreign concept to her. Panthers are solitary animals, so naturally, she was too. She moved out of her parent's home when she was 17 and started making money from Dainty Rebel. That was seven years ago.

"You know what, let's just create our own designs without outside influence; this camel toe shit is too much," Flora concluded, swirling around in her chair.

"Finally!" Willow exhaled.

Dainty Rebel started with customized shoes. As a teen, Flora used to draw on her canvas sneakers, which people noticed and wanted to buy. Now she had expanded her products to all sorts of accessories: shoes, jewelry, hairpieces, the works. Dainty Rebel was still a smaller company, a sole proprietorship to be technical. With no silly board of directors to answer to, Flora made the final decisions, and she was determined to keep it that way. Being based in her sweet Shifter town, life was perfect. Besides the trouble of having to come up with a new, awe-inspiring, and show-stopping collection.

❧

"WHAT ABOUT WE DO SOMETHING DAISY-THEMED, like killer daisies?"

Luxe, Flora and Willow's partner-in-crime, exuded earthy vibes in everything she did. Her blonde shoulder-length hair and taupe brown skin screamed "fairy" vibes. Flora remembered when she was nervous about going blonde because she was worried it wouldn't fit her dark-skinned complexion. After three months, Flora finally convinced her to make the change. Her prime reasoning on why Luxe should go blonde was how good Willow looked with her auburn hair. Sadly, battles with skin color were still a prominent racial problem among humans that spilled over to the Shifter world. Luxe didn't grow up in a Shifter community like Flora and Willow did, so that mindset followed her. Willow and Flora were positive influences for her, although Flora couldn't relate to how her dark-skinned friends experienced the world. "Light skin" privilege was a very real thing.

Luxe was a wolf Shifter. Flora never thought she would be so close with a wolf Shifter, especially a Luna wolf, a natural-born leader who stereotypically conflicted with the independence of a panther. It was an ordinary day when Flora stumbled upon Luxe in Shifter form on a sidewalk in town. Since then, Luxe was determined to become Flora's friend after finding out she was a Shifter like her. Shifting in public wasn't normal, but shit doesn't always go to plan when an animal takes over.

"We did that two seasons ago. We gotta spice it up, take it to the next level," Willow implored from her rocking chair in the backroom of Clothes Before Bros, where Luxe worked. The owner of the resale shop never had a problem with Willow and Flora hanging out with Luxe during her lunch break. A couple times a week, the girls all met to take their lunch break in the decorated backroom. Clothing racks filled the space, fairy lights hung from the ceiling, and fake vines lined the walls.

"Rings could work out, like literal metal rings That could be cool," Luxe exclaimed. She dashed towards a shirt from a nearby clothing rack. The blouse had metal rings connecting the sleeves to the shoulder seam of the bodice. While the top itself was ugly, the badass look of the rings could be the focal point of Dainty Rebel's new shoe collection.

"Brilliance flows from that gorgeous brain of yours, darling. Metal rings could be the next hottest trend, especially in shoes. The trending bucket hats already have them, so adding them to shoes would logically be the next step." Leaning in towards her notebook, Flora started sketching to draw inspiration from later.

"Now that that is out of the way, what's going on with this bright orange dress? It was quite an interesting choice to make this morning," Luxe said, looking Flora up and down. As ambitious as Luxe could be, her style was definitely more conservative than Flora's.

"I saw a picture of a traffic cone and felt the need to look the same. Regardless, I look good — and stop side-eyeing me Miss Cardigan-and-Tennis-Skirt hoe!" They all burst out laughing.

"So, are you going to tell Luxe about what happened at Lust Lane last week?" Willow said as she raised an eyebrow at Flora.

"What...happened, Flora?"

Flora twisted and twirled the ends of the braids that sat on her lap. "I only *think* I was followed when I left, and for that reason I drove to the police department before I made my way home to scare them off."

"Did you make a report?" Luxe questioned.

"A report on what, that I *think* someone was following me? You know they don't take those things seriously. Not to forget, we're not allowed to involve humans in Shifter business," Flora said leaning back in her chair. Flora hated to make her friends worry, but more than that she hated to let them think she didn't have things under control. She didn't currently, but they didn't need to know that.

Honestly, Flora was terrified. Some of the girls at the strip club had had stalkers and one of the girls was involved in an attempted kidnapping a couple weeks before. Thankfully, that girl's tough ass animal killed the attacker before they got to wherever he was trying to take her.

"Why not call the Council then; can they do something?" Luxe tried again.

"Not this early—an attack needs to actually happen, even then the chance of them sending someone to catch this *potential* stalker is slim," Willow informed. When it came to the Council, the rules and regulations were loose. They only stepped in when huge problems occurred, like a war between different Packs, needing to find killer rogues, or keeping humans out of nonhuman business. Protecting the existence of all nonhumans was their only concern.

"You need a bodyguard, then. Look, I know a guy who has a brother that could totally help you," Luxe said, phone already in hand as she started to make a call. Flora jumped up from her seat and grabbed Luxe's hand.

"No calls. If your guy is a Shifter, they'll want to know who they're protecting, what my animal is, and I can't risk it. They're too damn nosy."

"He won't ask. He's super private like that," Luxe said.

"Are they part of a Pack?" Flora asked, sitting back down, feeling more and more vulnerable as their conversation continued.

"Yeah, but it will be okay, I know the Alpha personally. He's the one that comes into the store sometimes."

Luxe had a huge crush on this Alpha for a while now since he came into the shop about a year before. From the pictures

Luxe showed Flora, tall, dark, and classically handsome describe him well but Flora didn't completely trust him or his Pack. Protection of the Pack was an Alpha's top priority; letting one of their own guard someone who is not part of their Pack puts them in danger.

"No, no, no — look, if it happens again, I'll give you a call and we can set something up with a bodyguard."

"You know we don't play that human shit, Flora. If there is any chance this could turn dangerous, then we need to handle it now. Not after you've been kidnapped, sold, or killed," Willow added in, her forehead creasing with stress and worry.

"Promise you'll call?" Luxe asked.

"Promise."

"Alright ladies, lunch is over," Willow announced. After hugging goodbye, Flora pulled out of the Clothes Before Bros lot and headed toward Dainty Rebel's offices. Flora loved that Rainfall Avenue paid graffiti artists to spruce up the exterior of businesses downtown. This Shifter town had its ups and downs, but its creativity was definitely an up.

"Make a right here," Willow insisted, staring out the window. Without question, Flora made the next right turn. Even though Flora trusted Willow, she still threw her a confused glance.

"Check the car behind us," Willow said. Looking out the rearview mirror, Flora felt the air become tense as her eyes started to shift back to the road. Tapping each finger on the steering wheel, she glanced at Willow. She continued to make three more rights before reality set in, her eyes growing wide. Flora saw the same car from the night she was followed leaving Lust Lane. But this time, she could see the man's eyes under the mask he wore.

Flora felt dread and fear surround her entire body.

"I'm going to the police station, call Luxe." A sigh of relief escaped Willow.

"I thought I was going to have to call her behind your back. You can be so stubborn," Willow mumbled, pulling out her phone.

"A promise is a promise, darling. I don't break my promises."

Flora just didn't think she would have to call her so soon.

❧ 2 ❧

DYLAN

"Dylan, don't you have something to announce to the Pack?" Jackson, the Enchanted Pack's Alpha, asked as he cooked on the stove.

Dylan's Alpha was young and often caught shit for it. Being the same age, Dylan knew older Shifters viewed them as pups compared to the long lives they lived, but his respect and love for Jackson as his leader ran deeper than what outside opinions could ruin.

"I got a job."

"It's about damn time," Eddie, the comedian and engineer of the Pack, joked. Though Eddie was only kidding, the words stung. Dylan was retired, and while the Pack thought it a good idea for him to retire, he felt lacking. He was used to being the highest earner in the Pack and went from that to the lowest earner. They all told him it wasn't a big deal. His previous job took great risks and more mental strength than he would've liked to admit. He worked with a crew of assassins for days at a time. One person can only kill so many people before their reflection stared back at them, screaming that they are no better than their targets.

"At Lust Lane," Dylan finished, picking at the grape bowl on the counter. "Why aren't these in the fridge? They're getting warm."

"They're hiring male strippers now?" Eddie asked, an eyebrow raised.

"No, Eddie, as a bodyguard, not that we shame anyone for their choices if that's what they wish—" Jackson said. His apron and beanie combo looked strangely normal in the Enchanted Packhouse. One of Jackson's top three Pack rules was acceptance of things outside the norm. They were a wolf Pack with a crow and a bear amongst their ranks, so it was natural to be considerably more open-minded.

"That's great that you've gotten back into the workforce, Dylan. So great I've already found another bodyguarding gig for you," Jackson smiled, his too-damn-white and too-straight-teeth shining in Dylan's face. He hadn't even started his first bodyguarding job and he already had another?

"Word goes around fast," Eddie commented, sliding onto a barstool at the island.

"What do you mean, Jackson?" Dylan asked.

"Well, a friend of mine, Luxe, called me a few moments ago. Her friend needs a temporary bodyguard. It would be just for a few days and shouldn't interfere with the Lust Lane gig," Jackson shrugged. Dylan had taken down bodyguards more times than he could count. But being one? He was nervous, anxious even. Knowing the extra gig was from Luxe made the job a lot more intense. Luxe was Jackson's soulmate, whether he knew it or not. Luxe was also a Luna.

"Who is Luxe's friend?" Eddie asked.

"Her name is Flora Larkspur. She's the owner of Little

Rebels, a fashion brand or something," Jackson informed. "She'll be here later tonight to meet you."

"Tonight?" Dylan asked. He looked up, shocked everything was moving so fast. His dark brown hair was surely mussed with how often he ran his fingers through it.

"Don't worry, Dylan; if you're as good a bodyguard as you were an assassin, everything will be smooth sailing."

"Yeah, smooth sailing," Dylan muttered. This time, he wouldn't have to kill anyone. He got to keep everything else about his old job except the part that tore at his core. Tore so deep he wasn't sure if he could ever recover. His life changed the minute he made his first kill, and ever since then, he didn't know how to stop. Killing had become his nature. He took the job as a bodyguard at Lust Lane to practice the art of not killing. To protect without murdering. Now the pressure was dire with the addition of another job, and he needed space.

Dylan made his way back to his room. His dark green high-top shoes reflected in the mirror. He was given the mirror from his parents as a going-away gift. If they could let their son move across the state to become an assassin and join a brand-new Pack that only had an Alpha, then he could learn how not to be a stone-cold killer.

He had the only bedroom on the first floor. Dylan was the first line of defense and anyone who tried to attack the Pack would never get past him. He needed to make this new reality a norm. Everyone he interacted with from then on would have to remain alive. He had a Pack depending on him, but having a killer like him in the Pack would only be another hit to their social standing. Not that Jackson or the guys cared too much about that, but Dylan did.

He bent down to take his shoes off at the door before launching into research. His gray walls and gray carpet calmed him enough to think rationally. He needed to be prepared for the meeting with Flora. He wouldn't want to make the Pack look bad by coming off as unprofessional. What do bodyguards wear? Where do they store their weapons? Do they carry weapons? He never bothered to search the bodyguards he'd come across before but now he was wishing he had.

Luxe rounded the driveway of the Enchanted Packhouse. Flora became encompassed in the uncomfortable feeling of being in an unknown area, increasing the anxiety she already had about this meeting. She was here to hire a bodyguard for a few days, a week, tops. This bodyguard was from a strong, loyal, loving Pack, a Pack who would probably kill her in retribution if this bodyguard died on the job. This situation wouldn't get that bad; she just needed to scare off the stalker. She could get through this.

Tilting her head up, her heavy braids in a high ponytail aiding in keeping her head up, which she most definitely didn't want to do. Flora's hands smoothed out her outfit. Confidence was key, and the start of confidence was a cute-ass outfit. That's what her mother had always told her, in different words, her mother wasn't one to use curse words. Flora stretched her legs out of Luxe's car, her signature anklet shining in the sunset. Her brand-new metal ring-inspired heels stepped onto the gravel.

Damn, the driveway was filled with rocks, not concrete.

Her heels were too high for that. She was going to trip trying to walk in the gravel, and the embarrassment brought a blush to her cheeks. She could throw up; the nerves were getting so bad.

"It doesn't matter. I got this, regardless," Flora muttered to herself. Taking deep breaths, she strode up to the porch. Jackson Enchanted, one of four Alphas living in the area, practically flew out the door toward Luxe and pulled her into a hug. A hug entirely too friendly for people supposedly "only friends". Jackson tucked his head into her neck, as a lover would. His smile was contagious. His skin was deep brown and his muscles locked Luxe into his hug — not that the girl wasn't loving every minute of it.

To Flora's knowledge, they weren't a couple, but that looked like it could change at a moment's notice. Another tall, delicious, but paler man stood on the porch. When Flora finally met his eyes, he was already staring at her. Lifting one side of her lips into a smirk, it was her time to turn on the charm.

"You know, you should think of upgrading this gravel driveway to a concrete one, it would be easier to walk on," Flora suggested, looking around the outside of the house, and pushing some rocks with the toe of her shoe. The house, of course, was gorgeous with its wrap-around porch and huge windows.

"You know, if you wore some normal shoes, you could have walked just fine on this gravel," the tall, too damn hot, snarky-ass white man on the porch replied. Brown floppy hair sat on the top of his head. Paired with brown eyes, broad shoulders, and slightly sun-kissed skin, he was a dream.

"Looking good comes at a price. Some of us pay it, some of us don't." Flora made sure to drop her eyes down his body. Of course, she was lying to herself, he was dressed nicely. He had a hoodie underneath a flannel, and straight-leg jeans, something she didn't normally find attractive. Flora being Flora, she didn't miss the silver chain hanging from his neck.

"Some of us may be paying too much. The 1800s called... they want their corset back."

"Ha ha ha, you are too funny, but it's actually a bustier top not a full-on corset."

She wore a fully white lace bustier top under a matching baby blue suit set, blazer and all. Sliding her hands into her pockets and straightening her back, Flora looked over to Jackson, who had this know-it-all smile on his face. "Anyways, I need to speak with you about someone who works as a bodyguard within your Pack. I need a big bad scary wolf to follow me around for a while."

"Yeah, you were just talking to him, but instead of conversing out here, let's head inside to my office."

Dragging her eyes back to the man on the porch, Flora bit the inside of her lip, glaring just a bit. Shit, he was supposed to be her bodyguard?

Jackson's office was in the middle of the house, and had no windows, unlike the rest of the house. Luxe and Flora sat across from his desk as Jackson took his seat and the man from the porch stood next to Jackson, leaning against the wall.

"So, can you introduce yourself as well as the problem you need assistance with?" Jackson asked Flora. It was straight to business and that was what Flora needed most.

"My name is Flora Larkspur, I am Head Designer and CEO of Dainty Rebel, a fashion accessory brand, and someone has been following me."

"That's it? Someone's following you, maybe they just think you're cute?" the guy in the back snapped, crossing his arms across his chest.

"Yes, because top-level flirting is to follow a woman around town and then dash off when you get caught...twice."

"Dylan, cut it out. You know how fast "following" turns into an attack."

"Attack?" Luxe questioned, her wide eyes running over Flora's face as if she was checking for scratches or bumps. Maybe Luxe shouldn't have been here for this kind of conversation, but Flora needed her. This situation could get ugly fast and Flora knew that.

"I just need someone to watch out for me, until all this stalker business surrounding the strip club blows over," Flora said, pressing her back into the chair. "So how much per day?"

"Don't worry about it." Even Jackson whipped his head in Dylan's direction. Eyebrows raised, Flora leaned forward out of her chair, staring. She hoped he didn't expect anything else. She had just met this man 30 minutes before.

Placing her well-manicured hands on the desk, she stood, leaning closer to Dylan. He matched her stance. She had to look up slightly to make direct eye contact, but that didn't lessen the fierce atmosphere of the room.

"I can pay, I will pay, with cash...only."

"I know you can pay by the shining anklet hanging above your left heel and the diamonds sitting on both your ears, but I'm offering my first-time services for free." She chewed on the offer.

Her eyes met Dylan's and she huffed. As annoying as he may seem, it was a damn good deal. She was a businesswoman after all.

"Fine. You start tomorrow." If someone offered something for free, the polite thing to do was to decline, but the smart thing to do was accept.

"We'll start at your place."

❧ 4 ❧

DYLAN

Dylan went back to his room. It was time to get to work. He would meet Flora at her apartment after Luxe dropped her off. Pulling out an overnight bag, he filled it with three outfits, a toothbrush, socks, a home alarm system, and weapons, in case shifting into his wolf wasn't an option. He turned to leave before nearly running into Jackson, who was standing in the doorway.

"You didn't sense me?" he asked, leaning against the frame.

The whole house was custom-made by the Enchanted Pack members. Jackson, being the only member who worked in construction, took the lead on the project. It was nice to live in a home that fit them.

"I did — I hoped you'd move."

"Why did you refuse her money?"

"Don't worry about it. I'll make it up some other way," Dylan said, suddenly worried that his Alpha misinterpreted him refusing pay from Flora. Scrunching eyebrows, he tried to move past Jackson only to be blocked again.

"I don't care about that; I just want to know why."

"I don't know."

"Dylan."

"It didn't feel right, the fear in her eyes. There is more to the story she isn't telling–which is fine, but she needs someone to watch over her. Now if you could let me do my job before the girls get too far..." Dylan answered before dashing out the door the second Jackson stepped aside. He couldn't tell Jackson the real reason he refused Flora's money, not yet anyway. Honestly, he was nervous and too insecure in his ability not to mess up.

He realized he had a major problem when he was working his last job as an assassin. Dylan was on the rescue side of a mission, yet, he killed almost everyone. He couldn't stop. In fact, he kept a couple barely alive so he could finish the job later. Flora unknowingly hired a crazed killer and in exchange for not telling her, he'd do the job for free. This would be a practice round to see if Dylan could work for the rest of his life without killing.

Dylan eased out of the mini parking lot on the side of the Enchanted Pack's home and caught up to Luxe and Flora within minutes. Tonight, he would scope out her home, look for weak points, as well as install an alarm system to her windows and front door. That much he could do confidently.

As he met the pair at the apartment complex, Dylan hopped out of his car, pulling his bag with him, and followed Flora up the stairs after her goodbyes with Luxe.

"How can I trust you, Mr. Enchanted?" Flora asked. Not slowing his steps at all, Dylan responded coolly.

"Call me Dylan."

"Okay, Dylan, how do I know you can do the job?" she asked, stopping outside her door and turning to face him. She stood shorter than him, but her energy matched his own. She wasn't playing and that made him unsure about his qualifications. It would be easier if the job was to find and kill the stalker, but she didn't hire a hitman — she hired a bodyguard.

"Experience from previous employment," he answered, staring her down keeping his stance strong and alert.

"Explain more, pretty boy. What was your previous job?" She continued to question him.

"I dealt with people who had done wrong by others, for others," Dylan explained, amused by the back and forth taking place. Lots of questioning didn't typically take place in Dylan's line of work. It always started and ended with "Will you, or will you not, take this job?"

"So, were you like a killer? An assassin? A super spy?" she whispered, tilting her head and crossing her arms. Her blazer tightened around her shoulders and elbows. Of course, her boobs started to pop even more in that tiny top she had on, but Dylan tried not to notice.

"Yes, an assassin, a hitman. I was whatever was needed. Now can I start my job or not?" He held the bag strap to his shoulder. With his line of work also came an extreme amount of patience.

"So, I'm letting an assassin into my home?" she clarified, keeping direct eye contact with him. Dylan could see the gears shifting in her mind, but she didn't have anything to worry about, he was on her side.

"Yes, to protect you," Dylan reassured.

Their staring contest continued. It was a battle of trust that he wouldn't lose. He didn't want to, therefore he wouldn't. He wanted this job more than he wanted to admit. As time passed, her composure started to relax as she blinked and unfolded her arms. Turning around, she unlocked her door, but abruptly stopped right before she stepped on the carpet.

"What's wrong?" he asked, stopping himself from falling over her.

"No shoes in the house past this point," she explained, pointing to the line that separated the tile from the gray carpet. She turned and stared once again at him, as he bent over to untie his sneakers. He set them down neatly next to a pair of high heels. Flora unstrapped her own heels before setting them down next to his, a smile crossing her face. Straightening her back, she walked towards the kitchen. Dylan once again followed suit, putting his bag onto the counter.

"Would you like water?" she asked, opening her fridge and pulling out a water bottle for herself. She looked back at Dylan. Eye contact seemed important to her, seeing as every time she talked to him, she made sure to meet his gaze.

"No, thank you," he responded, pulling out the alarm system and the booklet that went with it.

"I should've done this before you walked inside, but I'm going to search the apartment, so while I do, you can look through this information on the alarm system I brought for you," Dylan explained. Before she could even respond, he walked off. He looked at the windows, doors, and under all the furniture. Since she lived in a one-bedroom apartment, it didn't take him long to search the place. Finishing up, he came back to the kitchen island where Flora sat, legs crossed, booklet in hand. She looked up at him.

"What do you think? Do you like it?" he asked, taking a seat next to her.

"What do I think about the alarm system?' she questioned him.

"Yeah, I mean, if you don't like it, I can get a different one," Dylan shrugged.

"I would've thought you would just do whatever you

thought was right, no matter what I think," she explained, tapping her nails on the counter.

"That would be more of Jackson's style...being an Alpha and all. If you like the system, I'll install it tonight. It won't prevent someone from getting inside; if they want to come in that bad, they'll come in. An alarm will only make you aware that someone broke in."

Talking to her seemed normal, easy even. He tried to keep conversations short and sweet, but lengthy explanations just fell out of his mouth. Like she really needed him to explain how alarm systems work? He felt pressured to explain more thoroughly with Flora than he did with other people in general. She seemed to care about what and when he was doing things.

"Well, I like this system. Not that I know much about other systems anyway. If you trust it, so do I," she smiled, handing him the booklet.

"I'll get started then," Dylan responded.

SETTING UP THE LAST OF HER MANY WINDOWS, Dylan took a step back. As he was admiring his handiwork, Flora stepped into the room.

"All done?" she asked. By that point, she had taken a shower and was dressed in pajama shorts and a t-shirt. She dragged her feet across the room and landed face down on her black comforter. Dylan stared at her for just a moment, taking in her long, bare legs. He couldn't deny he found her incredibly attractive with her big brown eyes and light freckles that dotted her nose and cheeks. His attraction went beyond her looks; he began to realize he enjoyed being in her presence — a little too much for his liking.

He threw the window open, purposefully letting the alarm go off to dislodge whatever feelings were in his head. Scrunching his face, he refocused on Flora, who had jumped sky-high at the sound of the alarm. Letting out a short laugh, Dylan pulled out his phone to type in the code to disarm it.

"What the hell!" Flora howled, her hands fisting up at her sides as she stomped towards Dylan.

"We know it works," Dylan shrugged. Flora's eyes searched the half-grin on his face as if she was deciding whether to beat him up or not. Dylan took that as a sign to take a step back and make his exit. "Every time the alarm goes off, I get a notification on my phone, so if it goes off, I will come rushing over."

"Promise?" Flora asked, her body softening, arms uncrossing and her shoulders relaxing.

"I promise."

They stood at the end of the bed, staring into each other's eyes. Dylan took his promises seriously as hell, and this particular one would prove to Flora that he really had her back. He hoped she would begin to trust him enough to truly let him help her.

"Okay, time for bed. You look tired as hell," Dylan said, grabbing her hand.

Why he would even think to make physical contact with her, he didn't know. Taking her hand, he led her to what he assumed was her side of the bed, the right side closest to the window, with chargers spilling out of the extension cord on the nightstand. Once she laid down, he pulled the blanket up towards her. Knowing he needed to get out of there to save himself from the embarrassment, he rushed to the door. Before he left, he looked back to see her staring at him.

"I'll check the house without tripping the alarm, one more time before I leave."

Flora nodded before whispering, "Thank you, goodnight."

"Goodnight, Flora," Dylan whispered back.

❧

SLAMMING HIS CAR DOOR SHUT, HE MADE HIS WAY TO Flora's apartment. The last couple of nights proved to Dylan his car was damn sure uncomfortable, but he'd stick to staying in his car until she got used to him being around. It was a huge adjustment for him, so he assumed it would be for her too. He'd slept a total of five hours a night. The other four hours of the night that he was in his car were spent surveying the area. Between him and his wolf, they'd pick up if someone new was coming around at this point. Three days into this new job and he still felt as if he was going about it all wrong. Flora spent the last few days working from home, and today was the first day they'd go into the office together.

Being outside was great for his wolf, getting used to the regular scents of the people who lived there. He'd know when someone new came around based on scent. Her apartment building was toward the back of the complex, the back of it being surrounded by woods. He was sure it made a great view, but it also made his job harder. It was easy to blend in with the trees and bushes. He had a straight view into her apartment when he reenacted what a potential stalker would do to watch her from her windows. He waited at the doorstep, arriving earlier than his regular eight a.m. time to get ready for the day. He wasn't a sight to see first thing in the morning. He hadn't brushed his teeth or washed his face. Would he finally get to see a freshly woken Flora?

"Come in." She swung open the door.

Of course not. She was dressed, and her face was glossy. Like she'd put ... oil all over her face?

He wasn't sure. She looked as good as she always did. It was almost distracting. He'd come in at eight am, get ready in her bathroom, then move back out to his car and stay on watch.

"I need to get ready." He said, walking past her. The line between tile and carpet stopped him in his tracks. Kicking his shoes off, he rushed for the bathroom.

"I can tell," Flora said.

"I need five minutes."

"Take ten. I'll meet you at the office." Flora grabbed her keys and made her way toward the door. He turned to grab her arm. What the hell? It was their first day together leaving her apartment and she was already trying to escape him.

"Absolutely not. I'll drive you."

"No need. I'm perfectly capable of driving myself," she said.

"Flora, in order for this to work, you need to let me do my job," he explained.

"Dylan, this is a little much."

"Then why did you need a bodyguard?"

"A promise I made."

"Let me assess the danger. If it's not as serious as you say, I'll back off." With that, he went to get ready, hoping she'd take him seriously and not leave his ass. This was going to be a long day. They both had a lot to learn going forward. Hopefully, they'd catch on fast.

Her car was admittedly nicer than his, cleaner too since he'd been living in his. He hopped in the passenger seat of her car on their way to Dainty Rebel's offices. He figured this was against some sort of bodyguarding rule, but he figured he'd have to pick and choose his battles guarding Flora.

"We're supposed to be in a meeting right now, shit." She grumbled. That's all he gets before she's already opening the door of her office. He gripped her arm and sighed as they stood in the doorway.

"Flora, wait." He sidestepped her and looked down the hallway. He may have been overbearing, but Flora wasn't listening. How the hell was he supposed to do his job if she wouldn't let him take the necessary precautions?

"I highly doubt I'm in danger in my own damn building." She muttered, crossing her arms and tapping her heel. He didn't give her a response as he continued to walk her down the hall. "I don't think you need to be around when I'm at work."

"I'm only doing my job."

"I didn't know being up my ass was part of your job description."

"I didn't know complaining was a part of yours." Dylan was used to dealing with clients who weren't so terrified they hardly moved, let alone spoke, but Flora was a force of her own. Not only that but this was also an entirely different case. He was only guarding. He was to prevent danger from all angles. Typically, he was the danger, and the change of pace was welcomed. For now, this line of work would be enough. Granted, nothing had happened yet; he could see a future in this career path.

A male figure dashed down the hall at full speed toward Flora. Dylan didn't wait to see if he could recognize the man as an employee or friend of Flora's. He reached for the unknown man's covered neck. A dark fog of a tall figure was all he could see. The man's body was slammed against the nearest wall, and Flora's gasp brought Dylan back from his haze.

"Dylan, let him go now." If Flora was mad earlier, she was pissed now. Dylan could now see it was Michael, a fashion intern dressed in a black ensemble with a hood on covering his tear-stained face. Dylan had received a picture book of all employees of Flora's thanks to her personal assistant Willow. Though he wasn't sure he could trust her, it was the best information he could get at the time.

"Michael, what's wrong?" Flora's hand guided Dylan's arm away from the intern's neck, and she stepped between the two men. Taking a step back, his focus switched to Flora.

"Nothing really, harsh critique from superiors and all."

"Critique or insults? From whom?" Flora asked, tilting her head slightly. Dylan could see her shoulders tense, and her fingers gripped the intern's jacket. The man began to stumble over his words, and his face flushed a deeper red.

"Jessica." He mumbled. Unable to make eye contact, he tried to slip away, but Dylan moved to block the intern in. That earned Dylan a flinch from the man and a glare from Flora.

"Interesting, have a better day Michael," Flora said. She let the man go and continued toward her meeting, for which she was now very late for.

Dylan began to see that her company was her baby, and discipline was not exempt from her parenting style. Dylan was sitting in one of three meeting rooms. He wasn't fully listening to her as she went over her company policies on behavior and the consequences of not following them. Dylan was stuck on what had happened in the hallway with Michael. He felt bad for hurting the kid, but Michael could be Flora's stalker. Just as much as her assistant Willow could be. He wasn't ruling out anyone just yet.

Still, the kid was having a bad day, and he made it a thousand times worse. God, this civilian shit was hard. On his assignments, everyone outside his team was free game. It was only his first day, and being a bodyguard was significantly harder than being an assassin.

He looked toward Flora, back to the windows, then to each person's face. He'd continue to learn about every employee who walked these halls. If someone were planning to harm Flora, he'd know. He'd... protect her. That was his job here. To protect. He wouldn't kill them, but what would he do if he found the stalker? Then what? He'd have to do some more research to find out. Maybe the guys at the club would know. Dylan would ask during his shift tonight. He wasn't too sure how to proceed with guarding Flora full-time with his shifts at Lust Lane. Did he bring her with him? Drop her off at the pack house? Hell no, she wouldn't stay there. She'd probably sneak off, and then he'd have to track her ass down.

He had time to figure out how he'd proceed, at least. His first shift at the club wasn't till Thursday. For now, he'd have to take it one day at a time.

❧ *5* ❧

FLORA

"Stop, it's not safe," Dylan ground out, placing his hands over Flora's shoulders and maneuvering to walk in front of her. Ideally, a client would have a bodyguard in front and behind them, but Dylan was only one person, so standing in front was the best option in his mind. If something came flying at them, he'd be able to block it with his body.

With this potential stalker mess, Flora was on ten, her tension running high and her anxiety even higher. Having Dylan following her every move nearly every day for the past two weeks had been more stressful than what seemed helpful at first. She found herself constantly worried about him. Every night, he checked the alarms and slept in his car in the parking lot. Even though she offered her couch to him, he didn't want to push their boundaries.

When they walked around the Dainty Rebel office, everyone stared. Flora got stares before Dylan arrived but now it felt as if the stares had intensified. Dylan said he didn't mind but was he saying that just so she wouldn't worry about it? She constantly thought about him. Was he okay? Was he comfortable? It was getting ridiculous. Dylan was the bodyguard, not her.

"Look, I feel more comfortable and secure walking in front of you. I need someone literally watching my back," Flora explained, trying to get back in front of Dylan, who was using his wide stance to block her.

"Well, that's too bad since *I* feel more comfortable and secure walking in front of *you*." Dylan's snide voice fed Flora's growing annoyance.

"How about you just do as I say?" Flora tried. She shoved her hands on his shoulders so she could move him. Didn't he ever see celebrities walking with their own security team? The guards were behind them — actually, there were usually body-guards in front and behind *and* on the sides of the client. Damn that was a lot of guards. Only humans needed that many; she had Dylan, and he was an assassin, for Pete's sake. He was more than enough.

Trying to understand Dylan's reasoning was the first step in trying to get her way, but that soon turned into arguing because he seemed to only want to speak to her when they were arguing.

"How about you do what *I* say?"

"Stop using my words against me, Dylan. It's not funny. Isn't it your job to make me feel safe?" Flora complained.

"Nope."

"What do you mean 'nope'?"

"It's my job to keep you safe, not make you feel safe. Big difference," Dylan elaborated. In her opinion, his job should include both.

"Okay, let's compromise. Walk on my left side. The inside of the sidewalk," Dylan said, moving to the right side of the sidewalk. Huffing, Flora agreed and moved to the building's side of the sidewalk. She was meeting the girls at Clothes Before Bros for lunch.

Pouting, Flora glared up at Dylan.

"It's not the same," she grumbled.

"Well, what if someone attacks from the front?" Dylan asked, raising his arms in question.

"What about from the back?" Flora shot back with a roll of her eyes. Pulling her purse closer to her shoulder, she pulled down her fitted tank top. As Dylan pulled open the door for her, she stormed in and headed straight to the back room, where Dylan once again opened the door for her. As much as he liked to argue with her, he always remained a gentleman, which further pissed Flora off.

"Hello there, Flora. How are you, sweetie?" Willow asked, a smirk on her face as she stared down at her tablet.

"I'm doing okay, darling. Why don't you ask my shadow?" Flora snidely answered. Dylan just grinned as he pulled out her chair. But before Flora took her seat, she swirled around, grabbed another fold-up chair from the back of the room, and set it behind her own.

"Aww, that is so sweet, Flora. Seems like you really care for your shadow," Luxe teased, sliding into her own chair.

"Just because he's working on my last nerve doesn't mean he has to stand for lunch," Flora justified. Leaning forward, she laid her head on her crossed arms.

"Tired?" Willow asked. Flora was exhausted, mentally and physically. Her body had been running since she got up that morning, and between the many meetings she led, her legs began to ache. The stiletto heels she insisted on wearing did not help the pain in her calf.

"She hasn't had much sleep lately," Dylan claimed, taking his seat behind Flora.

"Neither have you, Mr. I'm Fine Sleeping in My Car Like a Damn Weirdo."

"How would you know?" Luxe urged Dylan. "Is that a bodyguard skill, to be able to tell from your car what your client's sleeping patterns are?"

"I can just tell," he answered.

"That's all we get? 'I can just tell,'" Luxe mimicked.

"Sluggish behavior, rushed and slurred speech, shaking, irritation, you know, the works," Dylan explained with a shrug.

"Ohh, so you've been keeping a real close eye on my good friend Flora, hun," Luxe said.

Instead of correcting her, Flora just winked her way before laying her head back down.

"How is juggling two jobs in a new field going?" Willow asked. The reminder brought an uneasy feeling in the pity of Flora's stomach. The few hours a week she was left alone or with the girls was a blessing as much as it was frightening. She was getting used to Dylan being there, and she was afraid that she'd forget how to look out for herself.

"It is what it is."

"Welp, okay then, it's time to talk about the trip coming up," Willow mentioned, finally making some eye contact with Flora.

"Trip?" Dylan questioned, crossing his arms and leaning back into his chair.

"I didn't think you'd be my bodyguard this long." As things were looking now, he'd have to go with her to Moonlight City, where she had a confirmation meeting with her lead production duo, Cassandra and Romeo Bray.

His eyes found Flora's, looking for an answer he probably should've been aware of way before this point. She could admit things weren't going to plan.

Distractedly swishing side to side in her chair, she was avoiding talking about the future with him. It made the fact that she wasn't safe anymore too real.

"What do you mean 'this long'?" His forehead creased with stress lines and his eyes narrowed slightly. "Until your stalker is dealt with, I am going to be here. Until my job is completed, I am going to be here. I'm confused why you would think otherwise."

"I mean, I thought having you around for a week would scare off my stalker, and life would return to normal," Flora said.

"No, that's not how this works. Where is this meeting?" Dylan asked.

"Moonlight City, Illinois. At Moonlight Production Factory. That's where we get our products manufactured," Willow explained.

"I have to meet the production team in a few weeks to confirm samples of the shoe collection I sent in last week," Flora said, picking at the end of one of her braids.

"Wow, that's around the corner already?" Luxe asked. It was just a couple of weeks ago that they were looking for inspiration for this collection.

"Yeah, the metal ring designs were approved by the rest of the design team and were pushed through to the production team," Flora jabbered on. She brightened at the topic. Any sign of being tired escaped her body and was replaced with passionate energy.

"Before I get to that meeting, I have a personal project to finish and get sent to them and it's stressing me out."

"Ah yes, the special edition stripper shoes," Willow exclaimed. "You've been working on those for a while."

"Yeah, and every time I think I get close, the shoe doesn't

have the right support, or the color isn't right and it's back to the strip club for inspiration." Flora threw her hands in the air to exaggerate her point.

"Is that why you go to the strip club every week...even though they've had all those security problems?" Dylan asked.

"Yeah, it wasn't like I thought I would get a stalker from sitting in the audience," she said slowly, suddenly examining the loose thread of her tank top. "Let's also not pretend it's a horrible thing to do. It's normally fun."

"Shit happens everywhere, nowhere is completely safe," Dylan said.

He wasn't really lying, though. Most times there was nothing a person could do to prevent being stalked. It doesn't matter what a person wears, how a person acts, or where a person hangs out at; bad people don't care about those things. At least, that's what she read from articles interviewing stalker victims.

Flora watched Dylan out of the side of her eye. He leaned forward in his chair to run his hand up and down her back. His touches were becoming more and more frequent, and she didn't want the small touches to ever stop. The comfort of having a protector allowed her to breathe. She didn't have to be strong around him. Flora relaxed into his hand, letting her shoulders drop. Her eyes shot to Luxe, who raised an eyebrow at the contact. The smirk on Luxe's lips made Flora blush, and she prayed Dylan wouldn't notice.

"Anyway, I only have one week to finalize these designs, and then the production team has a week to get samples ready by the time I get out there," Flora said, standing up from her chair. "Love you, girls."

Flora had a meeting with her finance manager. The math wasn't adding up correctly on her financial statements. The manager couldn't seem to do it himself, so Flora had to double-check the records on how much the company was spending. Annoyed and tired are not a mix of emotions Flora wanted to have when entering a meeting having to do with math and numbers. It was going to be stressful enough getting her manager to explain why she shouldn't fire him for being incapable of doing his job.

Outside, Flora started their short walk to her car, instantly moving to the side of the sidewalk closest to the building.

"I have to run a security check by the Club and you're safe enough at the Dainty Rebel office. So, I'll drop you off and head there." Dylan said, flanking Flora's side.

"That's fine," Flora shrugged, throwing her purse on her shoulder, and pulling down her sunglasses. Two weeks ago, she would have been overjoyed about Dylan giving her some space but now she was already counting down the minutes until Dylan would be back at her side, and he hadn't even left yet.

Just as they reached her car, Dylan yanked open the rear door of Flora's car and shoved her inside, slamming the door shut. Another man's arm came into Flora's view. Shock filled her as she felt the blood draining from her face. With trembling fingers, she locked her car door. Dylan pulled the man's arm, twisting it behind the man's back, surely on the edge of breaking it.

Suddenly, the man pulled out a small knife with his free arm. Noticing the gleam of the weapon, Dylan shoved him away. The man sprinted out of the parking lot at a speed only a Shifter could achieve. Dylan didn't watch to see where the man had taken off. He surveyed the area and something Flora couldn't see from the car must have caught his attention. Turning back to the car, he threw his body into the driver's seat of her car, pulling out of the parking lot. His eyes were glowing as he glanced at her through the rear-view mirror. "We need to get out of here."

"What about the girls?" Flora rushed, trying to pull her stuck cardigan from the car door. Seeing that she would have to open the door, she gave up and sat back as much as she could. Trying to press her back into the back of the seat to find some comfort. Tears were already welling up in her eyes and all she could think was what the hell had just happened.

"I'm calling Jackson; he'll send someone to pick up Luxe and Willow, just in case. Someone was behind the building by the parking lot, the attack was a distraction, a test, I don't know," Dylan quickly explained.

One hand held the phone, and the other gripped the steering wheel. He drove in a direction unfamiliar to Flora. She couldn't believe someone just tried to attack her. What if she was by herself? What would've happened if Willow or Luxe was with her? Why was this even happening to her?

"You're staying with me; I still have to go run that check at Lust Lane, so Willow has to cancel your meetings for the rest of the day," Dylan said. He drove around in circles, most likely to lose anyone who could be potentially following them. Tracing her fingers along the door handle, staring at the clean leather under her fingers, Flora finally let herself shed a few tears. Snuffles followed and soon she was silently crying in the backseat of her own damn car.

"Cry, Flora," Dylan said softly.

"How many times have you dealt with something like this?" Flora asked, her voice still small as her eyes searched for any threat outside the windows that could come at her. Gaining her strength and courage back, at a red light she swung open her door. Letting her cardigan fall free from the door, she got out of the car and slid into the passenger seat next to him.

"Don't worry about it; I signed up for this."

"That didn't answer my question. How many times?" Flora pressed, staring at him.

"This is the first."

"The first," Flora exclaimed.

"I don't protect, Flora. I kill," Dylan said frustration wrinkled his brows. She could tell he didn't understand why the question was so important to her. "I got you. It's gonna be okay. You're going to be okay."

"I know," Flora said, laying her hand on his arm that was resting on the middle console. "I know."

Harsh breaths filled the car. Tension weighed heavy between them.

"Why didn't you kill him?" Flora asked.

"That's not my job and not something I can just do blatantly in daylight." As his focus was on the road, his answers seemed more honest and less evasive.

Dylan looked down at the bruises forming on Flora's wrist. "What the hell is that?" he fumed. The bruises should have hurt but her mind was still racing, and she couldn't process the slight pain growing on the underside of her wrist.

"Eyes on the road, darling. I'd rather stay alive," Flora mumbled, circling a finger around the still-forming bruise.

"How'd that even happen? He didn't touch you."

"It happened when you shoved me into the car, and I landed on the seat belt buckle. It's no big deal; I bruise easily," Flora rushed out, staring out the window on high alert.

"You need to shift," Dylan growled, changing direction on the road once again.

Shifting between her animal form and her human form would heal almost any injury. The only injuries shifting couldn't heal were a missing body part or a bullet wound if the bullet was still inside her body. When it came to pain, both forms could feel it. Flora's panther would have the same bruises she had in human form. A wound would transfer between forms; shifting back and forth forced the body to accelerate the heightened healing properties of both forms. The only thing was, it was tiring as hell, and took just as much energy. It was like running with a car attached to your waist. Not impossible, but sure as hell not easy.

"I'm not shifting in front of you." She was firm on that. No way in hell would Dylan get to see her panther.

"I didn't know I was so rough," Dylan murmured.

"It's not your fault. It could've been a lot worse if you weren't there," Flora said gratefully. To think she was about to dismiss him from his duties a mere hour ago, thank goodness she didn't say anything out loud. Shivers ran up her body, fear taking the place of the strength she briefly had.

"You need to shift and heal in case there are any other injuries you're being stubborn about. We'll go somewhere private from everyone, me included," he said without sparing her another glance.

Flora accepted the conditions of letting out her animal. It had been too long anyway. As the realization of freedom occurred to her panther, it paced in excitement. Not being able to protect Flora angered the hell out of her panther and a good run, climb, and prance was in order. Flora stripped her fingers of all her rings, gold earrings, and necklaces, dropping all her jewelry into the cup holder between her and Dylan.

"Why do you even wear all that shit? What happens when you lose control and shift?" Dylan asked, putting the car into park and leaning back into his seat. The movement sent his woodsy smell wafting into Flora's nose. Filling her senses with him, his presence became encompassing and hard to ignore.

Flora turned her body so that she was facing him, with a hand on the door handle, practically jumping to get out and shift.

"The jewelry will pop off when I shift. I don't wear or design jewelry that could potentially hurt my or anyone's animal. Plus, that particular complaint is funny coming from you."

"From me?" he asked, amused. A smile graced his face, his deep brown eyes glowing, showing that his wolf was beneath the surface.

"Yeah, you. I spotted that silver chain around your neck the first time we met, and I haven't seen you take it off since."

"Should've known you would spot something like that, Miss CEO," Dylan teased. He exited the car and ran around the car to open her door. "There are ten acres here for your animal to run and play. This is Enchanted Pack land. The house is on the other side of the ten acres. So, keep that in mind if you wish to continue to keep your animal a secret. Don't go too far."

"Is this okay...I don't want to get you in trouble," Flora asked, unsure of roaming on the marked territory. Without permission, the Pack could legally kill her for being on their land. Property and territory lines in the Shifter world were enforced; if a Shifter crossed them, it was taken as disrespect, which was more than enough reason for murder. Flora wasn't taking this privilege lightly.

"Jackson okayed it; it's no problem as long as it is back here and away from the other Pack members."

"So, don't run into them?" Flora guessed.

"For your safety and theirs. You don't know all their animals and we don't know yours." Dylan turned and sat inside the car, keeping the door open. He'd wait there, she guessed. That would be good enough for her.

"Are you *sure* this is okay?" Flora asked.

"Go shift, baby girl."

With that, Flora entered the wooded area, walking deeper between the trees until she found a spot to undress in. After neatly folding her clothes, her panther began to take over. Nearly at the speed of light, a black panther appeared in the place Flora's human body once stood. She shifted between forms a couple of times, just enough to heal her bruises before she let her panther run. Flora's human mind shut off as her panther ran as fast as her legs could take her, switching between running and climbing trees.

Her muscles ached in a way she craved. The smells of leaves and mud excited her panther, and it made Flora smile inside. Her panther loved to climb. She could climb trees all day long if Flora let her. She couldn't shift often or for long while living in an apartment complex. But this land was full of trees and branches strong enough to carry her weight — her panther was living the dream. Jumping from one branch to another, the happiness from one form was shared to the other.

After a while Flora's panther sadly gave Flora back control of their body. Animals typically control the animal form and let the human control the human body. Getting dressed, Flora walked back to the car where Dylan sat exactly where she left him.

It wasn't a big deal when someone found out a person was a wolf or bear Shifter, so why did her panther have to be so scary? Flora knew; it was all she'd been told as a kid. Secrets saved lives. In order to keep her panther safe from the dangers of the world, she had to keep her a secret.

Panthers were strong and solitary animals. Animals are more aggressive than humans; naturally, so are Shifters. Fighting can be fun and playful with the right people. At some point, someone found they could make a quick buck hosting neighborhood fights. After a while, it got serious, and people got greedy. Fighters started getting paid less and wanted out. Except that wasn't an option anymore. It changed from fun and playful to life and death. That was the birth of the SBM and the fear of panthers.

"You didn't try to sneak a peek?" Flora asked, giggling as she walked up to Dylan's open door. Most people do, but her panther must hide pretty damn well if they never found out what animal she was. She wished it didn't have to be such a secret.

"Nope, you wish to keep that aspect of who you are a secret. It won't stop me from guessing, though," he stated simply, looking up from his phone. Most people try to guilt her into telling, but there was no sign of resentment or bitterness in Dylan's eyes.

"Thank you," Flora said slowly, reaching her hand out to his silver chain necklace, pulling it from out under his black long-sleeve shirt he always wears.

Dylan's face flushed red at the closeness of Flora's body. Her cream-colored outfit followed the wind, blowing away from her body. Dirt from the car door stained the right side of her pants and cardigan.

"When did you get this?" she whispered. Staring at the simple chain, and dragging her nails across each link, her nails made contact across the skin near his collarbone.

"When I got my first job, Jackson gave me the chain before I left. It reminds me no matter how far I go, there will always be a home waiting for me when I get back," Dylan reminisced, a small smile landing on his face.

"It's beautiful," she said, letting the chain drop back into place. "Show it off more. Be proud of it." Dylan just smiled, starting the car, and driving towards the strip club for his shift.

"Proud and loud are two different things, grizzly."

"Not a grizzly — you would've heard my footsteps when I shifted if that was the case," Flora commented.

He could guess all he wanted, but that didn't mean she'd tell him when he was right. Their guessing game didn't feel forceful or malicious. She couldn't help but smile every time it came up. What would he guess next? What random animal would he think she shifted into? As long as the game remained lighthearted, she let the game continue.

6

FLORA

Flora didn't really know what a "shift at the Club" would be like, but seeing Dylan standing by the back door, waiting to walk anyone who asked to their car was boring as hell. Pushing her dirt-stained cardigan open, the heat in the building began to bother her. She sat at Emery's backstage station while she was dancing. Four months into their relationship, Emery and Flora realized they were better off as friends and had been ever since.

Each station was set with a half-table, stool, mirror, and locker. Emery's station was closest to the back door and once she heard of Flora's little problem, she offered her stool to her while she went on stage so Flora could be close to Dylan. Opening her phone, Flora swirled on the stool, setting Emery's heels on the table. Just because Flora wasn't at work didn't mean she had to stop working. Eyeing all angles and dynamics of the well-worn pole shoe, she studied the structure and noted it in her phone. The last thing she wanted to do was make a perfectly cute heel that wouldn't be useful.

"Why is this passion project so important to you?" Dylan

wondered, leaning against the back wall. Eyes scanning the room, as he'd been doing for the last hour.

"Well, Emery and I met a while back. On a date, actually. When she found out I'd never been to a strip club, she invited me here. The first time I walked inside this club was to see her perform," Flora shared, continuing to take notes on her phone. "Of course, her performance was hot, but it was also inspiring. The acts here are more than being sexy, at least the good ones are. It's about the dance, the story they tell with their moves. I wanted to create a part of that story, so with the girls' help and excitement, we began working on a line of shoes that would enhance their performance."

Smiling, Flora knew what a good pair of shoes did to a performer. They could confidently dance with enough support from a sexy shoe they helped design. It lit Flora up with excitement. She couldn't wait to see them on stage.

"Have you tried?" Dylan asked, raising an eyebrow, a smile forming on his face.

"Pole dancing? Yes, I don't have the strength required to hold myself up. It was fun though," Flora shrugged.

"Cool."

"Cool, that's all you have to say?" Flora asked. He didn't talk much, but he wasn't even curious about her ex-girlfriend? She was damn sure curious about any of his.

The girls met at a coffee shop and Emery, with her outgoing personality, started a conversation with Flora and they started hanging out. After discovering their mutual attraction, they went on a few dates. But as beautiful and intelligent as Emery was, that type of connection wasn't there so they both agreed to stay friends.

"You're not very talkative, Dylan." Flora commented, giving him her full attention.

"Not much to say."

"I don't think that is true, Dyl," Flora tested. His face scrunched, letting her know the nickname was a no-go.

"Think what you want, rabbit," Dylan smirked, finally meeting Flora's eyes.

"You really think I'm a rabbit?"

"No, but you just confirmed it for me."

❧

SLAMMING THE CAR DOOR SHUT, FLORA STOMPED UP her apartment stairs; Dylan followed suit. Stopping in the middle of the staircase, she turned around, jutting her hip and crossing her arms.

"Why do you refuse to just sleep on my couch? Is it not to your liking? What's wrong with my apartment?" Flora fired out. She knew sleeping in his car had to be uncomfortable as hell.

"Flora, your apartment is beautiful, but we've had this conversation. Boundaries are important," Dylan said.

"At least tell me why?" Flora pouted as she continued up the stairs.

"Boundaries."

Flora huffed, yanking open her apartment door. She moved to the side to let Dylan enter first, as she'd been doing since he came along. He glanced around the outside and searched the whole apartment before he allowed her to step inside. The warm breeze outside was nice, but if their arrangement lasted until winter, it would get too cold for him to sleep in his car.

"Would you prefer to sleep on a bed? You could have mine and I could sleep on the couch," Flora offered.

"Hell no — why would you even offer? You won't let this

go, will you?" Following her into the kitchen, he leaned against the counter. His long sleeve shirt pulled tight across his chest as he leaned back on his arms.

She was staring — hardcore ogling — and couldn't stop.

"No, I won't. Unless it is you that is uncomfortable. Don't worry about me being uncomfortable because I'm not. I would feel safer if you were in the apartment," Flora rambled.

Opening up about her feelings was too easy with Dylan. Things were different now that someone actually tried to attack her. They couldn't figure out who did it; damn scent blockers prevented the wolves from scenting whoever it was. Fear crawled up Flora's neck as the memory of being attacked came back. She wasn't alone yet, and she sure wanted to keep it that way. "If it makes you that uncomfortable, then I'll call Willow or Luxe to stay in the apartment with me. I'm sure it's no big deal."

"Don't," Dylan spoke, reaching for Flora's hand. "I'll stay in the apartment, but keep in mind that I'm here. I respect your privacy, so don't accidentally shift."

"Is that what you're worried about, me breaking my own secret? I won't shift...out of comfort for the *both* of us," Flora pointed out, rounding the couch, and pulling out pillows and blankets. "So, do you want the couch or the bed? I don't mind; both are comfy."

"Couch," Dylan responded awkwardly, tapping each of his fingers on the counter as she laid out the blankets and pillows. Shuffling his feet slowly toward the couch, he sat on the edge.

"See? All comfy," Flora said, feeling accomplished. She was overdoing it with the plethora of pillows and blankets, but she just wanted him to be comfortable.

After "good night" and a last-minute security check, Flora headed to her own bed. A giddy feeling flowed from her stomach and into her chest. She hid a bursting smile from Dylan.

Dylan was in the apartment. If something happened, he would be right there and that feeling let her fall asleep peacefully for the first time since she'd spotted her attacker.

❧

THE NEXT MORNING WOULD SET THE TONE FOR THE rest of Dylan's stay. Waking up, she tried to go through her morning routine as she normally would. Yet she couldn't help trying to be somewhat quiet. Flora hadn't meant to wake Dylan, but she could tell she already did. Even with her music playing, she could hear his footsteps through the house, another noise that brought her comfort. She stopped listening when she heard him reach the bathroom, giving him privacy. She blushed thinking of an early morning Dylan, fresh from sleep. He'd be hot, too hot. His hair would probably be messed up and his voice would be all groggy yet smooth and deep and — she was snapped out of her daze as she knocked her phone off the dresser.

A knock sounded at her door as the phone hit the ground. Opening the door wide, she motioned Dylan inside and patted her bed, so he'd take the hint to sit down. He didn't even enter the room. He only checked on her with a searching gaze.

"I was just checking if you were okay. I heard something fall," Dylan said. Seeing she was okay, he tried to make his exit out of her room, but Flora wasn't going to let him escape so easily.

"That was my phone. Anyway, we are going to the office today to finish up the work I didn't do yesterday, *and* I have lunch with my mom," she said, twisting a braid between her fingers.

Dylan scanned the state of her room despite her rambling. In stereotypical girl fashion, her rocking chair was filled with failed outfit ideas. She threw another strapless bandeau on top of the pile. Dylan smiled, probably wondering how many clothes she could possibly fit on that chair.

"I don't meet the families of the people I work with," he said. He was fidgeting now, his eyes darting around the room lingering on the window and the hem of her robe.

"You don't have to meet her if you don't want to," Flora assured, trying to push down her disappointment. "But I need to tell her what's going on; she'll be more pissed if I don't, and she finds out some other way." A pissed mommy panther is a dangerous mommy panther, something Flora knew all too well.

He sighed, noticing her deflated mood. Dylan looked over towards her "I'll be there."

"Yay!" Flora yelled, picking out a loose pair of dress pants with a matching oversized blazer.

"Do I need to look fancy?" Dylan asked. He stared at the clothes on her bed, smoothing his hands over his hoodie.

"Throw a blazer on top, you'll be fine," Flora winked, picking a fitted long sleeve top to go under her outfit.

◈

SIDEWALK ARGUMENTS NEVER SEEMED TO ESCAPE their day-to-day routine. They'd fallen into the habit of Flora walking on the 'inside' of the sidewalk and him on the outside, but she still liked to tease him. The pair walked up to the restaurant and, upon seeing her mom, Flora smiled bigger than she had in a while. She was incredibly close with her mom.

Today they had matching dark hair and blazer suits. While the women exchanged hugs, Dylan offered a polite handshake, and Flora could tell he was unsure of what formalities he should take, unaware of her mother's animal. Different animals had different behaviors and manners, so Flora felt guilty that Dylan came in underprepared. She didn't even think about it before that moment.

"This gentleman doesn't know your animal, I see. Looks like you were listening to me all those years." Flora's mother laughed, taking Dylan's hand and giving it a shake. "I'm Lola Larkspur." Taking her seat, Flora's mom pulled on the end of her blazer, looking polished as she always did.

"You know, some things stick," Flora agreed, as Dylan pulled out her chair and pushed her in before taking his own seat.

"How is Dainty Rebel? It's the closest thing I have to a grandbaby," Lola joked as they placed their orders.

"Great — profits are higher than ever despite everything going on. We got a huge investment pushing our projects forward," Flora said, sneaking a glance up at Dylan. His focus remained split between her, her mom, and their surroundings. Without a glance back at her, he lightly laid his hand on her shaking thigh under the table. Startled at first, she quickly recovered, sliding her hand over his. They were still testing boundaries around each other. With one phone call, they went from complete strangers to seeing each other 24/7.

"Always straight to the point. My loving Flora, what's going on?" Lola smiled, reaching a comforting hand on the table. Lola's tight smile made Flora hesitate to tell her everything. She didn't want to stress her mom out yet her warm hand reminded her of her mother's strength.

"I thought it was a one-time thing. A guy from Lust Lane

following me home hoping to get lucky. Then it happened again, except I was going to work. Then recently…" Flora started, pushing around the fries on her plate with a fork. "Soon after I met Dylan, this stalker attempted an attack, or kidnapping, I'm not sure which. He couldn't get close enough before Dylan took care of the situation and got me out of there."

"He killed him?" Lola asked, eyeing Dylan.

"No, the attacker ran off. Dylan's top concern was getting me to safety," Flora said, hoping to remove any doubt her mother could have about Dylan. Flora trusted him completely; in fact she needed him. No one could replace him, and she needed her mother to know that. Lola was a woman on a mission. She could be cutthroat when she needed to be and wasn't afraid to fire anyone. Her hardheaded teenage daughter included. Working beside her mom as a seamstress in her teen years was a hard-learned lesson on doing what you have to do. Flora didn't prioritize her duties of sewing up buttonholes, so her mom cut her loose. Little did teenage Flora know she'd hate a fast food job even more than her seamstress job.

"Why didn't you just kill the attacker?" Lola questioned Dylan. While the Council laws of the paranormal community were loose, they were still laws. If Dylan had killed the attacker on unclaimed land, meaning no alpha ruling the land to decide if to punish him or not, he'd be sent to The Council. Unclaimed land is more dangerous than claimed land; dealing with Alphas or Lunas was easier than dealing with The Council. If Dylan was sent to the Council and he provided a justifiable reason for the kill, he would go on without punishment. If the reason was anything less than acceptable, then he'd be sent to Shifter prison.

"There was someone hiding behind the nearest building. If

I went off to chase after attacker number one, potential attacker number two would have a wide opening to do whatever they wanted to Flora. As she said, keeping her safe and alive is my top concern," Dylan explained, staring directly at Lola.

"Could Flora not have fought attacker number two?" Lola asked, a challenging spark in the upward turn of her smile.

"Mom —"

"She could've. I don't know her animal, but after the few weeks I've spent with her, I know she can defend herself," Dylan said, leaning back into his chair. "But that doesn't mean she has to."

Flora bet he could feel Flora's searching eyes on the side of his head.

She wasn't sure how she was supposed to feel about his words.

"Well, with that being said, you have my stamp of approval. And with the look Flora is giving me, it doesn't seem you need it." Lola giggled as her daughter looked away, the tiniest blush appearing on her brown skin.

"Where is daddy dearest these days?" Flora diverted, sipping on her straw.

"You know how he is, darling, off on another work trip," Lola said. Her mom was obviously hiding the truth from Dylan, but Flora wasn't sure why she was making it so obvious. Flora watched him interact with her mom. His shoulders relaxed, and by the end, he was actually smiling. To think he was so nervous before lunch.

Lola was a gem, and Flora was grateful for her company. She'd missed her family more than she wished to admit. They talked for hours about anything: Flora's favorite reality TV show to the spring-cleaning Lola had planned seven months in advance. It was just what Flora needed to ground herself amid all her problems.

"Alrighty mom, thanks for coming out," Flora said, pulling her mom into a hug.

"Dylan, you take care of my baby," Lola said.

"Of course, Mrs. Larkspur. It's not just me, though; it's a Pack effort as well," Dylan confirmed, taking Flora's hand in his.

"Please, call me Lola, but Pack effort?" Lola asked, glancing towards her daughter.

"Yes, I've yet to be introduced to them all, but after meeting their Alpha, Jackson, and knowing Dylan and Luxe trust them, I can tell loyalty and a sense of family run deep."

Flora gripped Dylan's hand just a touch tighter.

Dylan's chest puffed out in pride at Flora's praise of his Pack. Smiling, he looked down at Flora, teasing her.

"Alrighty darlings, I'll be on my way," Lola laughed as they parted ways.

Turning toward Dylan, Flora shined her smile up at him. "So, how was meeting my mom?"

"Just as expected."

"Oh, now you're at a loss for words?" Flora asked, a short laugh coming from her.

"What do you mean? She was just like you, or you're just like her."

"Just like me? What am I like?"

"Powerful, elegant, caring, you know?"

"You know?" Flora asked.

"Beautiful," Dylan complimented.

Flora looked up to see a light blush cover his face. She gave him a shy "thank you", becoming aware of the hot, sweet energy that hung in the air around them.

"Beautifully annoying," Dylan teased.

"You calling my mom annoying?" Flora questioned, the fire rising in her eyes.

"Nah, that's all you, porcupine."

"Not a porcupine," Flora yelled as she skipped toward their car.

"Beautifully annoying, my ass," Flora mumbled, opening her apartment door. Laughing as she stepped aside, she let Dylan go in first to conduct his usual search. Letting someone take such an immense amount of control of her life had been internally difficult. Having the security of someone watching her back offered more comfort than she imagined it would. In the end, or even just for the time being, it was worth it.

Her eyes scanned back and forth outside; this was one of the only times she was left partially alone. Currently, Dylan was physically away from her, and the pressure was on. She pressed her back into the rough textured wall between her apartment door and the next. She'd never met her neighbors, but maybe she should spend some time getting to know them. Making friends normally was a bother but as Willow and Luxe grew closer to her she thought maybe it was time to branch out. Be friendly for a change.

"Clear!" Dylan yelled out. He flipped on the lights as he

walked back to the door to take off his shoes. That was another thing she had to let go of. Wearing shoes in the house was a pet peeve of hers but to search the house, Dylan had to be ready for anything. Shoes stayed on until he was done, she decided. Leaving her fears at the door, she scurried into her apartment, slamming the door shut. Locking, unlocking, then locking it again, she pulled on the door handle to make sure it was secure before relaxing.

She unlatched her heels, walked inside, and dropped onto the couch.

Her animal was restless. Normally, she could go a week without having to shift but now that she was in constant danger, her animal felt a need to come out more often. Curling into the fetus position, Flora groaned. She closed her eyes, trying to relax.

"What is that all about?" Dylan asked, taking a juice from her fully stocked fridge. Getting food for Dylan was a pain in the ass, now that he was staying at her place 24/7. Not because it was an extra expense — in fact buying him food was fun and filled her with a sense of pride. What made the task annoying was that he wouldn't ask for anything. Flora had to walk around the entire store and pick things up for him based on his long stares and second looks.

Getting to the self-checkout was a whole other issue because he wanted to pay for everything. Flora bought the food to fill up *her* house; they were *her* groceries. Once, after arguing in front of everyone at the self-checkout area, Flora let him pay for her groceries. Now that she knew what he liked, she would go by herself the next time, she told herself. Once she could go anywhere by herself, of course. But if she could go out without him, then she wouldn't need to buy Dylan food because he wouldn't be around. The sudden thought of Dylan not being a part of her life fueled the dread already taking over her stomach.

"Nothing's wrong." Turning on the TV, she tried to distract herself. Her panther pawed at the front of her mind, whining constantly. That little panther needed to run badly.

Flipping through the channels, looking for anything to drag her mind away from her panther, Flora laid back and stretched her legs out. Other people's problems normally did the trick, so she put on reality TV. A human family with rich people's problems always distracted her for at least a few hours.

Suddenly, Dylan stormed into the room. His dark blue flannel-covered arm reached over Flora. She looked up at him. His nearness set her body off, she could feel the sweat building on her skin. Why did he get so close? Did she smell good? He sure did. He was practically on top of her, and Flora's body itched for him to just drop his weight on hers. Take charge of her beyond her security. She gazed into his eyes, only for the moment to go from sweet to sour, as he snatched the remote sitting beside her and switched off the TV.

"What the hell, Dylan?" Flora grumbled, reaching her arm out for the remote.

"You think I can't tell?" he asked, using his arms to prop himself against the back of the couch. Scooting so that she was sitting up, Flora just looked at him with an eyebrow raised in question. "You need to shift, why deny it?"

"I didn't want to worry you." she said, curling Dylan's blanket from that morning around her body. Dylan's scent filled her lungs. She continued to relax as the fuming Shifter stood in front of her. His glare could make anyone scared, but goddess, he was cute when he was mad at her. All riled up over her. It made her panther want to purr, too.

"Why would it worry me?"

"Because you, being you, would find somewhere for me on Pack land to shift and I'm not part of your Pack. It's wrong for me to shift on your land," Flora said. Embarrassment was evident in her tone, though she wasn't sure why.

"It's not wrong."

"It should make Jackson uncomfortable, especially since he doesn't know my animal — he's got a Pack to protect."

"Okay, then we'll go somewhere else," Dylan shrugged, dragging her by her ankles to the edge of the couch. "I have another place."

Getting up, Flora followed Dylan who stopped in the kitchen. "Do you have anything normal to wear?" he asked, gesturing at her wide-legged trousers and blazer.

"What I wear *is* normal, for me anyway. You're going to make me insecure if you keep commenting on the way I dress," Flora teased, posing one arm on her hip. But really she *was* teasing him; not a drop of insecurity about the way she dressed flowed in her veins. She liked to look and feel expensive, period. Nothing anyone had said before had bothered her but for some reason, she hoped Dylan thought she was cute, attractive even. Anger at her previous thought overtook her. Why was she caring about what a man thought of her?

"You know I look cute, Dylan. Do I seem like the type to need fashion advice from someone who wears hoodies every day?" She winked at him for effect. His eyes lingered on her body before the corner of his lip lifted.

"Go change into a t-shirt and sweatpants or something; you're not going to a dinner party," Dylan teased, leaning against the counter as if waiting for her. The glint in his eye told her they were on playing grounds. She smiled back. Despite his words, his cheeks were rosy.

Normally, she wouldn't have given his command any

thought, but he was sort of right. Deciding it would be better to strip out of loose clothing, she changed into a long sleeve crop top and a pair of baggy sweatpants.

"Better?" she asked, giving him a twirl.

"Very." He interlaced their fingers before escorting her out the door.

After an hour riding in Dylan's car, they pulled up to a single-floor house, surrounded by a forest of trees that excited Flora's panther. Though she didn't want to bother Dylan, her panther was riling up inside, and pacing back and forth within her mind. Dylan hopped out of the car and led Flora to the backyard.

"This is where I stayed during my assassin jobs. No one but my boss and my crew could find me here. It was perfect. I had a roof over my human head and plenty of room for my animal to run around." He walked up the stairs of the back porch, settling his lean body on the dirty couch next to the door. His outdoor furniture consisted of a couch and a coffee table, covered in dust and dried leaves, with the metal bits rusting away. Maybe it was a good thing Flora changed her clothes.

"*Was* perfect?"

"Was. It was perfect before I started missing my Pack. I needed them and once we put up safety precautions around the house, in case my work ever followed me home, there was no way I would live alone full time again." He ran a hand through his fluffy hair. "I'll stay here, and you can run and play and do whatever your animal likes to do."

Looking around, Flora gingerly took a seat next to Dylan on the couch. Overwhelmed with gratitude, Flora looked out to the open forest, unable to speak freely while looking directly at him.

"I couldn't live very far from my family either. As a teen, I couldn't wait to move out of my parents' home, imagining all the freedom it would give me. In the end, being too far away felt worse and I moved closer to home."

"Where did you go?"

"Not too far. I got an apartment in Detroit. I lasted two months before I moved back to Rainfall Avenue. It's no secret that I don't have a lot of friends, but without my parents, I was lonely."

"Loneliness has claws that dig deep, dragging you to where you need to be."

"Tell me about it," Flora sighed. Her time away from her family wasn't horrible. She worked, went home, and repeated that same routine every day. She was missing one piece to her puzzle that would've made her life perfect, and that was companionship. If she hadn't come back, she wouldn't have her parents around the corner or have met Willow or Luxe, or even Dylan. "Thanks, Dylan, for everything."

"Anytime, Flora."

With that, Flora walked toward the forest. Running her hand along the tough tree branches, she appreciated the privacy it gave her. Dylan grew on her like the leaves on a branch; the more she thought of him, the bigger the leaves would grow and one day she'd have to accept that the leaves would fall. There was an immense amount of trust between them. It shocked her to even think about the amount of dependence she had on Dylan, which he seemed to take in stride. Since the attack, she was relaxing bit by bit and Dylan's normally snarky ass just rolled with the punches. This may have been his first job as a bodyguard, but he was damn good at it.

Sensing that she was deep enough in the forest, she undressed. It was finally time to let her panther out. Flora's panther takes off as her human consciousness gave her panther full control.

She started with her favorite activity, climbing up a tree. Jumping from branch to branch, she climbed up another tree and ran to do it all again. Flora's panther was playful, but unfortunately, she had to play by herself since Flora didn't know any other panthers in the area. She tried to play with forest animals when they were younger, but due to her size and strength, she'd accidentally kill them. Doesn't stop her from letting out a whine or a sad roar when she gets into one of her moods. Knocking into trees and swiping at bushes, she could be vocal sometimes.

Flora's panther caught a whiff of another Shifter on the property, and a protective curiosity overtook her. She slowed down, weaving through trees to spread her scent around the area. Scent-spreading worked as a warning that if her panther crossed paths with another Shifter, shit was going down.

Dylan relaxed on the outdoor couch of his old house's back porch. Playing a mindless game on his phone, he tried to waste as much time as possible. Thanks to his bodyguard job, shifting into his wolf to scout outside Flora's apartment every day gave his animal enough time to run and wear out the constant energy that all Shifters have. Due to the comeback of non-Shifter wolves in Michigan, it wasn't rare for a human to spot one, so Dylan's wolf being out didn't upset the humans who saw him. Flora, on the other hand, didn't have that luxury. From the random scratches he found around her apartment, particularly on the couch and table legs, Dylan could tell she used to shift inside her home. Shifting inside a confined space was not the same as being able to run free outside. Seeing that she didn't get the opportunity to run free often, he made it his mission to provide it for her.

The wolf in him howled at the satisfaction of caring for another. Dylan's wolf was a protective motherfucker. He loved to fight for his own. It didn't matter the person, the animal, whatever — his wolf would fight anything if it meant protecting his family. Flora had snuck her cute little ass into his atmosphere and while he wasn't sure if he'd consider her family yet, she damn sure was getting close. He was as attached to her as his wolf was and that would bite him in the ass when the job ended. The number-one rule in his line of work was to never get attached. You can't save everybody; you can't rescue or repair every broken down or injured creature you come across. Not getting attached saved him from the heartbreak that could have followed literally anything going wrong. He wasn't perfect, but subconsciously he held himself to that standard.

Providing space and time for Flora's panther to run free gave him a sense of pride. Protecting and providing is the Shifter way — always had been. It was ingrained in their DNA to do so. It came naturally and so, when a Shifter felt they weren't doing their best to protect and provide, their mental health would take a dive. Anger and restlessness would build and build until they eventually went rogue. Going rogue was a mindset more than it was a physical change; a biological way of a Shifter feeling they failed at life.

Dylan had begun to feel that way. Beside his urge to kill, he was terrified of going rogue. Before Flora, he felt his mind slipping at times and that's when he started applying for jobs again. He began to find peace within himself while hanging around Flora. As independent as she was, he still found ways to take care of her and that satisfied him more than he would've thought. He couldn't find that satisfactory feeling with his Pack. They always did things for him, saying "Oh no problem, I'll do it" or "Relax Dylan, you've done enough for us." He was supposed to be second in command to Jackson, not them. It weighed on Dylan; he always felt as if he was walking on eggshells, and one day his Pack was going to snap and kick him to the curb.

Dylan's assassin days weighed heavy on the other Pack members. Maybe they felt as if they owed him for the sacrifice he made with every mission he went on. He wasn't sure but they covered everything, from bills to dinner each night, and even when Dylan would offer to do anything, he was shot down. The problem was that he loved his job. He got to choose which assignments he'd take. Which people he'd kill. Dylan often chose jobs where he was saving someone; often someone about to be traded or trafficked into the SBM. With the life-saving part he tacked on his assassin role there was a motivation, something deeper, making Dylan take every job he could. He enjoyed the act of taking a life. The Pack was babying a sadistic killer and didn't even know it.

Then came the question of whether or not to tell them how he felt. It came up every time he got back from a hit. Murder was seen as horrible even in the Shifter world unless the reason was deemed reasonable. During his time as an active assassin, Dylan realized he didn't always need a reason. He could kill just because and that's when he finally quit. It could be dangerous for a Pack with a ruthless killer as a member and he couldn't give Jackson a reason to let him go, so he never told a soul. He'd keep his secret for as long as he could.

As his senses suddenly sparked up, Dylan began to repeatedly tap the armrest of his couch. His chest felt heavy. Listening to his instincts, he walked into the forest. Something was wrong and judging by his wolf's reaction, it had to do with Flora. Shifting into his wolf, his brown paws beat the ground as his wolf took control, using her fading scent to track her down.

Watching from the shadows, Dylan's human consciousness took over in his wolf body. He searched for Flora's scent, but with different scents filling the air, he decided to search for just one — blood. Since he couldn't smell any blood, he decided it was safe enough for Flora to run around. Dylan turned around to head back to the house, but before he could, he spotted a creature in the open clearing in a couple yards front of him. Bushes and trees slightly blocked his view of the creature but not enough that he couldn't tell what it was. Circling in the clearing was a black panther. One of the most dangerous Shifters in the world was getting ready to attack another wolf on the other side of the clearing.

As Dylan sniffed again, he picked up another Shifter's scent, one different from Flora's. Confused about whether the panther was Flora or not, Dylan shifted into his human form. He yelled out Flora's name hoping that the panther was hers and wouldn't try to kill him. The panther jerked its head in his direction. Her tongue stuck out slightly as her tail swung from side to side. From the eye contact they were making and in the response to the name-calling, there was no doubt now in Dylan's mind that the panther was Flora's. Dylan shifted back into his wolf, standing back as the other Shifter, another wolf, got closer. Sizing up Flora's panther, getting in her way was a death sentence Dylan wasn't ready to fulfill.

Growls from the other wolf Shifter made Flora's panther tense. Her hackles began to rise, and her tail stopped swinging. The goal of the wolf Shifter was to attack, which switched Flora's panther mood completely, from joyful to defensive in a moment's notice. Flora's panther could see a fight was imminent; the stranger wolf's presence and purpose were clear. Dylan's wolf mentally scratched from inside, begging for control. His own growls filled his mind. As much as both Dylan and his wolf wanted to protect Flora, she needed to protect herself, fight for herself. Shifters' animals were proud of protecting their humans and families. Inserting himself in the fight before it even started would be overstepping Flora's panther's boundaries. Dylan would stand back and watch in case shit hit the fan.

The panther continued to circle around the newcomer, her shoulder blades rhythmically moving up and down as she strode around waiting for the other wolf Shifter to make a move. The wolf jumped from its spot behind the trees, landing on Flora's panther. In an instant, Flora whipped it off her back by shoving her body weight to the left. She wasted no time swiping her paw across the wolf's face, her claws leaving a trail of blood behind.

The wolf fought back, growling, and launched its jaw into her shoulder, whipping Flora around. Dylan stood still behind the fight, getting ready to jump in to help Flora if she needed him. Flora's panther escaped the wolf's jaws and landed a death bite of her own. The wolf went limp under the powerful bite of her panther. Letting it hit the ground with a thud, her panther walked toward Dylan's wolf, rubbing her head around his neck with affection. He was frozen to his spot. He didn't want to make any sudden moves and set her off. He was strong but panthers were on a different level. Flora backed away and began to run around again, not quite ready to shift back to human form. Dylan's wolf took that as a sign to search his land for any other shifters before heading back to his spot on the porch, letting her run free.

In human form, Dylan pulled up his jeans and sat on the porch, letting the last of the sun sting his chest. Warmth filled the chill from witnessing a fight nested in his chest.

Flora's a panther.

He'd met a panther.

Flora's a damn cat.

Shaking his head, he couldn't believe that the woman he was protecting was a panther. An animal that could rip him apart, as she demonstrated with the other wolf. Which he'd have to come back and take care of the body later... That also meant reestablishing his territory lines again and what a pain in the ass that was to have to do again. A man could only piss so damn much.

Why did she need protection when she was one of the strongest animals among Shifters — an animal most known for their fighting skills? Pulling his loose hair back, he made a call to Jackson, letting him know there was a loose shifter on his land. Sure, Dylan's home away from home was miles away from Enchanted Pack land, but Jackson needed to be ready if Shifters were getting brazen and crossing land borders so carelessly.

He wasn't quite sure what to do, let alone think. Swiping back and forth through apps on his phone, his mind focused on Flora. He wasn't supposed to find out what her animal was. Would she fire him now? Kill him? He couldn't tell. His mind continued to race until the sleek, midnight-colored panther strode toward the back porch. He stood slowly, meeting her at the end of the last step of the stairs. Dylan stood in amazement at the panther walking up to him. Kneeling in front of the panther, he left himself open. He wasn't all the way sure this wildcat wouldn't kill him, but based on the fact the panther wasn't running *at* him, he would take his chances. The panther rubbed her body all over Dylan as if marking him as...family?

Confusion filled Dylan as the panther purred, licking his face. Flora might not have liked him very much, but her animal sure did. Dylan gave her a few pets, returning the affection she was giving. Pride filled his chest again. Being liked by a panther was an honor. Giving her a few more loving taps, she took off toward the forest where he assumed she would finish her time being in panther form.

9

FLORA

Slowing her run, Flora's panther knew it was time to give back control to her human side. Stopping by her clothes she had folded on the forest floor, her panther laid comfortably while the shift began. Her human hands unfolded the clothes and put them back on. A cloud of dread covered Flora's body. Fear that Dylan wouldn't be waiting for her when she got back. Once people found out she was a panther, any sort of friendship or trust instantly disappeared and it crushed Flora every single time. She'd only known Dylan for a short amount of time, a couple of weeks max. Dylan didn't seem like the judgmental, run-from-fear type but on the topic of panthers, Flora couldn't be sure. She pushed her long braids over her shoulder as she shyly made her way back to the house. This was the one gray area in her life that made her insecure to the point where she couldn't hide it. She avoided this conversation with nearly everyone in her life, Willow and Luxe included. But Dylan weaseled his way in and found her most well-kept secret within a couple of weeks. She watched him as she approached the house from the tree line. He sat silently, comfortable, and still shirtless, as she neared. He was there. He'd stayed.

"So, you met my panther," Flora stated, sitting next to him on the old couch. Looking anywhere but at Dylan, Flora focused her attention on the pressure of the cushion on her back, creating a bubble of safety around herself.

"I wasn't going to say anything," he responded, trying to get Flora to make eye contact with him. She could feel his eyes searching for her own, but she kept hers focused directly in front of her.

Dylan stood suddenly, stooping down on one knee before her. His arm gently came up to the side of her face to bring her gaze to his. "Your animal doesn't change anything for me."

"It doesn't?' Most people in the Shifter world hated panthers and either wanted to kill them or sell them to the Shifter Black Market. Their history of participating in cage fights (voluntarily or not) ran too deep and terrified people. Panthers were always strong and solitary animals. It made them valuable to the Shifter community. It pained Flora to know that this fear was created by what was supposed to be fun and playful neighborhood fights. But, of course, bids got higher, and people became greedy. Fighters started getting paid less and wanted out. Except that wasn't an option anymore. It changed from fun and playful to life and death. That was the birth of the SBM and cage fighting.

"Nope."

"What if I was a turtle or a dragon?"

"Are dragons even real?"

"Who knows, with fairies, witches, and beyond, I wouldn't be too surprised to stumble across a dragon Shifter."

"But yes, Flora, even then. Nothing changes."

Smiling, Flora took her hand and placed it on his bare

shoulder, appreciating the muscle underneath his slightly tanned, naked skin. She couldn't overlook the pause that followed the physical connection. She liked the newfound nakedness of his chest and wasn't ready to let it disappear, so she yanked his shirt that was laying across his thigh and took off for the car, giggles escaping her lips as she climbed inside.

Dylan swaggered not far behind.

He really didn't care about her panther, and he didn't leave. She could hardly breathe. The excitement tore through her body as she slid into his car, smiling like a fool.

"Come on slowpoke, we've got shit to do," she yelled before shutting her door.

IT WAS SIX IN THE MORNING WHEN FLORA ENDED HER tossing and turning and finally made her way out of bed. A regular workday normally excited her but with meetings on top of meetings with some more meetings on top of those killed some of the joy of running her company. She wanted to be curled up on the couch watching TV.

Flora reached for her phone and instantly regretted the decision. A headache brought on from the brightness of her phone screen was already beginning to seep in. Flora found her way to the chillingly cold kitchen and pulled open the fridge door, looking for her usual breakfast foods. Setting fruit on a plate and a pastry in the toaster, she leaned against the counter.

Dylan knew her animal, he went as far as to come up close and not get his head bitten off. According to him, he didn't get bitten, and she couldn't see any bite marks, so he must have been telling the truth. Her panther wasn't normally an attacker, but Dylan was unknown to her. Her panther had never met him before. Flora guessed meeting him as a human first was enough for her animal.

Walking over to the couch to check on Dylan she leaned over it just like he did the other day when he called her out on her shit. Her hands pressed against the back of the couch as she hovered, trying not to wake him. Dylan was not a morning person whatsoever. He was grouchier than normal before nine a.m. Giggling softly, Flora slid his open sketchbook from his limp hands, examining the page he was working on the previous night.

Looking back at her were the eyes of her panther, her dark gaze shining bright even on a sheet of paper. She bit the inside of her cheek, trying to get her lips to stop trembling. Flora didn't know where to start digesting her emotions looking at that drawing. Tears welled behind her eyes and onto her eyelashes making it difficult to see the artwork. She wiped the tears away before they could fall, wanting to stare at the drawing for hours. No one had ever made her panther look so beautifully graceful. Her fur looked shiny and clean. There were no horrors to be found on the page.

"Sorry, it's not finished yet," Dylan said gently, grabbing the sketchbook out of Flora's hands. A blush covered his face; she was unsure if he woke up that way or if he was embarrassed that she saw his work. Smiling Flora leaned in closer to Dylan, invading his personal space.

"Why be sorry?" she asked, raising an eyebrow in question. Teasing Dylan had to be one of her new favorite pastimes. Something about getting under his skin enticed her.

"I — I don't know, you just weren't meant to see that," he stammered, closing the sketchbook and making his way to the kitchen. Following closely behind, Flora reached her hands onto his broad shoulders, stopping him in place.

"Dylan."

"Yes?" he asked, frozen in place by the feel of Flora's hands on him. He could've kept walking, letting her hands fall from his shoulders, but he stayed.

"I love the sketch you made for my panther," Flora said. Heat was building up in her own cheeks. There was no stopping now that she had started. "No one looks at a panther that way, let alone draws one so beautifully. Thank you for drawing her."

Letting her hands fall down his back, she felt each curve and mound of his wide back, not slapping his ass like she suddenly wanted to. Flora gathered herself, sliding past him back to her breakfast. These hot feelings coursing through her body landed in spots that they most definitely should not have. The man drew her animal, and she was ready to jump his bones. Was that all it really took for her?

Not saying anything, Dylan remained still for a moment before continuing to the kitchen. Flora was now super aware of where he was in her apartment, her body attuned to his every move.

"I have work today," Flora stated trying to fill the silence of the now overheated room.

"I know, me too. All day, right?" Dylan asked, even though he knew her schedule like the back of his hand. He dragged his hand down the handle of the fridge, before pulling it open. Flora watched his eyes search the contents. Biting the inside of her lip, she needed to pull herself together.

"Yeah, I'm going to get dressed," she informed him before rushing off to her room. What better way to pull herself together than to pull together an outfit? After her morning routine filled with 10 different skin products and a hair oil for her scalp, she pulled out one of her go-to outfits, an all-black number: wide legged dress pants and a tiny top. She paired the ensemble with her most comfortable black heels and silver jewelry.

"Is that even appropriate for the workplace?" Dylan asked, dressed in a similar hoodie and flannel combo as the first time she met him at the Enchanted Packhouse.

"In *my* workplace, it is," Flora said, giving him a twirl of her outfit, but really just wanting to see the movement of her pants flow as she spun.

"Okay, well, you got a jacket or something? It's cold as shit," Dylan asked, looking for a jacket for her. She had an oversized shawl at the office that would do just fine. Leaning on the back of her couch, she crossed her arms.

"Well, are you done questioning me or are you going to ask if I have a bra or underwear on too?"

Dylan played off the potentially inappropriate question with a cough before wordlessly walking out the door. Pushing herself off the couch, she followed behind him once again, getting a nice view of his ass in his jeans before she walked faster to be beside him.

❧

After her morning meeting of prepping her shoe designs for sampling finished, Dylan sat in a chair in front of her desk, sketching, while she worked on her computer, entering the last notes on the shoe sketches before sending them to her team.

After having many failed attempts to design these shoes, her special project, the stripper collection, would finally move to production.

"Okay, so the sketches are sent, and the sample should be

ready for pick-up in a few weeks when I go on my trip out to the production factory," Flora mumbled as she emailed the design team and Willow.

"I wanna see your panther use this," Dylan said, pointing to Flora's custom-made mini jungle tree on the left side of her office. The same one Willow pointed out, Flora knew it would stick out here but there was no room for it in her one-bedroom apartment.

"What if my panther isn't so nice this time?" she questioned. She knew he saw her fight the other day but fighting and meeting were two different things, and she was surprised her panther didn't try to attack Dylan in the heat of the moment.

"I'm sure she likes me."

"Oh, really?" Flora asked, finding herself leaning into him.

"Yup, she was feeling up on me, loving and licking me, too," Dylan said, tracing his hands where her panther must have licked him. Flora wasn't sure if she should take him seriously or not with the joking tone he was using. Playing along, she decided to turn the tables on him.

"Would you like it if I did that?"

"Technically, you did," Dylan's smirk irked her. He normally blushed at her sexual tactics, not served it back to her. The mental image of her licking Dylan's body caused heat to pool inside her for the second time that day. Changing the subject, Flora cleared her throat before responding.

"Anyways, shifting is not allowed in the building."

"Then why is this here?" Dylan asked, turning to look at the jungle gym. For a fake tree, it was pretty realistic.

"Because when I am *alone*, I break the rules," Flora said, tapping her fingernails on the arm of her chair.

"Such a bad girl," Dylan tsked.

"Only for you, Dylan," Flora winked, adjusting the thin straps of her top, an unconscious habit of hers.

"Do you have time to shift?"

"Dylan, no."

"Flora…" Dylan sang, finally relaxing into his chair with his sketchpad lying in his lap.

Willow popped into Flora's office; her head full of auburn curls. "Don't forget your meeting at three today with the production factory."

"That's why I love you, Willow. What would I do without you?"

"Crumble, perish, maybe miss your production meeting, who knows," Dylan answered.

Willow giggled as she entered the office, sitting next to Dylan in front of Flora's desk.

"I don't think Cassandra or Romeo would let you miss their meeting," Willow said, closing her iPad and pushing her glasses up.

"Cassandra and Romeo?" Dylan asked.

"Be careful who you mention around Dylan," Flora joked her gaze meeting his, "He might start thinking they're my attackers."

"Wait, what?" Willow exclaimed, straightening her back. "Did you ever think I was the attacker?" she asked Dylan.

"Yes, anyone could be the attacker. Most commonly it's someone the victim knows," Dylan nonchalantly said.

"What changed your mind that it wasn't me?" Willow asked, leaning against the arm of her chair, more curious than offended.

"You're too smart; this person attacked in broad daylight while she was with me," Dylan simply said, tapping his fingers on the desk. Flora noticed his habit was similar to hers. Chuckling, she looked away, newly interested in the painting of a pond in a jungle hanging on the wall.

"Well, thank you," Willow said, a smile covering her face as she looks away trying to cover her face with her hair.

"That's no surprise; Willow's too smart to be caught doing something dumb like that," Flora teased her friend.

Though if Willow for some reason wanted to kidnap or attack someone, that someone would be in a world of trouble. With Willow physically and mentally strong, Flora was sure her animal was, too. Add passion and intelligence to the top of the Willow cake and that was one badass mix.

"Okay, okay guys. I'm outta here," Willow said, making her way out of the office.

"Love you!" Flora shouted before the door closed behind Willow.

Turning her attention back to her computer, she sighed, setting up her camera for the next meeting. Being all the way in Moonlight City, a good three hours away, meetings with the production team were mostly held online.

"Dylan, can you bring my ring light over?" Flora asked, pointing to it across the room.

Without hesitation he grabbed what she pointed at and set the mini light on her desk, trying to find a plug.

"Where the hell?" he mumbled, searching the extension cord by her desk for an available outlet.

"I just plug it into my computer." Flora took the cord from his hand, enjoying the little contact they made. "Thanks though."

"So back to this Cassandra and Romeo business."

"They own the production factory out in Moonlight City. Both are lovely people who are incredibly kind. Sure, they're bossy some times and smothering at others. But they have no reason to try to harm me. They are as invested in my business as I am. Cassandra and Romeo are married and seemingly happy. They built a shoe production factory in their thirties. They lost their daughter a few years back but seem to have bounced back."

"You noticed you said 'seem' quite a few times?" Dylan asked, his suspicion rising.

"I used "seem" like twice, Dylan. Plus, I don't really know these people. I occasionally have lunch with them."

"Let me attend the meeting."

"No."

"You're preventing me from doing my job to the fullest."

"Dylan," Flora whined, setting her ring light to the right position for her call.

"Flora, let me attend the meeting."

Debating for a moment, Flora weighed her options. There was really no harm in letting Dylan attend the video call. "Is there a way for you to watch without them knowing you're there? We'd have to do introductions and they'll have tons of questions, and I don't have the time or energy for that."

"Let me call Felix, he'll know how we could get that done." Dylan said already typing away on his phone.

"Now, who is Felix?" Flora asked, if only just to be a smartass.

"A Packmate. He's a tech genius who would know how to add me to the call without the other participants knowing." The crushing reminder that Dylan was part of a Pack upset Flora's solitary nature. Panthers didn't grow up in Packs, let alone join them as adults. Not that she wanted to; most Packs didn't stray from their own species. Even if they did, the chances of them *letting* her in were slim to none. A panther's reputation of being too strong for an Alpha to lead was too much to overlook.

Being romantically involved with Dylan would mean him leaving his Pack, assuming Jackson wouldn't let her join their Pack. She didn't want to put Dylan in a position where he'd have to choose between them. Joining the Pack seemed like the next reasonable solution but a panther in a Pack was unheard of. Inserting a panther in the mix was probably too much risk for him to take.

Dylan probably didn't like her like that anyway.

Flora flipped through her notes of each design, as he got his phone set up for the call.

Minding her own, Flora wiped her hands along her pants. Knowing that Dylan suspected Cassandra and Romeo to be her potential stalkers made her paranoid and she couldn't even figure out what to think about it all. Pushing it away, she pressed the call button on the video conference system. Appearing on the camera she put a smile on her face.

Cassandra and Romeo popped on the screen with a great big hello. The owners of Moonlight Production were in their late 40s, Flora guessed, and had been married for decades.

"You've got your braids back in, honeypie," Cassandra pointed out, her honey-toned finger pointed at the screen.

"Yes, Cassandra. I put them in a few weeks ago," Flora said, pulling a few of her black braids forward.

"Beautiful, just like our little girl," Cassandra mumbled looking Romeo's way. Flora stole a glance up at Dylan, trying to read his face, which of course was as blank as a damn whiteboard.

"Thank you," Flora smiled, bringing her attention back to the couple on the screen. "So, how did those new designs look? Is there any note that should be made before sampling?"

"These are perfect, honeypie. The structural issues we had before are fixed within the design and we can produce the samples for you, no problem. Thanks to our personal investment," Romeo said, his gray eyes shining through the screen.

"I can't say how grateful I am, for you putting a part of your savings into funding this extra collection. I really couldn't have gotten it done without you," Flora thanked them. The length of time the pole shoe collection was taking to get through production really ate at her revenue and shit was sinking faster than she could've imagined.

After bidding farewell, Flora ended the call. Her eyes found Dylan's with a sharpness. She knew he would give her his opinion on the lovely couple who had given *her* no reason to be suspicious of anything for years. "What do you think?"

"How long ago did they lose their daughter?"

"Three years ago. Why does that matter?" Flora asked.

"How old was she?"

"I don't know, 18, maybe."

This was making her uneasy. Clueless was not a normal state of mind for Flora and it was making the atmosphere hot with uncomfortable tension.

"How old are you?"

"How rude," she joked. "What does that matter? You know we age faster than we look after 20." In the supernatural world, older was better; didn't matter if you were a man, woman, binary, in-between, a lion, or a squirrel. Ages 21-35 were considered young and dumb, and the years were often filled with embarrassment and being talked down to by elders.

"You're right," he said, holding his chin in his hand. "It doesn't matter. You look anywhere from 19 to 27."

"You should apologize."

"What?' Dylan asked as if snapped out of a daydream.

"You never ask a woman her age," Flora explained. Asking for an apology was only a distraction. She wasn't sure if she wanted to know what Dylan thought about Cassandra and Romeo. She had known them since the founding of Dainty Rebel and didn't want to think of them betraying her, let alone trying to hurt her.

"I'm sorry; I should have never asked a lady her age," Dylan apologized, a small laugh escaping him as he leaned back into his chair.

"I forgive you. Ready to go get something to eat?" Flora asked, grabbing her purse.

"I'm always ready to eat."

10

FLORA

"Walk on the inside of me, Flora."

"Even inside a restaurant?"

"Even inside a restaurant," Dylan confirmed, guiding Flora to walk alongside him so that he was between her and the wall that was lined with windows. Flora assumed he thought maybe someone would try to shoot her through the glass or something. It was like him knowing her animal changed the way he acted around her— which initially scared her — but Dylan turned overwhelmingly protective of her. It was his job, of course, but having him walk into the bathroom with her and listen to her pee with only a stall door separating them was embarrassing.

Walking into Eleanor's Diner, Flora's eyes instantly searched for Willow and Luxe. Finding them in one of Eleanor's classic red vinyl booths along the wall of windows, she strode away from Dylan. Surprised he let her walk ahead, she walked even faster in case he changed his mind. Flora spotted Jackson sitting a few booths away from the girls. He must be here for Dylan, she assumed, sliding in across from her friends.

"Hello, ladies," Flora smiled, feeling a sense of relief sliding over her body. Seeing Willow and Luxe, the closest friends she'd ever had, brought her a peace of mind she hadn't had in a while.

"Hello, *Mrs. Enchanted*. Do you two always walk together now?" Willow asked, sipping on her iced tea, swinging her finger between Flora and Dylan.

"It's not a big deal, he's just doing his job, and it's Ms. Larkspur, *Ms. Buttercup*."

"The same job he refused compensation for? The same job where he was supposed to watch you from a distance but decided to watch from up close?" Luxe smirked.

"Yes, the same one." Flora suddenly felt flushed with the realization that her and Dylan's relationship was vastly outside the contracted behavior between business partners, once again highlighting why she needed to destroy these seemingly small but frantically growing romantic feelings she had for him.

"More like a boyfriend, even," Luxe suggested, throwing a wink Flora's way.

"I wouldn't say that," Flora denied. She distracted herself with the menu she'd already memorized from her previous visits to Eleanor's. She'd been going there a lot since she preferred the diner's cooking over her own.

"Whatever you say, girly."

Running a hand through her straightened ash-blonde hair, Luxe tried to steal a glance behind Flora, ogling the man she'd been crushing on from a few booths down. Flora turned to find Dylan had taken a seat with Jackson, sitting where he could still watch her without craning his neck.

"How are things with you and Jackson?" Flora asked, setting the menu aside, eager to switch the topic off of herself.

"There is no 'me and Jackson'. He's not interested," Luxe pouted. Luxe was a beautiful girl who was a "head first, feet later" kind of woman. She must have had deep feelings for Jackson if she hadn't asked him out already at that point. She didn't usually have a problem asking guys out, so Flora wondered what was really going on there.

"He rejected you?" Flora whispered, surprised beyond belief. "I swore I thought he liked you more than a friend."

"I would've thought he was head over heels for you," Willow added. Jackson didn't act like a guy who just wanted to be friends with Luxe. Letting his Pack member be a bodyguard for a friend of a friend without compensation or a favor of any kind was a huge tell he had feelings for Luxe.

"It was years ago."

"Has he smelled one of your farts? Cause the shit you let out be deadly," Flora joked, trying to lighten up the mood.

"Flora!" Luxe nearly shouted, covering her face with her hands. "He hasn't fully rejected me; he says it's not the right time." She looked out the window, her 'girl in love' gaze following the clouds outside.

"Darling, I'm sorry some men don't know a good thing standing right in front of them," Flora said with a sigh.

"Yeah, maybe he uses a two-in-one in the shower or something," Willow commented, pushing her glasses down her nose. Willow had never talked or showed interest in men, or women, literally anyone before.

"What does that have to do with anything?" Luxe asked.

"That should go without saying, Luxe," Flora giggled. She subconsciously looked for the wavy-haired man behind her.

"Why do you separate shampoo and conditioner?" Willow continued on, suddenly serious.

"Because they do different things?" Luxe said.

"So how could they be in the same bottle, but wash and condition hair at the same time?" Willow asked, confusion written all over her face. "Something's wrong there; how clean and conditioned could someone's hair really be if they used a two-in-one?" Willow elaborated, frustration filling the edge in her voice.

"Oh, you know what? You're so right," Luxe agreed. Shaking her head, she continued, "But no, Jackson uses a shampoo and conditioner — no two-in-ones."

"So there goes Willow's logic. Maybe Jackson's just crazy."

Flora didn't believe that puppy dog-in-love sitting a few booths over hadn't made his move yet. It wasn't like an Alpha to not take what they wanted. Flora turned back to glance at Jackson to see his head turned toward their booth, an eyebrow raised in confusion.

"I forgot about super hearing; let's change the topic."

"So, Willow, is anything going on with you, girly?" Flora asked. Nothing was ever really new with them since they talked nearly every day, but filling the silence was a terrible and uncontrollable habit.

"It would be better if I knew you were safe and staying with me."

"That's not necessary; you know protecting me is Dylan's job, not yours." Flora met her friend's concerned gaze. Willow had brought this up before, but Flora rejected the offer. Though it might have sounded like a good idea before she 'hired' Dylan, now that they were together all hours of the day, she deemed it unnecessary to put Willow in potential danger like that. More than she already had anyway. Who knew what her attackers already knew about Flora?

"Is Dylan staying in the apartment with you, cause if he's not..."

"Yes, actually he is," Flora cut Willow off from beginning her rant of worry. Dylan actually agreed to stay in her apartment recently, but if she could just get him to eat her food, or at least let her pay for his own...

"Where is he sleeping?" Luxe suggestively asked, wiggling her eyebrows.

"On the couch, smartass." Flora blushed suddenly, wishing the questioning would stop. Thinking about Dylan was something she did all the time but was definitely not what she should be doing just then. The whole point of this lunch was to get some separation from the guy. Now it seemed not only could she not stop thinking about him, but her friends also couldn't stop talking about him, either.

"Is that all?" Luxe urged from the other side of the dull, white table. Rolling her eyes, Flora crossed her arms, and glanced back at her friend.

"What more could there be to tell?"

"Oh, I don't know. Maybe if this is turning out to be some romance movie where the girl falls in love with the big strong guy protecting her..."

"Yes, because it is totally realistic to be falling in love while at the same time being targeted and attacked by an unknown psycho. Love and intense anxiety go hand-in-hand," Flora teased, earning a chuckle from both the girls. The real fact of the matter was that they weren't too far from the truth and that scared her shitless.

11

DYLAN

"How has it been going? Not too difficult protecting Flora and managing your job at Lust Lane, is it?" Jackson asked. Dylan's eyes stayed trained on Flora as she made her way to her table, taking his seat only after she took hers. She needed space and he'd give her as much as he could. A space surrounded by her friends and his. He would focus on the space they occupied together, not the words that flowed from her mouth or the way she'd rest her head on her hand.

Dylan ran his hand through his hair; this was supposed to be separation time for them, but it seemed like all he could think about was the woman a few booths away.

"No problems," he reported, letting his dark brown eyes search the area, as he did every five to ten minutes in any new, open setting he and Flora were in. With the attackers still unidentified, they could have quite literally been anyone in the room.

"Okay, good. I wasn't sure how'd you do working two jobs at once, but since the club doesn't need you every day, I hoped it would work out."

"I miss the Packhouse," Dylan said mindlessly. Though he enjoyed being with Flora, way more than he thought he would, his Pack was his home, and being away for so long worried him. He didn't want the Pack to get used to him being away. An irrational fear of being left out or alone crept up on Dylan after seeing his Alpha again.

"We miss you, too. It's important to keep the Pack together," Jackson responded. He leaned against the wall of windows, further bending his legs to fit his 6'3" frame within the booth.

"I don't think it's just one person behind this," Dylan said, picking up his straw and dropping it into his cup. He didn't want to admit it could be a bigger operation than just a lonely guy with a borderline obsession in Flora. That would be way easier to handle than a group of people after her. Dylan could see the interest — he himself had the interest. Flora was a beautiful woman with her warm, creamy skin, dark brown eyes, and thick thighs. Who wouldn't want to be with her? The question was why go to such extreme lengths to get her when a conversation could've gotten her attention? Unless it wasn't about affection but something else.

"In the parking lot, there were two people there. One tried to grab her, and the other waited behind the building as backup. They were using scent blockers, too. They were way too prepared for this for it to be something small."

"Hmm." Jackson knew this opened up a huge can of worms. The only thing that came to Dylan's mind was cage fighting. Someone could have found out what her animal was and saw dollar signs. If this was the case, then the issue could potentially never be solved. Even if Dylan killed the group trying to capture her, another group would replace the dead one and the cycle wouldn't end.

As much as he wanted to pick Jackson's thoughts on the

cage fighting matter, he couldn't. Revealing what Flora's animal was wasn't his place, even in regard to his Alpha. Betraying her like that would completely break whatever was going on between them and in his heart, he wasn't ready to let that go. Being around Flora was something he would severely miss when this problem was resolved.

"You know I'm here for you. The Pack is here for you, so don't forget to reach out," Jackson said. Dylan knew he could reach out for help at any moment, but he'd wait until he absolutely had to. This was his job. He'd taken out whole cage fighting rings, big mafia-like operations, and corrupt Packs with his old crew. Maybe he should reach out to them if his prediction was right. In the end, though, he knew he could handle this with or without them.

"I've got this, but the minute I don't, I'll call."

"We'll be ready."

Dylan ordered food, trying to take his mind off of Flora and her situation. Cage fighting was incredibly dangerous. If someone was targeting her because they knew she was a panther, this changed what he had to do. Collectors got desperate around panthers. The only way to get those guys off Flora's back was to kill them all. Every single collector that had knowledge of her panther would have to die. Trying to relieve some of the weight building on his chest through a deep breath, he directed his attention to the beautiful woman sitting across the room.

He'd do it. Something in his gut told him he'd do in a heartbeat whatever it took to protect Flora. He would kill every man and woman involved in this fighting ring. No exclusions or exceptions. She had stuck her pointed heel in the ground and swung open the door of his soul.

"You're falling for her," Jackson whispered, staring Dylan

down from his side of the booth. Energy filled the small area around them. Alphas naturally had power radiating from them, one demanding submission. While most Alphas let the power fill a room, Jackson tried to hold it back when it wasn't necessary. It allowed him to create tighter bonds with the members of his Pack, giving them the choice to follow him instead of forcing them too.

Why he was exuding power threw Dylan off. "You haven't stopped looking at her since you sat down. Not in just a protective way but in a..." Jackson paused to think of the right word, "hopelessly in love kind of way."

"You a songwriter now? Somebody call Leo Enchanted, he's got a new partner," Dylan tried to joke and move the topic away from Jackson's prying nature, but that Alpha energy started to get to him. Honesty was going to start spilling from him any minute. He wasn't even sure Jackson knew he was doing it. What would get him so worked up about being romantically involved with Flora?

"Got jokes now?" Jackson replied with a laugh, looking back at the girl's table.

"I wouldn't say love."

"Well definitely more than *like*."

"Maybe somewhere in between," Dylan said, dragging his eyes away from the woman he knew he'd been obviously staring at the whole time.

"Be careful," Jackson said, turning serious. "She is not one of us, so keep that in mind. People judge hard on that kind of shit."

Dylan knew Jackson got a lot of heat for having a mixed-animal Pack. The Pack was mostly made up of wolves, but they had a bear and crow as well. Both Dylan and Jackson wouldn't have it any other way, but that didn't stop others from feeling the need to give their two cents; even going as far as to challenge them. Fighting for his Pack was nothing new to Dylan, but Jackson hated the way others made his non-wolf Pack members feel. Adding Flora to the mix would stir the pot even more. A personal battle for not only Dylan but the Pack. Was it selfish to still want her? Was Jackson truly upset about it? Dylan's Pack meant everything to him. Jackson had to know that, right?

The person any of the Pack members fell in love with and wanted to mate would have to become part of the Pack. And mating was basically supernatural marriage. Supernaturals lived a long time and mated for life. It was a big deal to find a soulmate, and Dylan was beginning to think that maybe, just *maybe,* he'd found his.

Dylan's eyes floated back to Flora. His potential soulmate was currently being flirted with. A tall Shifter leered over their table, smiling and laughing as if the attention was welcomed, and based on Luxe's face, it wasn't. As the man flirted, Dylan tried to stay rooted to his seat. He wanted to scare the man away for even talking to his woman. But he had to weigh his options on whether dealing with a pissed Flora was worth it. He decided to wait it out. She didn't need him to jump into every seemingly normal conversation she had in public.

He settled on a glare. At first, anyway. Using his enhanced hearing, he focused on the conversation taking place. He gripped the table, trying his hardest not to jump up.

"Um, no I would not like to get a coffee with you. Thank you for the offer." Flora was trying to be polite, but the niceness in her tone slowly started to slip away. The Shifter wasn't a bad-looking guy, Dylan thought. Fairly tall, muscled, and in a crisp dress shirt. Hopefully, for Dylan's sake, Flora was more into a sour-patch-kid kind of man instead of the classic businessman type.

"How about lunch another time?" he asked, leaning down closer toward her, towering over her as if that would change her mind.

"Can't take a no, big guy?" Luxe sneered from the opposite side of the table. Her own Alpha energy filled the area. Anyone with eyes could tell she was becoming pissed and *fast*. Hey eyes were glowing, showing her animal was near the surface and just as angry as Luxe was. Disrespecting someone in the presence of an Alpha was almost a death wish. If death wasn't an option, then it was surely asking for an ass-kicking. Alphas were creatures who valued respect. The minute respect was gone was the minute things become hostile.

"I wasn't talking to you, sweet cheeks."

"Sweet cheeks," Luxe barked out. "That's the best you could come up with?"

"Look, you little —"

Dylan couldn't take the banter anymore. The male Shifter wasn't a huge threat, but disrespecting anyone, especially women (add an Alpha woman on the top of that cake), was a no-go, and it was time to put a swift end to it. Making eye contact with Jackson, he nodded his head giving Dylan the okay to do whatever he felt he needed to do.

Standing from the booth, Dylan swiftly pulled out one of his many little black spades. Feeling the cool metal in his hand, he took a deep breath before getting into the throwing position, feet shoulder-width apart and pointing forward. Like a string pulling his arm forward he let go of the knife, sending it flying through the air before landing on Flora's table, right in front of the man's hand.

The guy jumped back, hands in the air as a surrender. Luxe was too pissed to move, no jumping or no backing down. Walking up to the table, Dylan looked the guy up and down. His shirt stretched tight as he pulled the blade from the table. Wiping it with his shirt, he put it back in one of his many weapons pockets.

"Okay, pretty boy. It's time to leave," Dylan said, keeping his face emotionless. He didn't necessarily want to spark an ego-fueled fight, but he wouldn't be opposed if the asshole swung first.

"Pretty boy? You got to be fucking kidding me."

"I'm not, and you got a pissed-off Alpha ready to hand your ass to you on a silver platter." Dylan paused and looked back to Luxe, asking "Alpha?"

"I prefer Luna, thank you." she said confidently.

Female Alphas preferred the title "Alpha" as much as they did "Luna", so they seemed just like men, but it was always polite to ask anyway.

"So not only have you pissed off a Luna, you've also pissed off me and the woman you tried to ask on a date. Do you see the situation you're in right now?" Dylan tried to reason with him, giving the guy an undeserving out.

"Whatever, she wasn't all that anyway." The guy tried walking away, but before he could get very far, Dylan grabbed the back of the stranger's head and slammed it against the nearest table.

"Next time, just walk away quietly," Dylan whispered before pushing the guy forward and out the door. "Enjoy your lunch, ladies."

"Alrighty, Prince Charming," Luxe giggled, seemingly in a better mood.

Dylan looked back to a flushed Flora, whose brown freckles

seemed to be shining against her skin. Sending her a wink, he rejoined Jackson at their table.

"Definitely more than friends, my guy," Jackson muttered with a deep laugh.

"Okay, I just need to do a few more checks over the structure, then I will be ready to officially confirm these sketches to the production factory for sampling," Flora muttered, the Lust Lane special shoe collection splayed out in front of her.

"Then the hardest part will be done?" Dylan guessed, sharpening dull pencils from Flora's desk.

"Yes, exactly," Flora said with a sigh. As much as she wanted to get these designs done and over with, she couldn't afford to get them wrong again. The budget for this project was running thin as was her patience to continue. Even with Cassandra's and Romeo's investment, she had to count her pennies. As much as she loved the idea of this project, it hurt to send back bad samples and she didn't want to continue disappointing the girls at Lust Lane and herself.

Why was this so damn difficult? She should've been done with this months ago. A whole year of designing and sampling slipped past her, and she wasn't sure how to interpret it. Was she just not as good of a designer as she thought?

"Lean back, Flora." A monotone voice broke her train of thought. Jumping from fright, her eyes shot up to Dylan's.

"What?" she asked.

"Relax, press your back into your chair." He said it as if it was common sense for him to even notice something like that. Following his instruction, she leaned into her chair wordlessly, pressing as much of her back into the chair as she could. Taking a deep breath, her heart began to beat normally again.

"Dylan, are you single?" Flora blurted out.

"I notice one habit you have and you're in love? Never thought it would be so easy."

"Answer the question, Dylan."

"Why?' he asked, a smirk growing on his face. Flora flushed, embarrassed she wanted to know the answer.

"Because, asshole, your girlfriend, mate, whatever would be pretty upset with you spending so much time with me." She hoped he'd buy the lame ass excuse she was selling. Rolling a pencil between her fingers, she silently hoped that there was no girlfriend or soulmate in the picture. That would rip her own soul out, crushing it into a thousand pieces.

"Did you see any women at the Packhouse?" he asked, leaning in closer to her from his chair across her desk. Looking off into space, as if thinking, she tried to recall the ten minutes she'd spent in the house. There was no recollection of any female presence in the house besides hers and Luxe's.

"No, but I didn't even meet the whole Pack so how would I really know?" She raised an eyebrow, challenging him. Taking the bait, he stood up, making his presence felt in the room. Flora knew he was second-in-command, a right hand to the Alpha; but this feeling was different. He was pressuring her to listen, to get closer. She was drawn to him. Even with her internal body heat rising, shivers still ran down Flora's arms.

"No, I don't have a mate...or a girlfriend," he said. He kept his eyes trained on hers for what felt like five minutes before he slowly sat back down, that damn smirk still on his face. She knew he got to her, and he knew it too. Flipping her hair off her shoulder, she turned toward her computer. While she had plenty of things she could be doing, she pretended to write an email.

"I have a question, too."

"What is your question?"

"Have you fallen for me yet, Flora?"

Flora began to choke on air, the shock taking a firm hold of her throat. Dylan handed her a water bottle. Taking a sip, she glanced over at him. Would he be disgusted if she had a crush on him? Did he actually care? Would he be happy? Who the hell knew — his stoic, chiseled face wasn't giving away shit.

"I'll let you get away with that one, Flora Larkspur." He laughed, the same sound that made her heartbeat faster.

Flora rolled her eyes jokingly.

"Damn," he muttered.

Damn? What does he mean by 'damn'? Damn, she doesn't have feelings for him? Damn, he really missed a bullet with that one? Feeling lost, she focused on her computer screen, trying to forget the conversation that took place.

"Okay, so what do you think about Hale from the printer room?" she asked, trying to change the subject. She looked for any reason to avoid answering the question, even if that meant going through their potential suspect list.

"He's on my list of suspects. He was staring a little too hard."

"Maybe he had a crush?"

"On you? That would only add proof to the pudding."

"No silly, you," Flora said, laughing at the shocked expression on his face.

"On me?" he asked, pointing to himself.

"Yeah, he's gay and loves a bad boy dressed in black." Flora laughed at the idea Dylan didn't think he was attractive to his own gender. Who wouldn't fall for the dreamy bad boy? Flora sure couldn't stop herself.

⚜

"Hey, um, I forgot my phone in the car; will you be okay getting in?" Dylan asked, patting his pockets.

"I'm a grown woman, Dylan. I can handle it," Flora said with a nervous laugh. She'd seen Dylan do this a thousand times. She could check her own apartment. Even so, the fear built up with each step she took alone up her apartment stairs. She could hear her car door open, and knew Dylan wasn't far. But why did she feel as if she was completely alone?

Flora steadied her hand on the doorknob before unlocking it. She walked into the apartment, searching as Dylan normally did before finding herself back in the kitchen. That wasn't too bad: checking the windows, in closets, and under furniture, running her hands along surfaces and under lamp shades for recording devices. The search came up clean, as it had been for the last three weeks. Setting the keys down on the black countertop, she plopped onto the barstool at the kitchen's mini island. She let her head collapse into her arms, wondering where this all started. From being stalked to needing a bodyguard, being attacked, and not knowing what would come next.

Tears welled up as frustration built from her throat. Flora's body shook with each silent sob. The embarrassment she felt for having to need protection became overwhelming. Since when was the protection from her panther not enough? Since when had she actually *needed* someone else? Sitting in the kitchen the silence rang in her ears begging for any small noise. Being alone had become a double-edged sword. On one side, Flora could unleash the cries she'd been holding in since that morning. On the other, she was open to attacks from anyone — her attacker included.

Consistent tapping noises filled the kitchen. Wiping a tear away, Flora dragged herself off the stool and listened, trying to figure out what made the noise without moving too much.

"Enough, Dylan, this is not the time," Flora's shoulders rose with tension. He'd never joked like this before, but she really hoped it was him. Thinking for a moment, she realized that she didn't hear the door open, and that Dylan hadn't come in yet. Looking around Flora listened to the sound, it was repeated over and over and getting louder as seconds passed. With shaky sock-covered steps, she walked toward the window in the living room, following the sound. With trembling hands, she opened the curtains an inch, and peeked out the window.

She let out a scream and fell backward onto the floor. A medium sized rock bounced off her window. Scrambling back, she bumped into the couch, sending another wave of terror through her body. A pounding on the door made her jump.

"Flora, I'm opening the door. It's Dylan," Dylan's panicked voice yelled from outside the apartment. He shot into the room, eyes searching for danger. Seeing Flora curled up on the floor with tear-stained cheeks, he darted toward her.

"The window! Someone is trying to break in," she screamed, pointing to the only window with the curtain open. She focused on the sound of Dylan busting open the window, checking for someone, anything that was out of the norm. Once he deemed the apartment was safe, he ran back to her.

"They must have run off when I came in."

By that point, Flora was curled up on the hardwood floor behind the couch, facing away from the window. Her legs were pulled into her chest as she firmly pressed her back into the couch. Her eyes tracked Dylan's movements, trying to find something to focus on. Dylan took a deep breath before taking a seat next to her, his legs spread out on the floor. Moments passed, as they both sat there staring at nothing. Silence welcomed them as Dylan regulated his breathing and Flora's thoughts raced.

"Before you run deeper into the darkness of your mind, tell me what happened," Dylan suggested, still not looking her way.

Flora took a deep breath of relief at the sight of Dylan before starting to explain. "I saw someone-outside my window."

"How did you know someone was there if the curtains were closed?" Dylan asked, confusion clear in his voice.

"Tapping. They were throwing rocks at the window. I went looking for what was making that noise."

"First problem: next time, just call me."

"I just told you someone was outside my window. Shouldn't you go look for them?" Flora snapped. She closed her eyes, but immediately re-opened them, realizing that not being able to see just made her feel worse.

"I would if I could smell them. I opened the windows during my search to catch a scent. I didn't," Dylan grimaced, dropping his head in disappointment. If only he'd been faster getting up the steps, or if he'd searched the outside first maybe he would've caught the guy. Knowing that neither option would lead to success, and that he took the correct steps to handle the situation, Flora stopped trying to blame him. She couldn't help her Negative Nancy thoughts getting louder and louder in these situations.

"Well thank you, Dylan, for rushing to my aid. This is more serious than I've been letting myself believe."

"Anytime. It's my job."

The digital clock on her countertop ticked away the silence that passed by, neither making a move. Flora stared at Dylan then, hot emotions taking a hold of her throat. She needed to take all this more seriously. Someone was out to get her, for what she had no idea. The sooner she accepted that, the better she'd be prepared.

"I think you should come with me tonight," Dylan said, getting up. He checked the time on his phone. It was 8:45 pm, time for his shift bodyguarding the strip club.

"I agree, being alone is the last thing I want right now." Flora's smile didn't reach her eyes, but she made an attempt.

Standing, Flora reached her hand out to Dylan. She was going to be out late, and for once she wanted to be comfy.

"I wanna change."

"Be my guest."

"Will you stand outside my door?" Flora asked, tapping her hand against her hip, nervous to even ask her bodyguard to do such a thing.

"Was going to." He grabbed her hand and followed her to her room, dutifully stopping outside the door to wait as he said he would.

With that, she went to change out of her office attire. She dressed down, in a matching black sports bra and leggings, paired with leg warmers bunched up at her ankles. In her foyer, Flora laced up her black and white high-top sneakers and stared at his black boots as he walked out the door. How long did germs take to transfer from the bottom of a boot to the carpet?

Dylan abruptly stopped just in front of the door with his hand on the knob. He stood still for a second, contemplating something. All she could think about was getting out of her apartment.

"You need a jacket," Dylan insisted, leaning against the door, crossing his arms as if ready for a fight. "It's cold as shit out there. The last thing Miss CEO needs is to catch a cold. 'I don't need no protection' Flora is annoying already; imagine taking care of a sick Flora." She felt like Dylan was staring at the bags under her eyes and she couldn't keep her shoulders upright anymore let alone be bothered with being insecure about her face.

Shock colored Dylan's face as Flora agreed to wear a jacket without a fight. She was still frazzled and listening was just easier. Taking off her shoes, she re-entered her bedroom and grabbed a baby pink zip-up hoodie.

"Wait dumbass, Shifters don't get sick like humans do," Flora said as she slid the oversized jacket on. Meeting him back at the door

"Wrong. Normal human diseases and germs don't *usually* harm us, but that doesn't mean we shouldn't protect ourselves; Shifters can still get a cold."

"What do you mean, wrong? I've never heard of a Shifter getting a cold or any other human diseases," Flora claimed, thinking he was just pulling her leg.

"Wrong," Dylan said again. Taking a deep breath, "My dad died from cancer."

"Cancer?" Flora whispered, reaching for his hand. His eyes filled with emptiness. Flora took her fingers and interlocked them with his, pressing the back of his hand to her face. "I'm so sorry."

She couldn't help the pity and sadness that filled her. She

wanted to ask why his dad's Shifter body didn't cure his cancer but figured she shouldn't. It happened and that was reason enough to be careful.

"It's okay. Just wear the jacket," he said shortly, moving his eyes away from hers. "Please."

Without a word, Dylan zipped up the soft hoodie, being extra careful to not make contact with the exposed skin of her stomach. Flora could see his cheeks turning red. It made her feel better, distracted even from her fear of being watched. Their heavy breaths and the sound of her zipper broke the silence. Dylan refused to make eye contact as he swiftly turned around and left the apartment.

Flora smirked, following close behind him. Flora was an attractive person, from the way she looked and dressed, to the way she carried herself. She knew the attraction other people had for her. The problem was the attraction she'd never had towards them. Picky was an understatement when it came to the people she chose in her life. Batting for both sides of the team, she once thought she would have more potential lovers but that simply wasn't true. A small giggle escaped her as she remembered telling her extremely attractive friends that yes, they were hot but no, they weren't her type and no, she wouldn't go out with them if they were into girls. Standards, types, interests all still played huge factors for bisexuals and everyone else in the dating game.

"What's so funny, kitty cat?" Dylan half-smiled, opening the car door for Flora, a show of chivalry from the big scary man himself.

"I'm not a kitty cat, wolf."

"How'd you know I was a wolf Shifter?" Dylan asked, shutting her door before sliding into the driver seat and pulling out of the apartment parking lot. "I don't remember my wolf meeting you. I was conscious when that other wolf Shifter attacked you. My wolf only saw you..."

"I was only assuming since I know Jackson's a wolf, but you just confirmed it for me," Flora winked. It was only fair she knew his animal, she figured, since he knew hers. While she'd always thought he was a wolf, she wasn't 100% positive. Shifters could be anything. While the personality of Shifters' animals could leak over into their human interactions, no one could ever be absolutely sure.

"The 80s called: they want their leg warmers back," Dylan joked. Flora rolled her eyes, scrunching the off-white leg warmers to achieve her desired look. Inspired by social media, she thought to try the trend out and she thought it was cute.

"You're just mad I make them look cute. Like slouch socks."

"Slouch socks," Dylan questioned. "I've never heard of slouch socks. Are you for real right now?"

"Serious as hell Dylan, look it up," Flora said laughing again.

Once they got to their destination, Dylan opened Flora's door for her, holding a hand out to aid her out of the car.

"How incredibly caring of you, Prince Charming," Flora teased, taking the smooth hand he offered. Interlocking their fingers, she wanted to be closer to him. Physically, mentally, it didn't matter; she'd take anything at that point. The little chivalrous things that Dylan did always made her heart flutter faster, making her blush. Men just didn't do those types of things anymore.

"Anything for the demanding princess of Rainfall Avenue," Dylan played along, moving his hand to guide Flora to the doors of Lust Lane.

13

DYLAN

"Do you think that being here is safe?" Flora asked, taking a seat at a little round table stationed towards the back of the audience. He didn't like to intertwine his two jobs but in his line of work, it is what it is. Today's shift was short: a cover for a buddy who was running late. It was only the beginning of the night when ladies got their solo time on stage. Not giving them a thought beyond safety, he pushed Flora's chair in. Surveying the main floor, he didn't see anything out of the ordinary tonight, but that was the point, right? Whoever was taking these girls took them because it wouldn't look out of the ordinary here. Strippers come and go, whether they find better opportunities, quit, or take a break and that made the job of protecting everyone here more difficult.

Grabbing a nearby chair, Dylan pushed it to their own table and took a seat. Today his shift at the club was to sit in the audience and look for suspicious activity.

"Yes, besides the Packhouse, Lust Lane is an incredibly safe place to be. Considering all the guards around, problems rarely happen within the club. It's what happens outside the club that's dangerous," Dylan explained, taking a sip of water from a plastic bottle. Leaning back, his broad shoulders crowded the space between him and Flora.

"Makes sense." Flora lightly wrapped her fingers around his water bottle, silently asking permission to have some. He let go and stared as she tilted the water bottle up, taking a sip before handing it back to him. Heat filled Dylan's cheeks; the dark lighting and gentleness of Flora's action stirred a whirlwind of hot emotion through him. Smiling slightly, Dylan tilted his head, gazing at the long braids flowing down her back, and her bright pink lower lip, begging to be kissed. His eyes scurried away. The thought of dropping everything and pulling her in for a kiss had come to Dylan's mind multiple times since he'd started working for Flora, and every time it did, he got embarrassed. Even if an opportunity opened for him to act out such a fantasy, he didn't think he would take it. Could two people like them make it? He wasn't sure. What he was sure of was that he didn't like to play games when it came to his romantic relationships. That was probably why he hadn't had very many.

"Yeah, today's shift is short; I only need an hour of your time," Dylan informed her, resting one of his arms on the back of her chair. He was searching for a sign that his action made her uncomfortable, but instead found her relaxing more into his arm. Scooting her chair closer, she leaned her head on his shoulder and closed her eyes. It being midnight, it was no surprise she was tired. This businesswoman was usually off to bed around ten.

He stared at her. All he could do was stare at her. She looked peaceful amidst the loud music and strobing colorful lighting. Flora dressed in one of those kid-sized tops, what she liked to call a crop top. She'd taken off the jacket once they'd entered the club. She was beautiful, graceful, and he could only hope he'd meet a mate who was half the person she was.

"Enjoying the show?" Flora asked, rolling her eyes up to his. Dylan wasn't watching the show — he was watching her and now she knew it. He saw a smirk form on her face, and he could practically hear the chug of wheels in her mind. The hard-on he'd grown just from watching her wasn't hidden under the dark atmosphere of the club, and unfortunately, she noticed that too. Purring, she trailed her hand up his thigh. He choked, sitting up straight and shyly looking around the room. No one noticed, but if they did, they turned away.

"Flora, you're making it worse," Dylan admitted, shifting in his seat. Looking away, heat blazed on his face.

"Aww, Dylan, don't be shy now," Flora continued, crawling into his lap.

Straddling him, she dragged her nails up and down his chest leaving a tingling feeling behind. Rounding her hands around his big shoulders, she looked down at him, his eyes glittering under the lights of the club. Naturally, his rough hands landed on her hips, trying to keep her still. He kept his hands steady, not moving a muscle. Until her glowing eyes meet his. She was as turned on as he was and with a breath of relief, he started moving his hands, massaging her ass.

"Flora, don't play with me." Dylan's eyes began to glow too.

Running her tongue across her teeth, she curled her hands into his dark brown hair, massaging his scalp. Dylan's head fell back as she started to slowly rock her hips against him. Heat was all he could feel. The heat from her skin, heat from his, heat from the room. His heart pounded like it would explode only imagining what it would be like to kiss her. Just as the overwhelming feelings came to a peak, Dylan tightened his grip on Flora's hip before swinging her up and behind him. He stood before a stranger's hand could land on Flora.

"Can I help you?" Dylan growled, his arms flexing, reaching behind him and pulling her closer.

"Nah, man, I'm helping you. The boss is about to check on everyone and seeing you getting action in the middle of the room is asking to be fired." The slightly shorter, muscle-covered, bald man laughed. He pointed to the door labeled BOSS.

With a shake of Dylan's head in thanks, the man walked away. The realization of what they did fell hard on both of them. Dylan didn't mind being fired, not in the moment anyways. Flora's eyes whizzed back and forth in the club, trying to look anywhere but at Dylan. Dylan turned around, facing her, once again re-adjusting his dark-wash jeans. "Look at what you do to me, kitty cat."

"We need a new nickname. Kitty cat isn't going to work." Flora glared at him, but she couldn't hide a small smile. Dylan grabbed Flora's hand, checking the time and seeing his hour was finally up. Writing in the logbook, he marked down the single hour he worked and left with Flora by his side.

Through that intense moment they shared, he knew it wasn't the time to take the jump and kiss her. As badly as he wanted to, he wasn't sure if she really meant to rile them up like that or if the emotions from everything else going on affected her. Confused, he didn't want to make it awkward and ask. He kept quiet about his own questions and feelings as he drove them home.

Flora went straight to her room when they walked through the door. Dylan took that as a sign she was exhausted. Feeling deflated in more ways than one, Dylan took a shower and decided to go to bed. Laying on the couch, he stared at the ceiling. Falling in love wasn't part of his job and was extremely unprofessional. Taking out his sketchbook from the backpack he kept at her place, he began to draw aimlessly. He needed to let go; to relax and stop thinking of what could've been.

After several minutes passed, the image of a particular panther becomes clearer on the page. Shading marks covered his fingers. Admiring his work, he smiled. Flora's panther purred through the page as she did in the woods. Setting the book aside, Dylan finally fell asleep, thinking about the feeling of Flora on his body.

14

FLORA

Flora stretched her arms over her head, tossing in her bed. The sexual tension from last night went unfinished, and the disappointment sent her straight to her room when they got home. Flora was surprised Dylan let her go as far as she did. She was playing with him...until she wasn't. The minute she crawled onto his lap, feeling his arms around her hips, hands inching towards her ass, she thought his shyness was extremely sexy and it turned her on as fast as flipping a switch. Groaning, she turned over in her bed. Heat began to build again. She'd thought she'd be entering her yearly heat — the time when female Shifters' bodies tried to force breeding and mating — with how hot she was for Dylan. Deciding she couldn't do anything about her growing aches, she stood up, her oversized plain white t-shirt barely dropping to her knees. Another day, another opportunity for a toaster pastry. Those damn things were so addicting, she limited herself to one a day. Popping a s'mores-flavored one into the. toaster, she walked over to the fridge and pulled out some fruit. She thought her doctor would be proud of the balance of healthy and unhealthy that was her usual breakfast.

An arm appeared, reaching into the fridge beside Flora's head. Gasping, she spun around to make eye contact with a wide, naked chest. Her eyes connected with Dylan's before her wandering, downward gaze saw anything else it shouldn't.

"Stop smiling, midnight killer," Flora joked, tilting her head upward, teasing them both. Her lips inched closer and closer. Dylan just smiled, smoothly grabbing the container of eggs out of the fridge and setting it on the counter, mere inches separated their bodies.

"Actually, it's nine in the morning. I didn't mean to scare you." Dylan's head dropped down, his lips almost meeting hers. Slipping under Dylan's arm, Flora swung around in front of the toaster, plating her breakfast. "A toaster pastry and fruit again? Who even decided toaster pastries were a breakfast food?" Dylan teased, cracking an egg over a frying pan left on the stove.

Muscles flexed underneath his tight skin as he moved around her small kitchen, a sight Flora could get used to. Nothing was more attractive than a strong man who could cook.

A moment later, she had to take that statement back. This man surely was attractive, but he couldn't cook, not eggs at least. As Dylan tried to flip the egg, not only did it break but it missed the pan altogether, landing on the floor. Turning off the flame, Dylan threw an apologetic look towards Flora. She gave him a gentle smile before helping him clean the mess.

"Okay, rockstar, let me show you how it's done."

Flora cracked an egg into the pan, flipping it over skillfully with minimal effort. It was Dylan's turn to admire from his safe perch on the bar stool. She swayed her body a bit more than usual, arching her back just enough. She would attract Dylan, enough to want her. What did he like in a woman? Did he like someone who cooked? She shook her head, setting the plate in front of him. Leaning her arms on the counter, she pushed the plate closer to him.

"Go ahead, eat," she said, a smirk on her face. Dylan could only look up to her, him being shorter sitting in a chair.

"Thank you, baby."

"Baby?" Flora said, leaning in, before quickly leaning away. "Hold that thought, let me go brush my teeth."

Before she could get far, Dylan whipped out of his chair, grabbing her arm and pulling her in close. Closer than she was before. Close like they were at the club last night. He looked down into her eyes, softly smiling at her. *Take the chance*, she mentally yelled. She was about to. Take the chance of ruining everything, of interpreting the wrong signs, of kissing the girl. This was different. Flora was different, he was different. He had to be hers.

He landed his mouth just beside hers, catching the corner of her plump lip. Wrapping his arms around her waist, he landed another kiss on the other cheek, once again only touching a bit of her lip.

Being so close, she knew he could see the flush of her cheeks and lean toward him in her posture. He could probably read the disappointment on her face too. Heat clouded her eyes as she stared at him.

"I don't mind morning breath."

"You say that, but you haven't kissed my lips. How would I really know?" Flora asked, snaking her arms around his waist, and trying to see how far he'd take their flirtations today. She couldn't push him too far, she couldn't risk scaring him too early on.

"One day, I'll show you."

"Not today?"

"No, not today. I want you to be 100% sure when I kiss you that you want me, too. I need us both to be so desperate that we lose air and turn blue. When I kiss you, I want it to be our first time kissing each other and our last time kissing someone new," Dylan said, pulling away.

Stuffing his scrambled eggs into his mouth, he made his way to the bathroom to get ready for the day.

FLORA LOVED HER JOB. IT WAS A DREAM COME TRUE for her to design accessories. But coming home at the end of the day was just as much of a dream to her as her job. She'd been working on her home, turning it into her dream apartment over the last couple of years. All the renovations, decorations, and life she poured into her home had vanished in a couple of weeks, fear replacing that warm homey feeling. Her attacker took her safe place. Standing behind Dylan while he unlocked the door, a rushed feeling of fear washed over her body. Daylight provided security, gave her a sense of power by being able to see. Now that her apartment was covered by the darkness of night, things had changed.

Those feelings weren't there last night. She slept fine last night, what was different tonight? She wrapped her sleeve-covered arms around her body, stepping back from the door.

Dylan stopped after he unlocked the door, turning around to glance at her. He stared for a moment, and her cheeks flushed from the attention. With a gentle smile, he turned back around before disappearing into her dark apartment. She could hear his footsteps moving around inside her home, searching for anything suspicious. She paid attention to the sound of the windows sliding up and down, and the turning of door handles. She counted how many rooms he checked as he went.

"Safe," Dylan called out before he walked back to the entryway, taking off his shoes. Flora entered on unsteady feet, slamming the door shut behind her. Rushing, she slipped off her own shoes before curling up on the couch. Sitting upright, she leaned against the back of the couch, her knees up to her chest. She couldn't shake the feeling of being watched, *hunted*, the voice in the back of her mind reminding her at every waking breath.

"Flora, what's going on?" Dylan slowly asked, before sitting on the couch as well, too far away in Flora's opinion. "You've been off-balance all day today."

"Really?" She played it off, trying not to create problems that probably weren't real. Sure, she worked later than normal today, but only for a few hours. But that happens when someone runs a business.

"We stayed three extra hours at work today, you raced to the car, then were slower than an injured puppy walking up to the apartment." He raised an eyebrow. "At work you bounced your leg for what felt like hours and clicked each of your pens for just as long."

Okay, so yeah, she stayed at work over three hours late, forcing them to go home in the dark, which backfired on her. "I'm not sure; I can't shake the feeling."

Trying to be nonchalant, tears began welling in her eyes. Blinking furiously, she looked away from Dylan. Crying twice in the span of 24 hours was unusual for her, but this was a *stressful* 24 hours.

"Do you," Dylan started to move closer to her, "feel safe?" Resting his heavy hand on her knee, he searched her face. Tears dropped as Flora let out a sharp laugh. Flipping her hair over her shoulder, laying out on the couch she rested her head on his lap.

"In my home of five years, behind a securely locked door and double-checked windows with a high-tech alarm system...no, I don't feel safe."

"Let's go then," Dylan said, dragging her body to the edge of the couch and carrying her to her bedroom. Setting her down on her bed, he backed away towards her closet and pulled a duffle bag out. Confusion filled Flora's expression, the sudden simple answer to her problem being so easily spoken threw her into being even more unbalanced.

"Go where? I have nowhere else to go," Flora said, waving her hands around helplessly. He didn't get it; she couldn't go to Willow or Luxe or even her parents. The guilt that plagued her wouldn't let her put the people she loved in danger.

"To my old house, no one will be able to find it unless I give them strict directions. Jackson doesn't even know the way." When he shrugged, she could see his pec flex under his tight white T-shirt as he tossed her bag toward her. "Now pack a bag."

"We don't have to risk your safe place, Dylan. I'll get over it." Flipping over, she tried to drag her comforter up over her, but it was yanked from her grasp as her ankle was pulled to the edge of the bed.

"You can pack your bag, or I can."

Huffing a breath, she dragged herself out of bed before packing an overnight bag. He left, she guessed, to pack his own bag. He refused closet space, just like he refused to sleep in the apartment before she convinced him to change his mind. Maybe she could get him to use up some closet space whenever they got back.

Sitting on the bench in her entranceway, she perused her collection of shoes. Choosing a pair of sneakers over a pair of heels for now, since she wasn't going anywhere the next day, she put on her socks. A familiar, gentle hand, one she was growing to love, took the shoe from her hand.

"Let me." He kneeled, taking his sweet time wrapping his fingers around her ankle. She seemed to be on an obeying streak with Dylan. Sitting back, she watched him push her foot into her shoe like she was a princess.

"Okay, you ready?"

With a nod of her head, he took her hand and out the door they went.

After numerous twists and turns down bumpy dirt roads, they finally got to their destination: the little cabin in the middle of nowhere that Dylan called home. Pulling up to the gravel driveway, Dylan parked the car. Instead of opening his door, he sat back in his seat, looking over to Flora. Looking up at him, she released a deep breath, trying to relax. Reaching out for his hand, she interlaced their fingers, running her thumb over the back of his hand.

"How are you feeling?" he whispered.

"I don't know," Flora whispered back, looking out at the house. Was this safer? Was it actually safer, or was she messing with herself mentally?

Getting out of the car, Dylan pulled her door open. Walking hand-in-hand up the steps of the house, they stepped inside. Flora took her shoes off as he turned on the lights. Last time she was there, she'd only seen the outside, and her panther was in complete control for the majority of the time. The cozy atmosphere inside was a surprise to Flora. He had a cream-colored couch, with a basket overflowing with blankets. A red brick fireplace with a TV hanging on the wall above it. Candles all around on the end tables. It looked like a dream, a Pinterest kind of dream.

"Did you get an interior designer?" she asked, dragging her pink nails across the back of the couch. Dylan let out a laugh, turning back to face her. The trail of his eyes over her body left a path of warmth on her skin. She was in his home, under his roof, and about to sleep in his private home. Feeling shy at the thought, she looked toward the fireplace, anywhere, to not look at Dylan.

"No, I did this. No one has ever been here besides me." He walked towards the fireplace, switching a flip and turning it on.

"Not real?" Flora exclaimed, surprised but also disappointed that she wouldn't see him chop wood anytime soon.

"Nah, that's Jackson's thing." He smiled, trailing into another room. She followed, her footsteps creaking with the floorboards. The kitchen followed the same cozy aesthetic.

"Hungry?"

"What do you have?" Flora asked, wondering if he actually had food here, thinking he mostly lived at the Packhouse.

"Well, I got those pastries you like in the car."

"Toaster pastries?" Flora asked with a smile growing on her face.

This man thought of everything, of course she'd love those calorie-filled addicting monsters. It was a blessing she was a Shifter who had an extremely fast metabolism. Cause those would go straight to her already oversized hips and thighs otherwise. She already got shit for her curvy figure; imagine if she had to pay the price of eating an entire box of those bad boys in one sitting.

"Yeah, that's all I have though. Don't mind the dust or the

lack of food. It's been a while since I've been here," he said, slipping out to his car to get her treat.

How long had he had those? Where did he even get them? It didn't matter to her because the thought that he got them for her filled her with that same heat that followed all of their interactions.

Setting the toaster pastry box down on a nearby table, he opened it, taking one out for her. "I don't have a toaster unfortunately." He ran a hand through his hair, scratching the back of his neck before they both took a seat at the table.

"That's fine...you're not going to have one?"

He shook his head, just continuing to watch her eat. This felt extremely intimate. Watching and providing food was something mates did. She knew he knew that. Was he falling for her, for real? Were the feelings she had similar to his? Suddenly feeling an intense amount of pressure, she cleared her throat before looking up at him.

"Okay, I'm going to get your room ready." Getting up *after* she'd finished her toaster pastry, she noticed. Fighting her uneven breathing, and warmed cheeks, Flora went to sit on the couch, trying to calm down.

"He likes me?" she mumbled to herself, wringing her fingers out. "Like for real? No jokes?" Deciding to stop talking to herself where he could hear her, she distracted herself with the light of the fire. She'd dissect this mess of feelings later. For now, she needed to get mentally ready for her trip to the production factory in Moonlight at the end of the week.

15

FLORA

"I got you sleeping on the couch in your own place?" Flora said, walking down the hall to see the man who so graciously had been taking care of her sleeping on his living room couch. She hadn't noticed there wasn't another room and she had slept in his bed, all comfortable and relaxed. Surrounded by the almost faded smell of him and having the best sleep of her life, he had tried and failed to fit his tall, lanky frame on his little couch.

"There was another bed, but I wanted to watch the front door just in case," Dylan mumbled, pulling his blanket over his head. His knees folded over the armrest, much smaller than the one at Flora's apartment. The blanket bunched at his thighs exposed his legs. To say he looked uncomfortable was an understatement. Guilt flared within her, her footsteps bringing her closer to the too-generous man laying on a couch two sizes too small for him. Kneeling on the floor, Flora's eyes roamed his body.

"Dylan, you didn't have to do that."

"No, I didn't. I wanted to."

"Thank you," she whispered.

Moving the blanket from his face, she wanted to give him a good morning kiss, crawl on the couch with him, and just be with him. But she wasn't sure she was ready — wasn't sure that he was ready. Instead, she ran her hands through his hair, the brown waves moving with her fingers. Dragging her hands through the strands of his soft waves, she massaged his scalp. Relaxing, he closed his eyes, gently pushing his head into her hands. After a minute, she guessed he'd had enough trying to get closer to her because he picked her up and placed her on top of him. She straddled him, leaning forward to place her hands back into his hair.

She wasn't sure what this meant, how she was supposed to feel. Now she was flustered and confused. Memories of her grinding against him at the club filled her thoughts, warming her body up in more ways than just embarrassment. He kept his eyes closed and his hands on her hips, close to her ass. She was on his stomach now but was completely aware of what ventured lower. She tried not to think, but his little grunts and moans were making her skin feel sticky with a building sweat.

When it came to Dylan, she was almost sure he was her mate. Her growing love for him stretched from the depths of her to the cells of her skin. Her body screamed that he was her one and only every moment they spent together. She had doubts though; if Dylan was her destinated mate and he rejected her she'd be vulnerable to rejection: a Shifter's natural shutdown after being rejected from their soulmate. Flora heard rejection from a mate made them feel like their heart was aching with a pain so deep no healing abilities could repair. Most didn't want to survive or live with the pain. Death was easily welcomed after the first couple days of pain, and a Shifter would kill themselves before their heart could give out. At least, that's what Flora heard. It didn't happen often, so no one she knew seemed to know for sure what happened. Flora struggled daily on whether to pursue Dylan or not. She was sure she was giving him whiplash. There was a flame between them, but she didn't know when it would die, and that scared her most. Even after he left her life, her flame for him would still be lit and that heartbreak wasn't something she was ready for.

She pulled her hands away, sitting up, as Dylan opened his eyes. "Okay, I gotta call the girls, update them and then we have to leave soon," she said, hating the despair of leaving that house in that moment. If it wasn't for the fact she needed food, she'd stay until Dylan kicked her out. She dragged her body off his, his hands slipping from her hips to rest on his stomach. His longing look must have matched hers. Going back to the bedroom, she picked up the phone, group calling Luxe and Willow.

Luxe answered, her face appearing on the screen first, a mere second before Willow's. It felt great, reconnecting with them. It hadn't been long since they last talked, but the girls were like family. Sure, they weren't officially Pack, but they might as well have been.

"Okay, so Flora are you ready to tell us where you're at?" Luxe asked, pulling her phone closer to her face, as if to get a better look. Sitting on the bed, Flora looked around the cozy cream-and-brown room.

"I'm not sure I can actually tell you," she said, suddenly unsure of what she could and couldn't say. Dylan was letting her stay at his hideaway and the last thing she wanted to do was ruin his secret.

"Can you tell us who you're with?" Willow tried, her auburn curls bouncing with her stride. She was in the office, doing what—Flora couldn't remember. It was a good thing Flora wasn't the personal assistant; she'd do a terrible job.

"I'm staying with Dylan, something happened the other day, and I couldn't stay at my place. It's —," Flora explained, trying to find the right words, "Not safe anymore." That brought on a chorus of 'what happened' and 'are you okay'. Flora started from the beginning, explaining everything. From the rocks being thrown at her window, to her practically dry humping Dylan in a club. She'd never live that down, by the sound of their laughs. A weight lifted from her shoulders; venting about it helped. She felt she could really begin to understand what the hell was going on.

"Aren't you glad I introduced you to Dylan?" Luxe laughed, trying to bring light to the situation. Flora shied away with a roll of her eyes.

"More serious than I thought," Flora admitted, waiting for the 'I told you so's to continue.

"I should start a matchmaking business," Luxe went on, with Willow's encouragement. "I mean, look how well Flora and Dylan turned out."

"We're not together."

"Is that what you want?" Willow asked.

"It would be nice." She played it off, cheesing too hard and blushing that much harder.

"So, what's the problem?" Luxe asked, working away behind the discount rack at Clothes Before Bros.

"It's not just a fling, or temporary boyfriend-girlfriend status. It's serious for me."

"What about him?" Willow asked, continuing their interrogation.

"I don't know." Flora shrugged. There were moments she thought he felt the same and moments she didn't.

"I think you do, babe, but these things take time, it's only been like three weeks," Willow said.

Saying her goodbyes and hanging up the phone, Flora remade the bed, thinking of the phone call and trying to calm down before she'd face Dylan again.

A knock on the door startled Flora, her body quickly turning to meet Dylan's gaze.

"I'm ready whenever you are." No rushing, no insult about how long women took to get ready, nothing. Nothing but a simple, "I'll wait for you." Damn the flutter of her heart. She couldn't help but smile.

"Thanks, hot stuff. I need ten minutes." Turning on her heel, she raced toward the bathroom with her bag in hand. She didn't need to really do her hair, thanks to the braids, and her outfit was picked out yesterday, a matching set consisting of fuzzy pants and a bralette. Boy, did small boobs come in handy sometimes.

Walking out the door, a pair of clean white sneakers on her feet, Flora was ready, both physically and mentally, to go back to her apartment. At least long enough to pack a bag for her production trip out to Moonlight City.

❧

"How many outfits do you actually need, kitty cat?" Dylan asked. He plopped down onto the bed, stretching his frame along her covers. A posture very much in contrast to Flora's hunched shoulders.

"Being prepared for the 'what ifs' never hurt anybody," she countered, packing her fifth pant suit.

"Where do you even find so many pastel pantsuits?"

"I have my sources." Piling in five extra pairs of underwear just in case, Flora was finally ready to go. Zipping up the matte pink suitcase she walked out of her room and straight to the door.

"Hey, slow down a minute."

"What?" she snapped. The air was suffocating in the apartment, in her own home. She couldn't get away fast enough and the reminders of her attackers were being dug up from the depths of her brain. Her mother went through something like that once upon a time. She was kidnapped when she was still dating Flora's dad and while he saved her, it changed her. It explained the many locks securing their doors growing up. She didn't understand back then but boy did she now.

She thought she was okay; thought she could pack one last bag for her trip to Moonlight City without issue. Flora tried to push her fear to the back of her mind.

"Both hands on top of your head," Dylan demanded, blocking her exit.

"No, we need to go."

"*Now*."

Huffing, she complied; the faster she listened, the faster she'd get out of there. Placing each hand on top of her head, she looked at Dylan expectantly.

"Breathe in for six." She followed his instruction, inhaling for six counts. "Now out for eight." And out for eight. "Relaxed?"

She was at least a little bit more than she was 14 seconds ago. Nodding her head, she slowly turned and pulled open the door.

"Alright, little meow meow, let's roll," he joked opening the door wide enough for the both of them.

"Little?" laughed Flora, letting him take the suitcase from her. Settling into his car, she watched him saunter around the hood before sliding into the driver's seat.

"Ready?"

"As ready as I can be." His hand reached over to cover hers in her lap.

The drive was long and filled with strictly the driver's choice of music the whole way there. A mix of hip-hop and pop spilled from the speakers. Flora was sure the pop hits were for her, but regardless it was a good time. Much more fun than driving herself at least.

Finding the hotel easily, they walked up to the front desk. With Dylan by her side, she felt comforted. Something she wished she could normalize in her routine. Flora knew she couldn't get too used to him being with her; there would always come a time to say goodbye. As much as she'd love to prevent that from happening, she wasn't sure how to go about it.

"Room under Larkspur, please," Flora informed Mary, the receptionist, whom she'd became loose friends with after her frequent trips to Moonlight City.

"Ahh, I see you've booked a different room this time," Mary said, a half-smile appearing on her face as she looked between Flora and Dylan. "Did you get mated and didn't tell me?"

"No, not mated, we're —" Pausing mid-sentence, Flora looked up at Dylan. She wanted to say they were more than a boss and bodyguard, more than a friend helping a friend. But she wouldn't, couldn't no matter how bad she wanted to.

"She's my girlfriend. No bite marks yet," Shocked, Flora's jaw dropped before her eyes flew to Mary's. Smiling, she tried to play off the sudden surprise.

"That makes a lot more sense. Never thought I'd see the day Flora walked in here with a man. Here's your room key and enjoy your stay." Grabbing the key, Dylan smiled, leading Flora away with his hand pressed against her lower back, bringing a deeper sense of comfort over her.

"Dylan —"

"Shh — just enjoy it," Dylan smirked his ass off as they made their way upstairs.

Hand still holding her waist, Dylan pushed open their door. Flora stood in the foyer of their room, while Dylan searched for anything suspicious. This had become a habit, one she realized she'd have to break once this job was over. Saddened once again by the thought, she grabbed their suitcases. The deal was to share a room but not a bed. But apparently, she hadn't been clear enough with Mary when booking because there was only one perfectly made bed right in the middle of the room.

"What the hell?" Flora muttered, turning on her heel and pulling out her phone to call the front desk. Just as she was about to press call, Willow's name appeared on the screen. Answering her call first, she stepped back into the foyer.

"Have you seen your room?" Willow rushed out, sounding as if she was holding back a laugh.

"Yes, I have. Do you happen to know why there is only one bed?" Flora asked, tension filling her voice.

Willow broke, laughing a little too hard in Flora's opinion. "Luxe put me up to it I swear."

"Luxe?"

"Look, there are no other rooms. Just enjoy it, Flora, you know you want to."

"You both are going to pay for this."

"I'm shaking in my boots. Truly, have a productive trip,"

Willow said, hanging up the phone. Running a hand through her overgrown braids, Flora let out a huff before stepping back into the main room.

"So," Flora started, unsure of what to say exactly.

"So," Dylan copied, that damn smirk still on his face. While she was stressing on the call with Willow, Dylan had wasted no time getting comfortable on the single bed, taking his shoes off and laying back.

"Correct me if I'm wrong, kitty cat, but didn't we agree on two beds and one room?"

Sitting at the end of the bed, Flora took in the other furniture in the room. A couch sat in front of the bed with a TV hanging on the wall. Across the room was a mini fridge, a brown sleek counter with a closet, and another door that she assumed led to the bathroom.

"Luxe and Willow had other plans. Willow said there were no other rooms anyway, so it looks like we're sharing a bed."

"The couch looks perfectly fine," Dylan commented, sliding a glance at the couch. The white couch glared back, knowing from experience it wasn't that comfortable. Tilting her head to the side, she questioned him.

"I mean, plus you're small enough to fit."

"Dylan!" Flora yelled, trying to slap his thigh. He grabbed her hand before she could make contact, a glint in his eyes and a small smile gracing his lips. Flushing, Flora gently tried to take her hand back, but his grip tightened. Laying her hand on his thigh and resting his hand on top of hers, just like he did in the car.

"I'm not sleeping on the couch."

"I wasn't going to let you, Flora. I'm sleeping on the couch."

"You're not sleeping on the couch."

"Then where am I sleeping?"

"On the bed," she said, pulling pillows and extra blankets from the closet. "Watch this." She proceeded to build a wall down the middle of the bed with her supplies.

"The wall of separation. Unless..." Flora suggestively joked, throwing her back with a laugh. Testing the waters through jokes was her tell, trying to see how he would respond. He smirked again. What was she supposed to do with a damn smirk? Biting the inside of her lip, tapping her fingers on the bed beside her, she stared at the wall.

"Coin for your thoughts? Or however the saying goes," Dylan asked, proceeding to draw shapes on the back of her hand. Was that something? Was that a sign to keep flirting?

"Penny."

"What?"

"A penny for your thoughts," she corrected, moving her gaze to him.

"I asked first," Dylan chuckled, keeping hold of her hand.

"When did you get so funny?"

"When I met you," he whispered. The room went quiet; the heat from their gaze building a tension that was about to choke Flora out.

"Do you want to go shopping with me?" Flora asked.

She wouldn't call it asking him on a date, but she was trying to ask him to...be...with her. Physically, in her presence. She couldn't figure out what the hell she was doing.

"Of course, that's part of my job," Dylan said, deflating Flora's balloon of hope. Rolling her eyes, she slid off the bed, turning her back to hide the defeated look she knew her face would give away.

"I need new panties." Lie. She didn't, she had more than

enough, but she felt the need to get back at him. Without saying anything, he moved off the bed, following her out the door.

❧ 16 ❧

DYLAN

She didn't drag him to the undergarment store, but he knew he'd follow her anywhere, despite what he let her think. He couldn't deny the blush that crept up his neck when she mentioned it, though. Following close behind Flora, she looked through racks of clothing. Stealing touches was all his mind would let him do, for now. Brushing her arm, fingers, back, anything that wouldn't be deemed inappropriate. Dylan couldn't figure out how to proceed with his feelings. He wouldn't know until this attacker situation was over. Until then, he knew he had to wait. *If* he could wait, however long it was, was the real test.

"What do you think?" Flora asked, holding up another one of those tiny tank tops.

"Isn't it practically fall time now?"

"I could still wear it around the house, under sweaters," she said as if it was obvious.

"It's short but looks like something you'd wear," he said, distracted by the feeling of being watched.

Turning abruptly into his chest, Flora whipped on her

heel, looking up at him. Her hands landed flat on his chest, the shirt long gone on the floor between them.

"What's going on?' she muttered. Without his wolf hearing he probably wouldn't have heard her. Leaning his head closer to hers, his brown eyes pierced her gaze. She could read him so well...

"Nothing you should worry about."

"No, tell me."

Dragging her hands lower, not quite yet publicly indecent, but pretty damn close. Dylan could feel his eyes begin to glow, focusing solely on her.

"I don't have a good feeling."

"Should we leave?" she asked. Her eyes trailed over the room, landing on a couple of smiling girls giggling and eyeing them together. He could only smirk at the glare forming on Flora's face.

"No."

"No?" Flora asked, scrunching her face in confusion.

"Definitely not, that's what they'd want us to do."

Kneeling, Dylan picked up the shirt, and dragged his hand up her outer leg. *Two can play this game.* "Now, will you stop death-glaring at those girls; they're practically kids."

"Yeah, only when they know, for the time being, you're all mine," Flora purred in his ear, dragging her nails up and down his chest. He'd have her do that forever if he could.

Mine.

For the time being.

That last bit sucker punched him in the gut. *For now,* will hopefully change into forever, into soul mates. Dylan and Flora Enchanted. Flora and Dylan Enchanted. It had a nice ring on it.

Sadly, it had to wait.

Standing chest-to-chest once again, Dylan couldn't help but make the moment last as long as possible.

"Don't be shy, Dylan. Let's put on a show," Flora said, pulling his hands around her body. Right on her ass. Pulling herself closer to him. The blush on his face was as immediate as the nerves filling his chest.

"Flora —"

"I'm okay, are you?" she rushed out, searching his face looking for what he guessed was a sign she stepped too far. Smirking, he pulled her tight against him.

"You started it." He pressed a brief kiss to the top of her head. She smelled like warm coffee. Feeling encompassed by her smell and being was a state he wanted to live in forever. A beat later, he saw the teenage girls leave the store and glanced at Flora to see if she'd noticed. She didn't thankfully, meaning he'd get to hold her just that much longer.

Slipping from his hold at last, Flora stepped back, looking back at him once more.

"Ready?"

"Ready for what?" Dylan asked, confused.

"The next store, silly." He'd walk into every store, especially if they could reenact that moment in every one.

ॐ

He didn't want to sleep. He didn't even want to blink, let alone move. The day was over, and Flora had fallen asleep hours ago. Sleeping Beauty Flora put the princess to shame. All Dylan could do was stare. He knew; he knew like the back of his hand at that point. If killing the kingdom and the villain was all he had to do to keep Flora, he'd get it all done before kissing her awake. Flora's restful state was enchanting, and he wanted this peace to follow her forever. The wall of pillows remained for a few hours during the night, no thanks to her. She played a game of hot and cold, cuddling with her blankets one minute and getting too hot the next. Throwing her blanket down while also grabbing a pillow from their wall and throwing it on the floor.

A groan slipped from Flora's lips. "What are you doing up?"

"Nothing, go back to sleep." Listening without another word, her eyes closed as she flipped over and fell back asleep. Turning his back to her, he tried to sleep. Warm coffee perfume wafted to him from her side of the bed. Relaxing with each intake of the comforting scent, he drifted into dreamland, where the woman behind the scent followed him.

It wasn't long before a leg swung over him. The contact was abrupt, but the skin was smooth. His body jumped, and through his fuzzy mind, his sole focus was reaching for his dagger on the floor beside the bed. While drowsy, his defense was still on high and quick as ever. He straddled the threat's body, switching their positions. Aiming the dagger toward the side of the neck, he prepared for a swift slice. Flora jerked awake to the sudden movements, finding the shiny object resting against her throat.

"I'm not into knife kinks, Dylan," she joked. Her sleepy eyes met his. Opposite to his tense posture, her body was completely relaxed, her legs trapped between his. Still processing the realization of his dagger held to Flora's throat, he quickly sat up, still straddling her. He quickly put the knife back into its cover.

"I'm sorry," Dylan rushed out, trying to slow down his breathing. Proceeding to lie flat on his back next to her, he reached for the rumpled blanket by his feet. "I'm so sorry,

Flora. I wasn't expecting the physical contact and I panicked
—"

"No, I'm sorry. I mean I was sleeping, but —" She shrugged
as she moved to her 'side' of the bed, lying on her side with her
head propped on her arm.

After a few moments of shuffling from both of them,
Dylan decided it was okay to risk the peace. He removed the
completely useless wall of pillows and scooted closer to Flora.
Her body heat mixed with his own. He wrapped an arm tight
around her stomach. Tucking his head into her neck, he finally
felt comfortable. Dylan placed his hand under her head.

"It's fine, I wasn't prepared," he murmured, closing his eyes
once more, hoping she'd keep her body close to his. She did,
snuggling even closer than before. Dylan could feel her *every-where*. Pleased with the result of the missing pillow wall, he fell
back asleep, much easier than before.

Waking up again was a similar story, with Flora's body still
wrapped around him. He couldn't move and he didn't want
to. Her light brown arms wrapped around his waist as her
naked leg was thrown over his own. He was convinced he was
the luckiest man in the world. He hadn't ever had the chance
to be cuddled in someone else's arms. Honestly, after this, it
would be hard to go back to his old life without it. The
comfort wasn't something he'd wanted to ever let go of.

Her arms slipped away too soon, followed by her legs,
taking her warmth with them. Instead of turning over and
wrapping his body around hers, he got out of bed. Disap-pointed, he headed for the shower, hoping to get that warmth
back from the steam of the water. Running a comb through
his hair, he dragged his still tired body to the bag he'd been
living out of for the last month and pulled out his sketchbook.
With his mini pencil set beside him, he began to draw one line

after another. Shadows and curves developed into a drawing of his wolf playing, tussling with a midnight-colored panther. *Flora's* panther. He wanted this drawing of their animals playing together to become real. Shifting with others was extremely personal, something only family, Pack, and mates did. Of course, he'd want to do something as intimate as that with her.

He knew he loved her. She was someone who he wanted to spend the rest of his wolf Shifter life with. The only person he could stomach cuddling with. Or being intimate with in a public setting. Yeah, she was his mate. His soulmate.

Flora turned over in bed, her breathing becoming shorter. He let the pencil fall from his hands, focusing on the soft clank of the pencil meeting the desk. He tried to focus on anything but the movements of the woman behind him. Anything but her tiny pajamas, the mauve-colored silk of her bonnet, the freshly awakened face he found incredibly sexy. His focus was on the realistic drawing he'd just finished. And immediately aware of what he'd drawn, he wanted to hide it. Knowing Flora, it wouldn't stay hidden long. Maybe if he pretended not to care, she wouldn't come prowling over.

He should be proud, it was a great drawing, technically speaking. But the personal aspect of it, the hopes and dreams practically written all over it in big fat letters was too much to share. Even if she was the biggest hope and dream he had, he couldn't be sure she felt the same. He could break out in a sweat; the nerves of her finding this drawing and the heat of his hoodie combining to create a red-faced Dylan. He wasn't a nervous person, couldn't be with the job he had. But this panther had changed him in more ways than he could count.

He could feel her movement coming closer and closer with each breath he took. Here it was. The slight embarrassment trickled down his spine. Placing her soft hands on each of his shoulders, Flora looked over the drawing.

"Do you ever draw your Pack?"

A simple question, with a simple answer. An answer he didn't want to come face to face with. One glaring detail that set Flora so far away from his Pack. Something he'd never thought would come to light. Something that would never happen.

The answer was no.

He never drew his Pack members. Never felt the urge to. Never thought about why he'd had no problem drawing her but couldn't draw his Pack, his family, his brothers.

"No," he muttered. Her hands tensed on his shoulders.

"Well, that warms my heart that you'd draw me," she said.

She slid her arms down his chest, leaning her weight against him. Her warm coffee smell engulfed him once more as she tucked her head into his neck. He welcomed the silence, not sure what to say or what to think. Did he find something he'd love more than his own Pack? More than the people who saved him? Comprehending how he felt about Flora was too much. His potential mate turned into a potential lifeline, and he wasn't sure how to react.

The shrill of a phone broke the peaceful moment of groundbreaking realization. Picking up his phone, he walked out to the hallway, standing right in front of the room. There was no chance of letting anyone slip past him. Though he was dealing with a mountain of emotions, he was still on the clock.

"Hello?"

"Hey, man. A lovely little envelope with your name on it came in the mail today. From Lust Lane. Please tell me I won't find any photos of you working on a pole in here?" Jackson joked.

"You won't — wait, are there photos in there?"

Fear crept its way around his shoulders. Though there wouldn't be any photos of him on a pole, there might be photos of Flora treating him like one. To save face for them both, he prayed his little slip-up wasn't photographed.

"I don't know, I haven't opened it. I was only kidding. Is there something we should know?" Jackson responded seriously.

"No, just open it, Jackson," Dylan growled, losing patience. He doubted it was a photo of him and Flora, but prayed it wasn't. If it was, it would surely have 'you're fired' written on the back of it. Rubbing his hand over his forehead, the sound of ripping paper came through the phone.

"No inappropriate photos, thank God. Not something I'd want to see." Jackson was back to joking around at this point, so Dylan relaxed, leaning back onto the door. Letting out a laugh, he was relieved his privacy was kept private.

"Jackson, what was it?"

"A big fat check; how much do you want to give to the Pack?" Jackson finally answered. Within Packs, it was normal to give a part of your earnings to the Alpha to manage. Sometimes for groceries, emergencies, Pack gifts, rent, bills, whatever else that Alpha deemed important. It was a member's honor to give a part of their earnings to the Pack.

"All of it." Dylan shrugged; that was the whole point of him getting a job. He had enough for himself, from past assassin jobs and whatnot. The problem was not having enough to give back to the Pack. Now he had something to give — he was a participating and deserving member.

"You don't have to do that; you've done your part for this Pack," Jackson said as he'd done again and again. It didn't change the way Dylan felt. He used to bring in hundreds of thousands of dollars, even millions, when he was an active assassin. He was the breadwinner and he loved to provide.

"I know, I want to," Dylan stated firmly.

"Well, if you change your mind, let me know."

"I got to go, another day following Flora around," Dylan said, even though they both knew there was nothing else he would rather do.

"Be careful, brother; make sure you know what you're doing."

"Will do."

Ending the call, he wanted to avoid having the whole "Flora and emotions" conversation with his Alpha again. Back in the room, he found a freshly showered Flora sitting at the desk; her own sketchbook lay on the tabletop. His sketchbook, still open on the page he drew on that morning, was pushed to the side.

"How do you draw so well?" Flora grumbled, an incredibly rough copy of his own drawing on her paper.

"I'd have taken you for a tracer." He'd seen her in her office tracing blocks of different shoe or accessory styles before adding her own style and flavor. As she said before, it was about the original design, not always the original art, in her line of business.

"I tried but I didn't want to mess yours up," she mumbled, turning in her chair to look at him. "I need a distraction."

"From what?" Dylan questioned. Nothing was on the books as the meeting with the production team would take place the next day. Everything was ready: the sketches for both collections were sent in and the prototypes should have been made.

"I always get nervous before a production meeting," she said, slouching in the chair.

Dylan sat on the end of the bed. He wasn't sure how to help or how to comfort her.

"Okay, let's go out," he said.

"Are you asking me out, Dylan?" she giggled, looking suggestively at him over her shoulder.

"What if I am?" He was testing the waters, what-if's filling his thoughts. What if he let Flora slip through his fingers? Was he asking her out, not at first, but if she took it that way maybe she did like him after all...right?

She blushed and looked away, her fingers stiffening, and the air became thick.

"It's okay if you don't — I don't know. I could just —"

"I would love to go on a date with you, Dylan," she interrupted, a smile gracing her face, her eyes trained on him. "I wasn't sure you actually wanted to go on a date with me." She laughed, tapping her fingers on the back of the chair, facing him completely.

"Flora," Dylan scolded. "How could someone not want to take you out: beautiful, passionate, and caring Flora. Get outta here."

"Yeah, yeah, whatever. No takebacks; now I have to get ready."

"Again? You look fine." She was dressed down, in flared leggings and an oversized t-shirt. *His* oversized t-shirt. Since he noticed that little detail, he really didn't want her to change.

"You look amazing. Keep this on," he said, tracing his hand along the hem of the short sleeve.

"Where are we going?" she asked, turning sweetly sick, mischief dancing in her eyes. He bet if he didn't answer this question correctly, she'd change. What did she consider a t-shirt-worthy event? Tapping the side of his leg, he knew what but debated telling her.

"Let's stay here," he began, getting nervous as he went on. "And draw together."

"I can't really draw, Dylan." she said, confused.

"I'll teach you."

❧

"I NEED HELP," FLORA POUTED; HER RESPONSE TO THE rising eyebrow on Dylan's face. "More help."

The hotel room drawing date was t-shirt worthy (approved by Flora) and off-the-clock approved for Dylan. Moving behind her, he wrapped his arms around her body, placing his fingers over hers. This was in no way helpful to her, but it brought him closer to her physically. They started with shoes — she taught him how to draw shoes, and he taught her how to draw her animal. While learning how to draw would take more than one lesson, Flora was getting the hang of it quickly.

"Okay, I'll lead," Dylan murmured, dragging her fingers across the paper. He drew her animal, the black panther, like it was second nature.

"When did you get so good?"

"Practice. I've been drawing since I got back."

"Back from where?" Flora seemed hesitant to ask, and he knew the question would come up eventually, but it hadn't before now.

"You know I was an assassin. I'd do anything for my Pack. When Jackson asked me to join, funds were dangerously low, and it was just the two of us. So, I became an assassin. The pay was more than generous."

Unmoving, Flora listened, the drawing lesson long gone from her mind. His arms were still wrapped tightly around her.

"I worked with an organization who'd reached out to me when I was barely an adult. Before, there was no purpose for me to join, nothing to fight for. But after joining the Pack, everything changed. Jackson needed me as much as I needed him. So, I went on 30 jobs over the course of seven years."

He wanted to say more but before the conversation got too real, he wanted to be careful. Scaring her off on the first "date" was not part of the plan.

"How many people have you killed?" Flora wondered, still completely relaxed in his arms.

"Are you sure you want to know? There's no going back."

"Yes."

"Forty-seven."

"Forty-seven people," she murmured, dragging her nails in a calming motion down his arm.

"Yeah, forty-seven people."

"Any guilt?"

"Nope, none."

He had killed bad people; sure, it felt good to protect their next victims but that didn't erase the fact that he too had become...bad. It didn't change the fact he became like the people he haunted.

"I only took specific jobs, those targeting rapists, killers, anyone whom *I* deemed evil."

The silence between them was palpable. Did this change what she thought of him? He was waiting for the moment she'd tense up and pull away from him. But the moment never came.

"Good. Guilt would make all those deaths seem like they happened for nothing."

17

FLORA

"Dylan," Flora muttered in disbelief. Her eyes widened as she pulled the burnt pieces of what used to be a toaster pastry from the toaster. She tried to withhold her laugh, but the more her breakfast crumbled, the more she let the chuckles loose.

"Don't laugh at me; I was making those for you," Dylan said. He leaned against the counter of the mini kitchen in the hotel room.

"Yes, darling. That was very sweet of you. Thank you," Flora laughed, snuggling her way into Dylan's arms. Forgetting the toaster pastry; she rested her head against his chest, his arms coming around her hips.

It had been a month since she and Dylan first met, and she had grown attached to him. He was everywhere all the time, and she didn't want that to ever stop. She wanted to spend every minute of every day with someone who wasn't like her. Dylan came with a Pack, though, and she wasn't sure she'd fit in it.

"What is it like, being part of a Pack?" Flora rushed, her

words punctuated with a blush covering her face. He could probably guess why she asked the question, but she wanted the possibility of life after her stalker to include Dylan. That included his Pack.

Still, she wasn't trying to get her hopes up. What Pack would want a panther anyway? Panthers were too dangerous, too strong. It would be too much of a hassle for any Pack, let alone his. She knew the Enchanted Pack had a couple different breeds; it was what made them so well-known, but a solitary panther Shifter being part of a Pack was unheard of.

"Well, it's like finally being accepted for who you are by people who love you. Being surrounded by people who would lay their lives down for you. The bond created is stronger than a biological family's," Dylan said, running a hand up and down her back as he explained. She could feel the love in his voice when he talked about his Pack. She wanted that for herself.

"Could I meet them?" she whispered.

"Yeah, once we get back. I'll introduce you."

"How many members are there?"

"Seven, all guys. Are you ready for that?"

"With you? Yeah," she muttered, nuzzling closer. She wanted to be part of his life. He had been in hers long enough; it was time to see him in his element and see if they could work out if his Pack would accept her.

"We have to go to the production factory in an hour," Flora said, not letting go of Dylan.

"I know," he sighed. "I want to stay here a little longer."

"Is this a knife?" Flora softly asked. She dragged her fingers around the handle behind his back in an elastic belt he wore above his pants. She didn't pull on it, afraid of hurting him. Her arms were wrapped tight around his torso, and she had no clue how to handle such a sharp object, so she didn't try to.

"Yeah, well a dagger...go ahead and pull it straight out, then point the blade outward before bringing it between us," he whispered. He was still running his hands along her back, completely relaxing her.

Flora followed his instructions, taking a step back away from him. His arms loosened around her, but he didn't completely let go. The dagger had a jade-colored handle and silver vine-style engraving with a freshly cleaned silver blade. It was beautiful. How many people had he killed with this?

"You're so formal. Dagger, knife, same thing," Flora smiled, carefully putting the dagger back.

"Actually, a dagger is for stabbing, and a knife is for cutting and slicing," Dylan informed with a sly grin. Flora giggled, throwing her head back.

Dylan swooped Flora into his arms, carrying her to the bed and placing her sitting up against the bed's headboard. She watched as Dylan opened her suitcase, seeing the outfit she had packed for the day and laid it out on the end of the bed for her: a pink silk calf-length dress with a knit cardigan.

"No panties?" Flora asked, raising an eyebrow. Dylan's cheeks went pink as he shied away, taking a few steps back.

"Flora..." he grumbled, glaring at her.

"It's cute seeing you all flustered; it doesn't happen very often," Flora said, sliding off the bed and grabbing her clothes and a pair of fresh undergarments.

"Yeah, yeah, yeah...just hurry your pretty little ass up," Dylan murmured still flushed as he sat back on the bed.

"Little?" Flora asked, turning her head back to look at her definitely not little ass.

"Don't we have a meeting to go to in like five minutes?"

"When have you ever been pressed for time, Mr. Enchanted?"

"Since now."

With a hum, Flora wandered into the shower.

FLORA'S NERVES BEGAN TO TAKE OVER WHEN THE meeting room came into view. Not only was she worried about her designs, but the little problem of her stalkers niggled at the back of her mind. She wanted to assume she was safe, being out of town and with Dylan, but she knew better. At least *now* she knew better. That last breach of privacy in her apartment really set her off, and she hadn't been quite the same since. She prayed this new constant worry would fade once the problem had been taken care of.

"Ready to meet Casandra and Romeo?" she asked Dylan, who was walking directly behind her. He was in her shadow, and she was grateful for that extra layer of security.

"Of course, time to get them off my suspect list."

"Dylan," she winced, lagging her head back to ram into his shoulder. There was no way they were behind the attacks; what purpose would they have to be? None. She still believed it was someone who frequented Lust Lane, not someone she knew personally. While it could be wishful thinking, she doubted it was Cassandra and Romeo.

"Won't know till we find out," Dylan commented as he pulled open the office door. The older couple stood together. Flora adored the love between the couple. They'd been together for over 30 years and still were infatuated with each other. Cassandra was dressed in a sweater dress and pumps with her hair straightened to perfection. Romeo was outfitted in dress pants and a button shirt, freshly ironed, and his hair parted to the side and gelled.

"Cookies?" Cassandra's warm honeyed voice asked, pushing a plate of chocolate chip cookies forward on the conference table.

"You know it, Cassandra," Flora asked, a smile brightening her face as she reached for the gooey mess of cookies.

"So, who is this dashing young man here with you, Flora?" Cassandra asked as she proceeded to take her seat. Flora stared back at Dylan, unsure of how to answer the question. She wanted to say he was her boyfriend, but they only had their first date just last night, and jumping to conclusions wasn't her style.

"My bodyguard. Dylan Enchanted," she said, winking at Dylan.

"It's nice to meet you," Romeo spoke up. The pressure of Dylan meeting the two people who had her back in creating Dainty Rebel was daunting. The atmosphere in the room made her feel as if spiders were crawling up the back of her neck.

Shaking Romeo's hand, Dylan proceeded to offer his hand to Cassandra as well. Dylan's shoulders squared off the moment they got close. His brooding energy filled whatever space in the room that wasn't occupied with the discomfort of strict judgment. Sitting next to Flora, Dylan wrapped his arm around the back of her chair. She couldn't lie and say she didn't thoroughly enjoy her bodyguard's possessiveness, with whom she also happened to have one of the best dates of her life with a mere 12 hours ago.

"Let's pull out the prototypes," Flora said, clapping her hands together. It was time to see her next two collections come to life.

"THEY DIDN'T MENTION ANYTHING PERSONAL, NOT once during that whole meeting."

"Dylan, what if I don't want to know what you think about them?" Flora asked as she plopped down onto their shared bed. The meeting was great, perfect even. The prototypes for her next line of shoes were approved and ready for production. Cassandra went as far as to tell Flora how proud of her she was. The pride nearly dripped from Cassandra's pores and it warmed Flora's heart. It was unusual for the first designs to work out so easily, but they did for her metal rings collection. The stripper collection prototypes on the other hand were approved, but she needed to run them by Emery, Flora's favorite performer at Lust Lane, before she hit the green button towards production.

"You're right, I don't want to ruin the moment," Dylan said, laying over her body. Resting his head on her chest, they both blushed.

"Sorry, I overstepped —" He started to get back up, but she grabbed his shoulder to stop him.

"No, stay," Flora said, running her hands through his short waves. The comfort was welcoming. The weight of his body heating hers was a feeling she'd never want to let go of.

"A dime for your time," she mumbled, wrapping her other arm around his resting body.

"A penny for your thoughts?" he mumbled back, pressing in closer. The contact suddenly felt desperate, limited.

"How long will this last?" Going with the truth would hurt more, but she wasn't one to skip around it.

"How serious are your feelings?" he asked, turning his head to look at her. Smiling, she wasn't sure she was brave enough to tell the truth. They'd been on one date, and he had her hooked.

As many dates as she'd gone on, no one had made her feel this strongly.

This deeply. This desperate. Like how a soulmate should make her feel.

"Serious," she confided, meeting his eyes finally. The gaze was sizzling, the physical touch searing. "You?"

"More than you'd believe, kitty cat."

"More?"

"Definitely more."

More than enough to be soul mates?

She wanted to ask him. She held back the question this time. Laying in silence, she rested her hand on his head.

With that, Flora dropped her back onto the crisp hotel pillows. The warmth and weight of Dylan's body lying over hers lulled her into a much-needed sleep.

18

DYLAN

She was sleeping, breathing deeply. His own body moved as her chest rose and fell. Now that he was left alone with his thoughts, the silence began beating in his ears. Cassandra and Romeo Bray were high suspects on his list, and he knew Flora wouldn't want to hear it. It would crush her to know people who she trusted were after her. Dylan couldn't exactly prove it either, his wolf instinct pushed his suspicions.

Getting up he pulled out his notebook and pen. His phone rang and he answered it quickly, trying to silence it so it wouldn't wake Flora up.

"Hello?"

"Hey, I was just watching the surveillance at Lust Lane, and guess who I saw." Felix's low voice came from the end of the line. He was also an Enchanted Pack member who was hired at the club to set up security cameras and watch the feed until they could hire someone more permanent.

"Who?"

"Emery Sparks. Your girl's ex," Felix stated. "She was

meeting with two big guys. Found them on the dark web and they're cage fight collectors."

Shit. Holy shit. Emery was working with collectors. Flora's ex-girlfriend was involved in cage fighting?

"What was she doing with them?"

"Just talking. The cheapskate club owner wouldn't get cameras with a mic on them. Something about a breach of privacy," Felix said, clicking his tongue.

"Okay, did you do any more digging?"

"She's been in contact with someone under the name of WL. Nothing on him. But she's been talking back and forth with WL for about a year. About what I can't tell yet, it's all in code."

"When could you figure the code out?"

"This is some high-level shit, so probably a couple of weeks."

They weren't working with that kind of time frame. Anything could happen in a couple of weeks, and he was beginning to question Flora's mental state. One person could only take so much. He'd met Emery multiple times: walked her to her car, watched her interact with Flora. While he could never write her off completely, she seemingly had the same likelihood of being Flora's stalker as Willow and Luxe had. Chances were slim as hell. But slim still meant there was a chance.

"Okay, call me if anything else happens. I have to go," Felix said before hanging up. Dylan didn't know what his next steps were. Emery probably knew what Flora's animal was and figured she could make a quick buck selling her into cage fighting. Most people who found a panther Shifter would do the same. It was a damn shame what money could make people do.

"Who were you talking about?" Flora's sleepy voice startled

him. He schooled his posture and slowly turned to face her. She was still cuddled up in the fluffy comforter on the bed.

"We don't know for sure what's going on," Dylan began. He didn't want to tell her that her ex, who she still was close friends with, may be trying to sell her to the Shifter Black Market.

"Don't play with me, Dylan. Just tell me straight out."

"Emery was spotted talking to collectors outside of Lust Lane."

His statement was met with silence as he stared at her. She was processing and it was scaring the hell out of Dylan with each minute that passed.

"What do you know?" she asked, her sudden question a lighting crack to the tense atmosphere in the room.

"That's about all we know," Dylan left out the info on "WL" in case it would freak her out more. She wasn't supposed to be the one stressed out. Dylan wanted her to go on with her life as normal. Let him hold the weight of her reality.

"What are we going to do? I was supposed to meet up with her to finalize the prototypes for my collection when we get back."

"We'll meet with her together. It will be a good time to assess the situation further." Dylan decided it was a risk. A huge fucking risk he didn't want to put Flora in. But if they could confirm the stalker was Emery, they wouldn't be chasing a ghost anymore.

"Does she know what your animal is?"

"No, I don't think so."

"What about the other girls at Lust Lane?"

"No, I don't shift around there."

"Not even by accident?"

"I don't have that kind of luxury."

Damn, it didn't make sense. Even if Emery wasn't after Flora the other girls at Lust Lane were in trouble. Dylan looked out the window, what the hell was he going to do now?

"What are we going to do? The other girls —"

"Will be fine until we can confirm what Emery was doing. Innocent until proven guilty and all that shit," Dylan said. "Until we can meet with her, we'll let Felix handle Lust Lane."

Flora shriveled up in her blanket. He could practically feel her shrinking back into her corner and slipping through his fingers. He sat next to her grabbing her hand. Giving it a squeeze, he sighed.

"Let's continue our trip. Hold off on all this drama until we get back to Rainfall Ave and I'll have a plan by then. Okay?"

"Okay, I can do that," she muttered curling her body into his. If anything, he was right there to protect her. That would be enough for now.

❧ 19 ☙

FLORA

"Okay, what are we doing tonight?" Dylan asked, jumping on the bed in their hotel room. Flora had sat already, after a long day of doing...nothing. She was trying her damndest not to think about Emery so instead, she'd put her entire attention on Dylan and the reality show playing on the TV.

"I want to relax," Flora said, yearning to curl her fingers in his wavy, grown-out hair. She loved the intimacy that came with running her fingers through it and that they both enjoyed it. At least last time he did. He was always doing things for her, making her comfortable and safe and happy. She wanted to return the favor.

"We've been doing that all day though." He was restless and it showed. He could hardly sit still for two minutes. He'd checked the building's security ten times that day, but she could tell he was itching to do it again.

"How about we switch roles? What do you want to do, Dylan?" Flora asked, rolling over to lay her head on his chest.

The rough cotton t-shirt combined with the smooth muscles lying under it brought more comfort to her once again.

God, when did she become so bad at dating? Were they dating? Should she ask? No, she definitely shouldn't. No need to ruin whatever this was. At this point, Flora knew she'd do anything for this man. "You always do what I want to do."

"It doesn't matter to me what we're doing as long as I get to spend time with you," he mumbled. "We did a drawing session yesterday, so let's camp out tonight."

"Camp out?" Flora questioned. She was never much of a camper and being in the wild didn't seem the tiniest bit appealing.

"Yeah, staying in, snacks and movies, under piles of blankets."

"Piles of blankets? Do we have enough?"

"You brought three whole blankets with you; I'm sure we have enough." He laughed, that deep rumble traveling through her body. "We need snacks though, so get your little behind up."

"Gas station?" Flora asked. She was in a pair of sweats and one of Dylan's shirts, no bra in sight. Her small boobs didn't always need one, but the shirt was thin. Dragging her body from the bed, she searched around the room for something to cover up with.

"What are you doing?"

"Looking for something to cover up with. In case you didn't notice, I'm braless."

"Ahh no, I noticed," he said, flushing that adorable red his semi-tan skin could never hide.

"Oh really?" Flora asked, walking up to him slowly. The constant heat that surrounded them built. Biting the inside of her lower lip, she dragged her slightly hardened nipples down his chest. The lack of distance between them would have anyone questioning whether they should be working together or not. She tried to remember he'd spent so much time with her because she'd hired him. Because he had to. As much as it crushed her, the truth was a reality she would have to accept. For now she didn't have to, right? He seemed willing.

She wondered if she should step away. What if he felt forced this whole time? Tears welled fast behind her eyes as she made a move to step back. How unprofessional, how horrible she felt.

She wanted to have forever with him and here she was taking advantage of him? A harsh, dry swallow sliced down her throat.

"Dylan, I shouldn't have —" She moved to step away from him.

Growling, he wrapped his arms around her body, smashing them together. No air could get between them, just the way she liked it. His glowing eyes bore into her, light brown and captive. How badly she wanted to stand on her toes and kiss him. She waited for him to make the next move.

"Flora, I want to kiss you. I'm going to kiss you," he mumbled, waiting for a sign of refusal before leaning down and devouring her lips. Brushing up higher against his body, she met his lips with just as much force.

Finally, he'd kissed her. He kissed her. *He* kissed *her*. No backing away, no waiting. Now she knew just how his lips felt and now she wasn't sure if she'd be able to stop. Desperate to get impossibly closer, she ran her hands up and down his chest, deliciously trapped between his strong arms.

Flora's head leaned to the side as his lips traced down the side of her face and along her jaw. He was kissing her, hard and...loving.

"You don't feel forced to be with me in any sort of way, right?"

"No, you have no idea how much I want you," Dylan said between kisses all over her face now. Their heat began drifting away as the steamy moment turned sweet.

"Dylan," she laughed, as the attack of kisses continued. "I think it's time to get those snacks."

"I'm having mine right now."

"You deserve your cuddle time. Let's go to the gas station," Flora said, not making a move to break his hold.

"I guess, if I must." He rolled his eyes sarcastically and stole one final kiss, setting her feet back on the floor.

"You still need that jacket though," he said, grabbing his own hoodie over her head. "These nips are for my eyes only."

"Oh my God!" Flora shouted out a laugh, enjoying the intense smell of Dylan surrounding her.

"What are you getting, kitty cat?"

"Chips of course, and maybe a few kisses. Are those for sale?"

"Those are free. Just for you."

❧

THE CRINKLE OF THE BAGS PACKED WITH SNACKS, which Dylan refused to let her pay for, dangled between them as they walked back to the hotel. The crisp air wrapped around Flora's ankles as she picked up her pace to keep up with Dylan's long strides. Damn, she'd felt out of shape before but the chilling air and the cramping in her calves put her at a disadvantage.

"Oh my Lord, are we almost there?" Flora whined, stopping to bend over and stretch her aching legs. She guessed the use of a gym membership would've prevented this embarrassing moment of weakness.

"Come here," Dylan said shortly, grabbing her arm and singling her over his back. Her legs instinctively wrapped around his waist as she took the bag from his hands. He held her up by her thighs, giving her the most comfortable piggyback ride she'd ever gotten. Being a bigger set woman, hips and thighs and all, she didn't have the luxury of feeling small; well, before she met Dylan, that was. While his muscles didn't bulge out like a bodybuilder's he sure could carry the weight of one. Cold wind caressed her face as she rested her head on his shoulder, smiling the rest of the way back to the hotel.

"Dylan," she said as he carried her on his back through the hotel lobby and up to their room.

"Yes."

"What movie do you want to watch?" Flora asked for the third time since they got back from the gas station. The mild argument had been going on for the last ten minutes. She was trying to give him the chance to watch something he wanted. She'd forced him to watch endless hours of reality TV drama and it was his turn to pick something. The only problem was that he also felt that it was her turn to pick something since he planned their last date.

"No, Flora, what movie do *you* want to watch?"

"Oh my goodness, Dylan, you pick. I'm sure you don't want to watch my movies."

"Since when do you care? Flora, I like what you pick out, now pick something," he said, laughing as he plopped down on the floor in front of the small couch. Blankets piled around them, and the same pillows that once tried to separate them on the bed now lay behind them.

He was right though, Flora didn't care what others

thought, especially not when it came to her TV anyway. She watched her trashy shows proudly, but she wanted him to enjoy their time, too. As much as she did yesterday during their drawing date.

"I really want you to enjoy this."

"I will, I'm with you," he said simply. Wrapping an arm around her, he pulled her body closer so that their sides were mashed together.

Giving in, she grabbed the remote, turning on one of her many reality shows. Snuggling in, she laid her legs over his, getting completely comfortable. She fell asleep after one episode.

❦

Knocking on the door pulled Flora awake; the constant insistent kind of knocking that irritated the ever-living shit out of Flora.

"Dylan," Flora mumbled, tracing a lazy hand up his arm. He was sound asleep, his arms still loosely wrapped around her body. She didn't want to move but the knocking wouldn't stop. Sighing, she reached for the remote and paused the TV.

Untangling herself from Dylan, she stumbled toward the door. Even though he was only a few feet away, she was still unsure about answering the door. There was nowhere she'd be absolutely safe even with Dylan by her side, she'd learned that the hard way. Flora decided she'd only check who was at the door. Her stalker wouldn't give her the courtesy of knocking on the door, that much she knew. She peeked in the peephole and saw Cassandra. Relief washed over Flora as she pulled open the door.

"Hey, what are you doing here so late?" Flora asked, worry

suddenly warring with relief. Standing on the other side of the open doorway Cassandra just smiled, a sweet mothering smile. Except this smile sent chills down Flora's back. There was a crinkle around Cassandra's eyes that made Flora uncomfortable. Something was wrong. Before Flora could ask what was wrong, Cassandra took a swing at her, kitchen knife in hand.

"What the hell, Cassandra!"

Jumping back, Flora dodged the swing by mere inches. In a panic, she tried to slam the door shut. Cassandra kicked the door wide open as Flora ran into the living room. Romeo stormed in after with a chain swinging from his hand.

Hearing Flora scream out, Dylan woke up and jumped into a wide stance. He pushed Flora to stand behind him.

"I don't know —" Flora mumbled, gripping the back of Dylan's shirt.

"I got you," Dylan muttered, his eyes trained on the two intruders. Cassandra and Romeo looked damn near ready to pounce. Cassandra wielded her knife and the chain Romeo had was attached to a collar like a leash.

Flora fell to her knees. Shock and terror filled her senses, causing her panther to get riled up. Flora herself was not a fighter, but her panther definitely was. She couldn't stop the shift as her panther took her place behind Dylan. Growling and snapping her teeth, the panther was ready for a fight.

20

DYLAN

Cassandra blinked anxiously focusing between Dylan and the snarling panther. Only a couch separated them, and Dylan was unsure of what the hell was going on. It couldn't have been this easy. Why would they choose the most obvious time to try to get to Flora? Were they really the ones stalking her? And what for? Why — it didn't matter. Not right now. It was him standing between them and Flora.

Why the hell was he sleeping though? Why did she answer the door? He didn't want to blame her for the situation they were in; it sure wasn't ideal. Taking a deep breath, he held his arm in front of Flora's panther. Regardless, this was going to happen eventually. They were going to be face-to-face with her stalkers and he should be happy it happened when he was around to protect her.

Dylan's eyes shot from Cassandra to Romeo and back. She was obviously the head of their operation. Dylan couldn't decide if he should fight them or get Flora out of there. He should have been watching Flora; her panther was impatient and broke the ice by sliding past Dylan and jumping onto Cassandra. Romeo took that chance by lunging for Dylan.

Cassandra fell to the floor. With the black panther weighing her down, she stabbed her knife into Flora's side. Flora's panther ignored the pain, biting into Cassandra's shoulder. She ripped her shoulder from Flora's mouth with a scream.

Dylan swung at Romeo who dropped the collar in his hands to block the hit. As quick as Romeo was, Dylan was faster. Pulling his jade dagger from his waist belt he stabbed upward into the man's torso. Romeo groaned and backed away, giving Dylan enough room to jut his leg into the dagger sticking from Romeo's ribs, kicking it deeper.

Turning around, Flora's panther charged Cassandra again while the older woman tried to grab the dropped collar and leash. Taking another knife from one of his many holsters, Dylan quickly threw it. The sharp blade went straight through Cassandra's hand, the bloody blade shining on the opposite side of her palm. Seeing the leash and collar still on the ground, Dylan realized the goal wasn't to kill Flora but to take her. The dagger in Cassandra's hand slowed her down, giving Flora's panther an advantage while buying him time to take out Romeo.

Escaping to the kitchenette, Romeo pulled the knife from his side and Cassandra pounded her fist into the panther's chest before they rolled on the ground, trading hits. Finding a lamp, Romeo smashed it over Dylan's head to no effect. Dylan rushed forward and used his weight to plummet Romeo to the ground. After a series of punches from Dylan, Romeo passed out.

Dylan rushed toward Flora, but in his haste, fell to the ground, his feet entangled in something. *Fuck.* A light orange fox skidded away from under Dylan and straight out of the hotel room.

That must have been Romeo.

Turning his attention back to Flora's fight, he watched Cassandra shove the blade from her own hand right into Flora's side. Dylan desperately wanted to push the panther out of the way and take on Cassandra himself, but jumping in the way of a panther on a mission was a death sentence. Instead, he took his ninja star blades from his belt but hesitated, deciding the risk of hitting Flora was too high.

He had to break them up somehow. But jumping in front of a panther scared him shitless. She could get confused and attack him. Losing Flora scared him more. He had to go for it and pray the panther recognized him. He used his body weight to push the injured panther to the side, praying she wouldn't turn and bite the ever-living shit out of him.

Cassandra got up, seeing her partner in crime had left her, but she knew better than to run from a predator like Flora. Dylan charged at her. The goal wasn't to kill, but to capture. He reached for the woman, her hair slipping from his grasp as she retreated, running from the room. Deciding to finally go for the kill anyway, Dylan picked up his jade-handled knife from the floor, covered in Romeo's blood, throwing it at Cassandra's neck. She quickly shifted, dodging the knife. A white panther dashed out the door.

Cassandra was a fucking panther. Flora's panther tried to run after Cassandra but Dylan quickly closed the hotel room door.

"No, we stay," he muttered. His adrenaline was coming down and he hoped hers was too.

Normally an angered panther could've broken down the

door, no problem. But this one was injured and seemed to trust him. In any other situation, Dylan would've run after the attackers but leaving Flora by herself was a no-go. The animal tilted her head to the side as if asking why they weren't going after them.

"They didn't come to kill you; they came to take you. Getting you alone could be part of their plan and I can't risk you getting hurt again," Dylan explained, shaking his head and breathing heavily. Being concerned for someone else during a fight was always difficult, but Flora going up against another skilled panther terrified the hell out of Dylan.

Taking on two people at once hadn't been a problem for him before, but a lack of recent training must have impacted him more than he thought. This time, there was so much more on the line. He didn't care about getting scratched or taking punches. Flora being stabbed and attacked weighed heavy on him. She shouldn't have even had to fight at all, let alone be injured. His whole job was to protect her, and he didn't.

Stabs of failure hit Dylan's gut as he stared at the only being he was supposed to protect, freely bleeding on the ground. She wouldn't die. He knew the placement and depth of the repeated stabs were precisely executed not to kill her.

Ignoring that growing guilt, Dylan quickly locked up the room, checking windows, doors, and closets before turning around to the injured panther. Her eyes paced the room, her nose twitching from all the different scents in the room. The minute Dylan finished locking up, the panther visually relaxed. Circling around herself, she assessed her wound. She looked up at him, now kneeling in front of her.

"I need you to shift for me, Flora," Dylan whispered, petting her side and touching his nose with hers. He let the tear that had welled behind his eye drop. She was hurt because of him.

"Please, Flora."

Getting her to shift a few times would help the enhanced healing process kick into high gear. Her panther stared directly at him. She licked his cheek and shifted back to her human form. Since she'd feel her wound after shifting, the wince on Flora's face was no surprise. Seeing the blood and wound still on her side, Flora's body naturally shifted back into her panther. After doing that a few more times, her body completely healed up.

Flora lay on the floor, naked. No scar, no more bleeding, and no more pain. Dylan quickly pulled a blanket off the couch and wrapped it around her. Nudity wasn't a big deal in the Shifter world, but Dylan didn't know where Flora stood at that moment. He laid her on the bed, tucking the comforter tight around her.

He couldn't stop staring. He wouldn't heal unless she did. Breathe unless she did. He was captured by her; he needed her. For now, she needed as much rest as she could get after shifting so many times. Determining she was safe and well within his eyesight, he started to clean their hotel room. Picking up all the knives around the room, he put them away, knowing he'd have to pay for the holes left in the walls and furniture. The room was destroyed and covered in blood splatters.

Rattled up, he paced around the room, keeping his wolf at bay as Flora slept. He spent the rest of the night packing and cleaning. They had to move. Staying in the room they were attacked in would not be safe. Uncertainties filled Dylan. He felt incompetent.

Except this was bigger than a job. This was about Flora's safety. Dylan leaned against the counter, gripping it to the point it cracked. He needed help. This wasn't an obsessed stalker; this was a team of at least two criminals that wanted Flora captive. Two showed up tonight, but who knew how many people were working with the Brays.

He stalked toward Flora. It was time to go.

"Flora, do you want to take a shower before we leave?" Dylan asked, not really wanting to wake her. Rubbing her arm, he watched her turn towards him, tears running down her face. It crushed him.

"I'm sorry," she let out a sob, her arm gripping his for dear life. Shocked, Dylan leaned in, his other hand coming up to hold the side of her face. He tried to wipe all the tears as they fell.

"How could you possibly be sorry? If anything, I should be the one saying sorry."

"Because you could've been hurt," she said, her tears streaming more freely.

"Yet, I'm not. Thanks to your badass panther," Dylan said. "I should've been better at protecting you, Flora; you shouldn't have gotten hurt at all."

As if a switch flipped inside her mind, Flora shot upright. Placing both her hands on each side of his face, sincerity in her eyes, she said "I'm fine, you did a great job. If you weren't there, I would've been wherever they were trying to take me."

"Well, I'll have to stay by your side, then," Dylan said, looking up into her piercing brown eyes. "So that doesn't happen."

"Promise?" she asked.

"Promise, kitty cat."

Flora rushed for her bag before darting to the bathroom. The sound of the shower turning on made him laugh. Still a little shocked that she would feel sorry for the attack on her, he took a water bottle from the fridge. He needed a shower too, but leaving Flora alone and unprotected wasn't going to happen. Until he got her to the safest place he knew, they would have to deal with the growing funk coming from Dylan's body.

❧ 21 ❧

FLORA

"Dylan, for the love of God, please just take a shower. I promise not to answer the door for three minutes," Flora commented, trying to push the funk of Dylan's sweat and grime from the night before out of her nose. They were walking up to Flora's apartment after a three-hour car ride from Moonlight City. She tried not to say anything the whole car ride back, but damn did that man stink.

"Flora, once we get to the Packhouse, I'll take a shower."

Flora needed to get more of her things before going to stay with his Pack. A hot, soothing shower was hard to leave, and convincing him to bathe would give her more time to stall. Going to the Enchanted Packhouse scared the hell out of her. The invitation from the Alpha himself wasn't assuring enough. Pack culture was something she had no clue about. She wasn't sure if she wanted to learn about something she knew she couldn't be a part of.

Nerves built up in Flora's spine at the thought, still on edge from the attack just hours before. She was trying to keep her nerves to herself, trying to appear at ease and calm, but Dylan noticed from a mile away. He pressed his hand against her back as they walked up to her apartment. That little gesture provided an insane amount of comfort in Flora's mind. Breathing a little easier, she slowed her walk to be closer to him. Though being closer meant being closer to the smell of sweat. Dylan sure was sexy and sweaty earlier, but that sexy wore off when the man smelled like cow shit.

"It wouldn't hurt showering here," she mumbled, unlocking the door. Instead of waiting outside like she normally did, she followed Dylan's every step inside. Ignoring her own shoe policy, she kept her sneakers on. She was scared she might need to make a run for it. Being left alone wasn't high on her list of things to do unless it involved Dylan introducing himself to some soap and water.

Sliding the last closet door shut, both of them visually relaxed. Flora pulled her shoes off leaving them neatly on the shoe rack in her bedroom before pulling out two gym bags, thinking it should be enough for her stay at the Packhouse. Hopefully, this would all end soon and she wouldn't have to come back for more clothes or bathroom necessities, or anything because, in reality, she would never come back to her cozy, safe home. She'd have to break her lease, move out, and find somewhere new. The thought of skipping town ran through her mind but her friends and business kept her rooted. Plus, if she was being honest with herself, she loved Rainfall Avenue. Sighing, she pulled hoodies, dress pants, and blazers from her closet.

"You're going to put those in a gym bag?" Dylan asked, leaning back onto her bed.

Even with sweat dried on his forehead, Dylan was still a

sight to behold. With the new distance between them airing out the funk, the sexy in Dylan came back. Huffing at the fact she was rumpling her nice clothes, she continued to neatly pack them in the bag.

"Yes, it's only a 30-minute ride anyway. I'll hang them up once we get there."

"So, you're accepting the help of my Pack and getting comfortable with the thought of staying at the Packhouse already?" Dylan teased, "I thought it'd take more convincing."

"It would if we weren't just attacked. This is bigger than a stalker who's in love with me or an ex-girlfriend who secretly hates me..."

"Emery is not off the suspect list, kitty cat."

"I have no idea why Cassandra and Romeo would want to...kidnap me?" Flora questioned. "Can you kidnap an adult?"

"Yes, you can kidnap an adult," Dylan said with a sigh. "Enemies could never get close enough to hurt you, hence why normally it's family and friends who do the backstabbing."

"I don't want to think about it anymore," Flora muttered.

"Do you want to be at the briefing? You don't have to if you don't want to."

"Yeah, I want to be there," Flora said, folding a mini skirt into her bag. Turning around she stood in front of her closet, wondering if she needed anything else.

"Don't forget laid-back clothes; we'll be training and sleeping too," Dylan chuckled, getting up from his spot on the bed.

"Together?" Flora flirted, the thought seemingly pleasing her insides. Only after a nice, hot shower for both of them. She couldn't quite wash the feeling of stained blood off her skin.

She grabbed some sweatpants, leggings, t-shirts and sports bras. With as much as she was packing, she felt as if she was moving in, adding more pressure to being a guest and stepping into unknown territory.

The ring of her phone pulled her out of her thoughts. Willow's name appeared across the screen and worry coursed its way through her body. Why was Willow calling?

"Hey, we're outside your door. You have this envelope sitting here. A flower too," Willow said. Jackson had called Luxe who in turn called Willow and said they also should stay at the Enchanted Packhouse. Thank God. At least she wasn't the only guest.

Flora rushed to the door but paused at the entry rug. She waited as Dylan opened the door. Without any words, he took the envelope from Willow's hands, stepping outside as he ushered her friends inside the apartment and shut the door.

"I'm sure it's for safety reasons," Flora said from down the little hallway of her entrance in her apartment. Seeing Flora, both Willow and Luxe rushed forward, crushing her in a group hug.

"Oh, my goodness, are you okay?" Willow asked.

"Don't you ever scare me like that again," Luxe said, lightly slapping Flora's arm as Willow continued to look Flora over.

"Didn't mean to. I swear I wasn't even going to tell you."

"That's even worse, Flora," Willow yelled, anger replacing the worry that once dominated her face. Laughing off the guilt of making them worry and now having to stay at the Pack-house, she led everyone to the kitchen. Dylan stormed in, note and flower in hand. Placing them on the counter for Flora, he looked as serious as ever.

"We have to go, now."

"Now?" Flora asked, picking up the note that must have been in the envelope. She paused, not wanting to read it. It was from Cassandra and Romeo, which meant they beat her and Dylan to Rainfall Avenue and that they knew where she lived. She took a deep breath and opened the folded letter.

Patience is key, as they say. Flora, do know we love you very much. We need you to come home. Fulfill your duties by coming to us. If not, then we will simply come and get you ourselves.

Love,

Cassandra and Romeo

"WHAT THE ACTUAL HELL DOES THAT MEAN? WHY the flower?" Luxe vocalized, reading over the short, creepy note. Flora shuddered, letting Luxe grab the note from her hands and watching her hands shake.

"An aster flower," Willow mumbled, lost in thought. "Patience?"

"Meaning they will wait us out. That note wasn't there when we got here; they could still be around, so we need to move *now*."

⁂

DYLAN GRABBED FLORA'S BAGS AND LED THEM ALL TO his car.

Willow, Luxe, Dylan, and Flora stood outside the Enchanted Packhouse. Flora never thought she would have to step foot on Pack grounds again. While Dylan unlocked the door, Flora watched Willow stare at the rocking chair tempting her from across the wooden porch. Willow tapped her platform Mary Jane heels, fidgeting. Flora knew of the love Willow had for rocking chairs, so much so Flora put a rocking chair in her own bedroom so that their frequent meetings were more comfortable for her. Flora couldn't take all the credit though, it was Luxe's effort of finding the perfect rocking chair that would fit both Willow's obsession and Flora's taste for comfortable modern design. Flora would be lost without them. She needed them as much as she needed Dylan. If anything, she wasn't as much of a lone animal as she thought.

The door shot open, revealing another man just as good-looking as Dylan and a gigantic smile. His eyes made direct contact with Willow's.

"I knew I smelled the tea-spilling girl outside. What are you doing here? I told you don't worry about it." Willow's face showed signs of recognition, confusion, then embarrassment in rapid succession. Willow's gaze fell to the floor as she shifted her weight from one leg to the other. Flora knew she'd have to pry juicy gossip out of Willow soon.

"Let's do these introductions inside, Eddie," Dylan grumbled, pushing the man inside the house so the girls could follow.

"I guess it is cold outside; what's going on here?" Eddie asked as he eased the crowd into the house, jumping over the couch to sit, and waving them into the living room.

"Welp, my stalker problem has gotten worse. My production crew has been stalking me, and now they've tried to kidnap me," Flora explained, practically floating over to the couch opposite of Eddie. Crossing her legs and straightening her outfit, she held her head up high. All she could do at that point was to look confident. Letting her negative emotions show was a no-go. That would only increase the worry Luxe and Willow had for her, increasing the chances of them getting more involved than they were already. This was *her* mess to deal with.

Dylan rested his hands along the back of the couch, standing behind Flora, and it felt as if he was standing over her.

"Not to be offensive, but if Flora is the one that was attacked why are Luxe and…"

"Willow," Willow answered shortly, crossing her arms before taking a seat on the other end of the couch.

"Yes, Luxe and Willow, here also? Actually, why are you all here?" Eddie added, shaking his head.

"How could I not be here to help protect my friend?" exclaimed Luxe, her gaze melting into a liquid fire of anger. If Flora hadn't seen her wolf already, she would assume Luxe was some sort of Hellhound. Hellhound Shifters were rare but with as quickly as Luxe gets heated, she must have a hellhound in her family tree somewhere.

Dylan sighed, "This is a lot bigger than we thought. I…I need help. I need my Pack. Her apartment isn't safe. The attackers know too much, including what her animal is —"

"And we know theirs," Flora murmured, sliding her gaze towards Dylan. They knew who and what they were up against. That was better than where they were a mere 24 hours ago.

"I can't do this alone."

"It's unnecessary to do it alone," Jackson said, striding into the room. Luxe visually softened her stance, sneaking glances at him. Flora could tell Luxe was hiding a smile. "Follow me."

They strode right past Jackson's office into the room next door. Flora's heels clinked as she stepped inside the room where the rest of the Pack was waiting. The Enchanted Pack consisted of seven men, including Jackson, Dylan, and Eddie. Meeting the Pack was a big deal in the Shifter world. It was like meeting your partner's parents; something as such required an enormous amount of trust between all parties. To think that Jackson trusted her, someone he only knew through a friend encompassed her in a warmth that filled her body, warmth of family and belonging.

Dylan slipped his hand into Flora's, leading her to the right side of the long oval table that sat in the middle of the room. There wasn't any decoration in the room, just the table surrounded by chairs and a projection screen hanging from one wall. Dylan pulled out a rolling chair for Flora, then pushed her in before taking his own seat between her and the head of the table, where Jackson sat. Luxe sat on Jackson's left and Willow next to her. Eddie took his seat beside Willow, sitting quite close to her. Willow kept her eyes down but couldn't hide the tiniest smile. Flora would've never guessed her friend was into the joker type, but Willow had never been as flustered around a man as she was with Eddie. What in the world happened between them?

"As you know, we've had a situation go bad, then worse. Before we get too far into it, it's about time we introduced ourselves," Jackson announced.

"I'm Jackson, the alpha of the Enchanted Pack. You know Dylan and Eddie by now. Next to Eddie is Felix, and next to him is Leo." Jackson said, pointing to the East Asian man covered in tattoos and muscles, Felix. Next to him was a South Asian man who was slim but lean with mid-length dark hair and stubble along his jaw to match.

"On the other side of Flora, are the brothers Ryder and River." The brothers had matching molten dark eyes, with dark, midnight-like skin. The younger-looking one, River, had short braids in his hair similar to Eddie's. Ryder, the older brother, had a buzz cut, just long enough for small waves to form in his hairstyle. One thing every Pack member had in common was muscle.

"So, let's debrief the situation at hand," Jackson said.

⁂

"Let me get this straight," Eddie began, confusion written all over his face. "Flora was followed on her way home from Lust Lane which led her to believe that the man following her just had no boundaries. Then it happened a second time at a store, and she called Dylan. So then, there was an attempted kidnapping at the parking lot, and a sighting outside her window. *Then* there was another attack at the hotel and now a note has appeared at her apartment."

"Sounds about right," Flora confirmed, shaking her head.

"You only now decided to get our help? Are you crazy, you should've called a long time ago." Eddie said, dramatically waving his hands as if it should've been common sense to seek their help. Was it really so common to seek their help? Packs were loyal to their members, but they weren't known to be saviors. She'd already asked them once and didn't have the nerve to ask again. She had to lay out everything on the table if the whole Pack was going to get involved. This she knew but man did her throat become dry and achy.

"I'm not part of the Pack. On top of that, I'm a panther. Let's be for real for a moment — who would've helped out a panther?" Flora said shortly, embarrassed about the whole situation.

She tried to be nonchalant about revealing her animal, but she couldn't even look any of them in the eye at this point. Asking these men and her best friends to risk their lives for her was a lot to take on. It seemed like this was the only way to get this problem resolved cause living life on the run was out of the question.

"We would. A woman in need of help can always get help from the Enchanted Pack," Jackson said, agreeing with Eddie. "Is there anything anyone wanted to add?"

"Considering Cassandra is still breathing after being caught under a panther whose intent was to kill, she obviously knew a thing or two about panthers. She was too skilled — too knowledgeable in fighting a panther, for an average Shifter," Felix pointed out, flexing his hands on his head. Intriguing tattoo designs climbed up his arm and around the base of his neck.

"That's where she and Romeo messed up. Cassandra knew how to handle a panther because she is a white panther. It's probably why Flora didn't kill her ass," Dylan says, glancing at Flora.

"So, what is Romeo?" Luxe asked.

"A damn fox," Dylan spits out. He was clearly still pissed about Romeo escaping from him.

"Flora, you're a panther Shifter?" Luxe asked her eyes trained on Flora. Flora could only nod. Luxe gave her a nod and a warm smile in return. One that said Luxe would keep her secret.

"So, what are we going to do?" Willow asked, pushing her glasses down. Flora couldn't decipher whether her friend's scrunched brows were due to her question or the fact she just found out her friend was a panther. Flora was glad to see her friends were going to be okay and safe in the Packhouse with her. Despite not really wanting to be there herself, it was nice to know that in the end she, Willow, and Luxe were safe and protected.

"We don't know," Jackson mumbled.

22

DYLAN

"You okay?" Dylan whispered, interlocking his fingers through Flora's as they left the meeting room.

"No," she muttered, her eyes blankly staring in front of her. He hated seeing this look in her eyes. One he's seen so many times before during his past rescues. But hearing her be honest with him was a guilty pleasure he could never get over.

"Come with me for a minute," Dylan said. He pulled her back down to the first floor.

He pushed open the door to his room, the comfort of it bringing a sense of home to Dylan's heart. He hadn't slept there for the last month and honestly, he just missed his bed. Their shoes reflected in the mirror that leaned against the wall by the door, just as he had left it. His wolf's hairs lay on the carpet from the last time he shifted in there. Watching Flora in his space, she took a step forward, just enough to admire her shoes in the mirror. Then a sharp look up to him, giving him the eye contact he now desired from her. Raising an eyebrow, she questioned him: his rules, his room, and how to proceed in his space.

Dylan only offered a shrug, he would let this woman do anything, to him, to his room, to his life. Whatever she wanted to do, he'd let her. She bent to take off her shoes, setting the black heels neatly next to the mirror. Her heels blended in perfectly like they belonged in his space. She dragged her feet on the dark gray carpet, sitting on the very edge of his bed.

"This is Dylan Enchanted's room," she said, looking around as if she missed something the first few times. Sketches of his wolf adorned the light gray walls, something that Flora noticed almost immediately. She openly stared at them, causing Dylan to blush. He wanted to rip them down but remained still.

"Since we've been staying together, in the same bed, would you like to…"

Dylan started to ask, but the sudden rush of heat pulsing up his neck made him pause. Fears of her saying no and him being embarrassed started coursing through his mind. His fingers drummed along his thigh as he tried to rein in his nerves. He'd never had such a problem with his nerves before. But Flora Larkspur made everything different. Made him different. He wasn't sure of himself anymore and he wasn't sure how to feel about it.

"Dylan," Flora said, edging him on to continue. Her eyes peered into his and held a heat that had no business lighting Dylan on fire like it did. She smiled, which was good, a win in his mind. Still, he wished he never said anything. They were on his playing grounds now. He had to make the first move and he was nervous.

"Doyouwanttosleepwithmeinhere?" Dylan tried again, forcing the whole sentence out this time.

"Say that one more time? I don't think I heard you," Flora

said standing up, a knowing smirk on her lips. She knew damn well what he had said, but for her, he'd try again.

"Will you sleep in here, with me?"

"Oh, like sex? Or just sleeping?" she asked. Her hands ran up and down his arms.

"Why not both?" he murmured, snaking a hand behind her waist and snatching her closer.

"Why not both?" Flora repeated. "I would love to stay in here, on this gray bed, with these gray walls, with the gray carpet and décor," she trailed off laughing as they looked around the room.

"Gray is a great color."

"It is. I do love it, but some other colors wouldn't kill you."

He pressed on into the room, lying in the bed next to her. Flora scooted closer, leaning her head on his chest. She gripped his shirt hard; he couldn't see her face, but he felt the tears dampening his shirt. He didn't say anything, just rubbed a hand up and down her back as the emotions flowed.

Finally. Finally, she'd let go, and thankfully she was comfortable enough to do so with him.

"I'm sorry, I just..." Flora cried, looking up at Dylan. Her tears glided over the many freckles that dusted her nose and cheeks.

"Nope, it's okay. It's all okay."

"But it's not, I'm crying. I'm under attack, why would... why would Cassandra do this to me? She was a person I could look up to. Someone who helped me, guided me. Why?"

"We don't know yet, but we will soon."

"Yeah?"

"Yeah." It was the only promise he could make.

"Thank you."

"Anytime. Anytime, seriously." He didn't want to go into

depth about how literally he meant what he said, but hopefully, she'd know.

"I need to go see the girls. We are taking my braids out tonight, so I might not sleep here tonight; we'll get done late and I don't want to bother you."

She's taking out her hair? What does that entail? How long does something like that actually take?

"It's fine if you do. I want you to bother me. You can come to bed whenever," he said, hoping to convince her to sleep there with him. It was incredibly comforting to have her by his side. Not only because it made her easier to protect but also because he simply wanted her there. She brought the warmth and comfort he'd missed since he'd started being an assassin, something he'd never thought he'd get back.

"We'll see. How do I look — do I look like I was crying?"

"I'm sure the girls won't care about that, Flora."

"I do," Flora said, wiping her face.

"Yes, you look like you were crying," Dylan admitted, giving her a pointed look.

"Okay where is the bathroom?"

"One is connected to this room, right there," he said, pointing toward the bathroom.

"Flora, how long does it take to 'take out your hair'?" he asked, pulling out his phone.

"My braids are waist-length, so normally six to seven hours?"

Six to seven hours? So he had six to seven hours to do what? What could he do in that time without her? Should he just go with her to take her hair out? No, she needed this time with Luxe and Willow...without him. Disappointed, he rolled over shuffling under the blankets after kicking off his shoes.

"What are you doing after you take them out?"

"I'll let my hair rest for a few days before I put them back in."

"Oh, okay," he said, an idea coming to him. If she's going to put them back in, maybe he could help her. If they take so long to take out, they must take as long to put back in, right?

Dylan opened up YouTube and began his research by looking up braiding videos. Typing 'braiding' in the search bar didn't work. Those braids didn't look like Flora's. He tried again, typing 'box braids'; he was sure he'd heard Eddie using that lingo. Still too many different types of braiding videos came up. One had six different ways you could start a box braid and he was getting nowhere.

"What kind of braids do you have?" Dylan asked, scrolling through videos.

"Knotless braids are what I'm doing the next go round. Something less straining since the break between styles is so short, why?" she asked, walking out of the bathroom and patting her face with a paper towel.

"Just wondering," he mumbled, typing 'knotless braids' in the search engine. That finally limited the types of videos that came up, thank God.

"Okay, can you walk me to their room?" Flora asked, a little bag she filled with hair products hanging off her shoulder.

"You could bring the party here?" Dylan suggested, knowing damn well what her answer would be.

"Dylan," she said pointedly with a laugh.

"Let's go." Dylan jumped up from the bed, saving the video tutorials for later.

THIS BRAIDING SHIT WAS GOING TO TAKE practicing. An intense amount of practicing. Dylan had sent a text to Luxe, asking to practice braiding on her hair but she declined saying she was helping Flora. Then who would he ask? He couldn't do it on his own hair, his hair was too slippery and short. Maybe Eddie would know, he had the longest hair in the house. Though it was hard to tell he had the longest hair due to Eddie's curl shrinkage, more lingo he learned, through the internet. All Dylan needed was some hair to practice on. Eddie was always asking others to do his hair for him so it shouldn't be a problem.

The hours spent on the internet could only do so much. What if he learned the wrong braiding style? There were so many different ones. What if she changed her mind and wanted twists this time? He didn't know how to do twists, which was a whole different ball game. Maybe he should let this whole thing go. Maybe he was overstepping the bounds of their relationship.

He just needed some practice. No pressure. If she didn't want his help with her hair, Eddie sure would. No harm, no foul if she said no. Dylan walked up to Eddie's door, pushing aside the mild embarrassment and dread that would soon follow, and knocked.

"Come in," Eddie hollered. Dylan stepped into the room, taking in Eddie's unbraided hair and the game controller in his hand. "What's up?"

"I need help."

"With...what?"

"Braiding hair."

"You want to braid *my* hair?" Eddie chuckled, surely getting the mocking and teasing prepared in his head. Dylan stood at the entrance of the door, stock still, almost too embarrassed to move. He had a goal to accomplish, and he was going to do it, damn it. "I don't wear the exact same kind as Flora and I don't add extra hair."

"I know." Dylan said, his skin flushing hotly. Of course, Eddie figured out why Dylan randomly wanted to braid his hair. "So can I or not, Eddie?"

"Of course, can you part?"

"Part?" Dylan questioned slowly, trying to remember if he watched a video on that specific section of the art of braiding. "Yes, but it's shaky."

"Good enough for me. I want four rows on each side in the front and five rows in the back," Eddie said, turning his bean bag so Dylan could reach his hair. Sat next to the little gaming spot was the surprisingly neat row of hair products he assumed Eddie used. All he needed was a comb, brush, gel, and ties.

"Hey, I'm tender headed, so be careful," Eddie laughed.

"Instead of focusing on what I'm doing, you need to focus on your game. You're getting your ass whooped," Dylan lied, opening all the required jars and placing everything neatly in rows on the mini table beside them. He read each label and set them accordingly in the order he would use them. If anything, he was prepared.

"Ha ha, funny guy. Get to braiding."

"So, he asked you too?" Luxe said from the open doorway. Her honey scent filled the room as she held the missing ingredient to Eddie's braids. She grinned; the wolf knew what she was doing.

"Practice makes perfect. Does it not?" Dylan mumbled, grabbing the water bottle from her offering hands. Flora's hair would be blown dried, but once again, so many different types of fucking braiding required so many different techniques.

"You're welcome," Luxe yelled as she shut Eddie's door on her way out.

"When is she going to become our Luna already?" Eddie commented.

"Whenever Jackson gets his head out of his ass," Dylan answered, as Felix joined the hair braiding party. He plopped onto another bean bag across from Eddie. His legs stretched well past Eddie's. Felix was the tallest Pack member at 6'4" and the extended ceilings they had to build were expensive as fuck, but they would do anything to make all their Pack members feel comfortable in their home.

"So, when are you getting your own head outta your ass?" Felix joked, staring down at his phone. The damn crow was always on his phone and always knew everything about every damn body.

"What do you mean?" Dylan asked, confused. Taking the comb to separate Eddie's hair into equal, large sections with gel.

"You and Flora.'

He should've known this question was coming. Only for the simple fact that he didn't know how to answer. Labels weren't something he and Flora set. He wanted to bring them up; he wanted to be her boyfriend, her partner, her mate for Christ's sake. But he selfishly wasn't ready to mess up whatever it was they had going.

"Exactly, Dylan, what's going on? Because it's obvious it's more than work going on between the two of you."

"I saw her come out of his room a couple of hours ago," Eddie edged on like a gossiping teen.

"I don't know what's going on yet," Dylan said using the rattail end of the comb to make a general part before slathering gel across the crooked line he made. He kept trying until he finally got the line straight. He wouldn't let Eddie walk around looking goofy with uneven parts.

"Well, you know you're a catch, right?" Felix's frigid exterior never gave enough credit to the love and loyalty he gave.

"That's not the point. The point is what if the feelings aren't there?" Dylan asked.

"They're written all over your face. What do you mean if they're not there?" Eddie said moving on from the game to eating the chips next to him.

"For me, they're there. For her...for her, it's in question."

"And why is that?" Felix questioned.

"Because what if these feelings arose in her because I protected her, continued to save her time and time again. It's like falling in love with the superhero and not the man behind the suit. How do I know she feels the same?"

"Know if she loves you?" Felix said, raising an eyebrow and a knowing look slapped across his face. It made Dylan completely frustrated that he didn't know. Something he couldn't figure out.

"Yes."

"You know the saying, if you love 'em, you gotta let 'em go," Felix said, looking over at Dylan's wounded eyes. He could barely go six hours without her, let alone let her go completely.

"And if they come back, they were meant for you. Or however that saying goes," Eddie finished.

23

FLORA

"Oh my goodness, I'm so tired," Willow moaned. They would have finished taking Flora's braids out way earlier since three pairs of working hands were tasked to take the braids out but with the number of snack breaks they took, it was currently three a.m., and they still had a quarter amount of braids to unravel.

"You can stop if you want, Willow," Flora said, taking the used braided hair and putting it in the grocery bag-turned-trash bag that they hung off a chair.

"Okay, so now that he's probably asleep by now, how are things with Dylan?" Luxe asked, still working on the braid in her hand. Her own blonde hair was swept up in a bun.

"I don't know, he asked if I would sleep in his room with him," Flora said, unsure of where she and Dylan really were in their relationship. She hadn't given it much thought; with the betrayal of Cassandra and Romeo, the last 24 hours had been mentally draining and she was barely holding it together.

"Well, he sent me a text about an hour ago," Luxe smirked, giggling as she grabbed another braid to let down.

"What did it say?" Flora asked.

"Oh, only if he could practice braiding my hair so he could help you do yours." Luxe revealed, wiggling her eyebrows. The blush was furious on Flora's face as the realization hit her like a dog pile of weighted stuffed teddy bears. How fucking adorable. Her assassin was learning how to braid hair just for her.

"Luxe, he probably wanted that to be a surprise," Willow side-eyed Luxe, laying on the queen-sized bed in the guest room they occupied.

"Oh, oh man, please be surprised when he tells you, damn," Luxe rumbled on. Slouching forward, she pouted as she continued working her slim fingers through Flora's curly hair.

"Of course, babe don't worry about it," Flora said with a laugh.

"Okay, *tea-spilling* girl, when did you meet Eddie?" Flora asked, her eyes finding Willow's through the mirror.

"Yeah, how could we slide past that?" Luxe commented, mock glaring at Willow, whose cheeks were flushed.

"I ran into him at the gas station is all."

"And?"

Huffing, Willow burrowed deep into the pillows by the headboard. "And, I might have almost fallen, and he might have saved me is all."

"Okay, cutie. We'll dive into this another time," Luxe said jokingly as she proceeded to tuck Willow in under the huge, fluffy comforter.

"Last braid, girly," Luxe said an hour later. Finally, Flora was ready to drop dead herself. She was more than ready to go see her prince charming, who was apparently trying to learn to braid just for her benefit. No guy had tried to learn to braid for her.

How cute. How caring. Damn, the feeling she wouldn't be able to let him go grew deeper every damn day.

"Okay, I'm going to wash my hair. Thanks for the help, lovelies."

After the scalding, cold much-needed shower in the girl's room, Flora dressed in the bathroom. Now to figure out where she was sleeping. Would Dylan care if she slipped into his bed at four a.m.? She didn't want to wake him or make him regret that he'd offered in the first place. But she really wanted to be wrapped in his arms. Surrounded by his body heat and woodsy smell. Damn, she was going for it. Step by step down the hall, praying she was heading for the right room, she tried the door handle, finding it unlocked, and slid into his room. His soft gray carpet made her smile; it was such a stark difference from the cold hardwood of the hallway. She gently lifted the covers on the bed, just enough for her to slip in. No wall of pillows could save Dylan from her. She wrapped her freezing hands around him, over his chest while hooking her leg over his. His aroma filled her senses and her shoulders finally unwound.

He'd noticed she was there. With a grab of her hand and a pull forcing her arm and body closer, Dylan snuggled into her deeper. No matter how long this lasted physically, this feeling would last forever.

❧

"WILLOW?" FLORA CALLED OUT, HEADING DOWN THE hall. The nerves were starting to eat at her. It was breakfast time, *Pack* breakfast time. The Enchanted Pack ate breakfast every morning together. This morning Willow, Luxe, and Flora were invited to join the morning *Pack* activity. More than invited, they were commanded by the alpha himself to be at the breakfast table with the rest of his Pack while they stayed at their house. For the sake of Flora's ego, she'd pretend Jackson invited them instead of demanding them.

When she awoke, Dylan was gone, and the bed was cold. Flora saw the paper invitation sitting on his nightstand, informing her to be present at breakfast. That's where Dylan must have been. Her brows furred together as she rolled her shoulders back, why didn't he wake her up and take her with him? What the hell was up with that? Her panther was uneasy, shaking from within. She was pissed at being left alone too. Time was running at high-speed as she got ready for the day. Not only was she being forced into unknown territory of Pack life, Dylan also left her high, dry, and alone. Her wildcat was pissed.

So now here she was, getting Willow of all people to come down to breakfast. A faint call back came from the room Willow and Luxe were sleeping in. Hearing Willow's voice, Flora quickened her steps, worry sitting heavy on her chest. Willow hadn't come down for breakfast. No whisper, no hurried rush, nothing. The whole Pack (plus Luxe) sat at the table and waited. They actually waited for Willow to make her appearance before they would pick up their forks. It was the weirdest experience Flora had ever had. She couldn't volunteer fast enough to go searching for the missing woman.

"Not to rush you." *But to rush you.* "We're waiting for you at the table for breakfast," Flora said through the door. What she really wanted to do was to bust through the door and make sure her friend was okay. Willow was always on time. Always. So, for her to not show up on schedule, left an uncomfortable feeling in the air.

"I'll be down in a minute. I'm so sorry," Willow rushed out, her curls a mess and her face holding nothing. She was a blank slate. The glow she normally had was gone and her eyes looked sunken in.

"Wait." Flora paused, grabbing her arm to stop her in the hallway. "What's going on?"

"I'll share at breakfast, I'm already late. Let's go." Willow took her hand and Flora just followed like a lost puppy. Willow was sad, something was tearing at her, so it was tearing at Flora too.

Taking their seats, everyone's plates were still empty. Not a single crumb was found out of place or by anyone's mouth. They really waited. Sitting next to Dylan, Flora's fingers followed the rim of her empty plate while she tried not to stare at Willow. Willow was taking short steps and her gaze was focused on the table as if she was in deep thought. Something was wrong with her best friend, and it sent chills down Flora's spine. She'd never seen her like this.

"Are you okay, Willow?" Jackson asked from his spot at the head of the table. Concern was laced in his voice. He took the first serving, placing a single pancake he'd made onto his plate. Pack members followed his lead, beginning to grab pancakes and bacon, filling their plates and Flora soon followed their lead of grabbing food and placing it on her plate once she got the hint.

"I have an announcement to make if you don't mind," Willow said, glancing around at everyone.

24

FLORA

Flora placed a comforting hand on Willow's thigh — this sudden need for an announcement was news to her as much as it was to everyone else. Luxe's eyes pierced into Willow's before they moved on to Flora's. She also had no idea what this was about.

"Go ahead," Jackson gestured to Willow that the space is open for her to continue.

"I have to leave," Willow rushed out, looking at Flora, regret and a slimmer of something else in her gaze. Something that looked close to heartbreak. Although they had been friends for a while now, they didn't dive into each other's past, but now Flora was wishing they had.

"Why?" Flora whispered.

"Something...something important...has come up back home and I need to take care of it." Willow took Flora's hand from her thigh and held it in her hands, squeezing as she spoke.

"Now, you know that is not the most ideal option. If you leave, we can't keep you safe from whatever Cassandra and Romeo have in the works," Jackson said. He couldn't order her to stay because he wasn't her Alpha. Though Flora wasn't sure if Jackson would do something like that, it seemed his Pack was free to make their own decisions. It was another stereotype the Enchanted Pack broke.

"I wouldn't go if I didn't have to," Willow confirmed. "My family needs me." There was no changing her mind about this; there was a resolve in her voice that Flora could read from a mile away. Whatever it was, it was serious, and she had to go. Flora could reason with that; she was coming back.

"Come back as fast as you can, please," Flora mumbled. She stood to pull Willow into a hug. The heavy tension sitting in Flora's chest became more and more unbearable. Why the hell was she so emotional? The tears she had to work like hell to hold back seemed obsessive.

Willow would come back.

"I will," Willow confirmed.

"When are you leaving?" Eddie asked, his low, toneless voice filtering into the conversation. He looked almost as distressed as Flora. Worry bushed his eyebrows together. His freshly done braids contrasted with the wilting emotion he was exuding.

"Now, or after breakfast."

"Are you going to tell us why you're leaving?" Luxe blurted out, her brown narrowed eyes shooting to Willow. As independent as their little group was, they hadn't been apart since they met five years prior. It was a foreign feeling to be left and Flora couldn't stand it. This felt wrong. Something was wrong and it was up to Willow to share what was wrong.

"I'd prefer not to, not now anyways. Maybe someday."

Damn, not only was she leaving, she wasn't going to tell them why. It seemed like another blow to the gut.

"That's okay, no pressure," Flora mumbled out quickly,

not feeling the assurance she meant to give. A large, warm, hand from the familiar man sitting beside her landed on her leg. He did nothing more than rest a hand on her lower thigh. No eye-contact. No fleeting moment, nothing. The hand lying on her thigh only lasted seconds. Cold air washed over her once warm leg, adding to the mountain of emotions she was feeling. What the hell was that?

She turned her attention back to Willow, the leaving member of their Pack — wait, no. Party? The leaving member of their party. She'd been in this setting for 24 hours and it was already getting to her head. Setting aside that worry, she continued eating, trying to get through the depressing first breakfast at the Enchanted Packhouse. The other members, Felix, Ryder, River, and...darn. Leo! Leo remained quiet, observing what was taking place.

When it came time to say goodbye to Willow, she had her bags ready and waited by the front door. Flora crushed her into a hug, tears spilling down her face. She cuddled her head into Willow's shoulder. Pulling away was hard. This was like moving out of her parent's house for the first time. That feeling she often got when family members left finally sunk down into her body. Knowing she wasn't going to see them for a while stung, everywhere. With Willow, the feeling was no different. It was no different.

"You're my family now, don't forget that. Don't forget me. Promise."

"I promise," Willow whispered back, holding onto the hug tighter. The same gutted feeling mirrored in Luxe's posture. Her hair pulled up in the same distressed, messy bun as Flora's natural hair was.

"I'll drive you wherever you need to go," Dylan said abruptly, picking up his keys. Without looking back, he followed Willow out the door. No acknowledgement was made towards Flora. Or anyone else, really. Flora and Jackson both stared hard at Dylan's car as he pulled out of the driveway.

"What was that about?" Jackson asked. He checked the lock on the front door again before turning to Flora. She could only shrug her shoulders. She wondered if she had done something. Did she say something that freaked him out? Maybe he realized she wasn't worth the hassle of being a mixed-breed couple. Insecurity never fit Flora but when it came to Dylan, boy did she begin to question herself. Her lovely panther, though she loved her to death, it seemed once again, she made her different. Why couldn't she have fallen in love with a panther Shifter? Maybe she wouldn't be going through so much feeling of loss.

❧

THREE DAYS HAD PASSED SINCE WILLOW LEFT. SINCE Dylan became a cold-hearted asshole. Since she'd started living in the Enchanted Packhouse. Two nights ago, Dylan stopped talking to her. Two nights ago, she'd taken the hint and slept in the guest room with Luxe. Two nights of feeling her heart shatter completely for the first time. No man had broken her heart like this before. She damn sure wasn't planning on getting to know this feeling any longer. She pulled on one of her blazers and wiped away the silent tears that stained the pillowcase. She was going to talk to the jerk down the hall.

At breakfast, they still sat next to each other. Though the space between them was mere inches, it felt like miles. Both parties refused to look at each other. Flora wasn't sure what brought on the act, but enough was enough.

"Okay, we've gotten comfortable enough with the new

additions, it's time to get started," Jackson announced when everyone had finished eating. "We start training today, ladies. Meet us in the training room on the second floor in one hour. After that it's time for everyone's animals to meet each other."

"Have you ever met a panther before?" Flora asked, highly suspicious of the events occurring that day.

"First time for everything right? It's safer if your panther and our animals know who friend and foe are and to be able to tell the difference with swiftness." This made her finally look at Dylan, who surprisingly was already looking at her.

"It'll be fine; I'll handle your panther."

"You'll *handle* my panther?" Flora asked, feeling as if her panther was being looked down upon and had to be *handled.*

"I'll take care of her. Read her signs, know when enough is enough," Dylan shrugged, leaning back in his chair, looking away from her again.

"Okay," Flora said, looking back at Jackson. The Enchanted Pack would get to meet her panther.

⁂

"I fucking hate training," Flora groaned.

"It's been three days since we moved into the Packhouse, babe. Eventually this was going to happen, and you knew it," Luxe said.

It was easy for Luxe, she loved working out, dancing, the whole-body moving thing, was her specialty. Willow and Flora, not so much. Thinking about Willow, she missed her so damn much already. She left without an explanation and that totally rubbed Flora the wrong way. She tried not to be hurt but why couldn't she have talked to her?

"Where the hell is Willow?" Flora mumbled stepping on the gym mats of the training room.

"I hope you'd miss me this much when I'm gone," Luxe said following Flora.

"When?" Flora asked. Was Luxe planning on leaving too?

"Never, you can't get rid of me, bitch."

The whole Pack was there. Jackson had demanded they all be ready for anything. The tension was bunching up on her shoulders and running laps around her mind. She couldn't understand why the whole Pack was involved, why Luxe and Willow were involved. Why Willow left and why Dylan was being so cold. While the added help and protection made her feel safer, it didn't take away the guilt of putting all those people in danger. Going up against a panther was dangerous, even if you were on the same side as one.

❧

"FIVE MORE."

"Five more what?"

"Don't play dumb, Flora. You've only done five and the deal was ten."

"Dylan, don't tell me five more push-ups," Flora gasped, falling on her stomach. Working out was never something she was interested in. The ache and burn in her muscles was not the motivating factor Dylan must have thought it was. He was especially on her ass and not in a good way. In fact, it was pissing her off more than anything.

Regardless, staying at the Enchanted Packhouse meant rules had to be followed, and if Jackson said they needed to train that's what she'd do. It was respectful to the Alpha of the Pack, something heavily pushed in Shifter culture.

That being said, the whole 'push-ups, running, burpees, and defense training' was kicking Flora's whole ass. Being sore was an understatement and a hot shower was in order *ASAP*. Exhaling, Flora stood up wiping her sweaty hands along her black shorts.

"Dylan —"

"Flora, don't '*Dylan*' me. Just do five more. It's the bare fucking minimum, how the hell do you expect to protect your-self if you can't even do 10 inversion push-ups, Flora?" Dylan snapped, the frustration busting out of his words as he moved along the mats, getting closer and closer to her. Towering over her with his tall frame and being loud as hell. This was it.

"Who the hell are you yelling at?" Flora asked, trying to keep her own voice soft and cool. She was hurt, emotionally and physically. Yelling was not only rude in her book but brought up unwarranted intense fear. A need to run, to escape, go somewhere safe. Yelling from the one person she was supposed to feel safe with was a fucking joke.

"You, Flora. How have you survived this long not knowing how to fight?" Still, he was yelling.

"I'm done." Turning on her heel, she strode to the door. Ready to pack her shit and leave. This wasn't going to work. If continuing to yell, bitch, and moan was all the communication he was going to give her then why the hell was she still there? "If you're going to be a cold-hearted asshole the whole time I'm here, then I'm done. I'm leaving. Consider yourself fired because I'm not doing this."

"There you go again, not thinking of your own goddamn safety, Flora. That's the fucking problem."

"Stop cursing at me!"

"You stop first."

"How mature, Dylan."

Flora let out a sharp laugh, turning back around to face him. Stomping forward she met him face to face. Anger coursed through her body. She could take care of herself — she had been for six years. She'd been on her own, moved out of her parent's place, fed, shifted, and clothed herself for six years, and just because she couldn't throw a punch, all of it is taken away?

No, it wasn't. She knew deep down that wasn't what he meant. But Flora was on a roll. She pulled her hand back and swung. Of course, trying to hit a trained assassin was stupid. He caught her wrist before kicking his leg under hers, bringing them both to the floor. Heavy breathing and a whole bunch of physical contact brought Flora to an angry flush. Looking away, she slowed her breathing down.

"What if I'm not there to protect you?" Dylan spoke softly. No more stress lines across his tanned forehead, only little amounts of frustration left in his posture.

"Dylan, I've never had to physically defend myself before. You can't expect me to be even a little good on day one."

"I know, I'm sorry. There's no excuse for yelling at you or getting angry."

"All I get is a sorry?" Flora asked. Sweat was sitting at the top of her eyebrows but that didn't stop her from raising them up in question. She needed more than a *I'm sorry*.

"Flora, I'm apologizing for acting like an asshole. I'm honestly scared. I'm scared I can't always protect you and when that happens, I need you to be prepared. I need you to survive this. I just can't see you get hurt any damn more."

"That's all you had to say Dylan. But know the next time you yell at me I'll let my panther take a nasty bite outta your ass. She hates that shit more than I do."

"Let's do those push-ups," Flora conceded, pushing his

shoulder back with a small smile. He stood up as she flipped over. She wasn't sure if the apology was for the last couple of days or just this moment, but it didn't matter. It was time to get shit done.

He squatted down, ready to count her reps as she got into the push-up position. Huffing, she sat back on her knees, her arms already shaking at the thought of having to do another damn push-up.

"Ready?"

With a nod of her head, Flora began the hardest workout move of all time. Bending at the elbows, she lowered her body to the ground. Slowly dropping her body to the ground, she used the last of her energy to bring her body back up. Okay, so she was only doing girl push-ups, or whatever Dylan had called them. But an actual push-up for someone who hadn't worked out a day in her life was too much. Her panther always fought for her when she needed her to. Which wasn't often. Flora didn't find herself in very many positions where she needed to defend herself. But Dylan was right, depending on her panther at all times was unreasonable, her panther needed to be able to depend on her as much as she depended on her panther. They were equals in their body after all.

"One."

"Oh my God, please help me through this," Flora prayed, guiding her body back down.

"Four more."

After four more, Flora left without a word to take a shower, caked in sweat.

DYLAN

"*There you go again, not thinking of your own goddamn safety, Flora. That's the fucking problem.*"

Except Dylan knew damn well that wasn't the problem at all. The problem was him. He couldn't deal with the fact that he would have to live a life without her; that one day soon she'd have to leave him behind and move on with her life. She'd forget him while he'd wish things were different for the rest of his life. The storm taking over inside made him push her away because why save the heartbreak for later? He could savor the bitter feeling swirling inside him and hope it'd turn into hate and secretly knowing it never would.

Except it was getting to be too much. He hated that she left his room, his bed. She started sleeping in Luxe's room when he started being an ass.

He stood outside their door. He needed to air everything out and let her decide what she wanted to do. She was a grown-ass woman who didn't need him to make decisions for her. He knew that yet he wasn't ready for reality. He knocked softly on her door.

"A moment," her soothing voice called out. His nerves rose by the minute. What if he'd messed up everything permanently? What if she'd realized that she wasn't really in love with him — could that happen within three days? Flora ripped the door open, dressed in her signature baby blue blazer set with a white what she called a "bustier" thing underneath. She was stunning, as always. She glowed and sparkled from the lotion she'd put on.

"Look, I'm ready to get this over with. And this whole 'meeting with each other's animals' thing scares me shitless, but I trust you. I trust you to do your job wholeheartedly. So, please, stop my panther from doing something that could get her, we, reported to The Council."

"Of course, Flora, but that's not what I'm here for," he said, smashing his fidgeting hands into his pockets. "I'm sorry."

"Sorry?"

"Yes, I'm apologizing. I've been a cold-hearted ass, as someone recently told me, and I'm sorry." He looked up at her. She stayed completely still as he went on, giving no indication of resentment or forgiveness. "I'm scared, my feelings for you are very real and very deep and I...I'm completely in love with you, Flora Larkspur."

"Dylan," she said, looking at him, a small smile on her face. "I love you."

Time froze, as he knew it would. Inside he was jumping around, his heart pounded with excitement. His cheeks felt completely flushed, but it wasn't the right time.

"How do you know that? How do you know it's not some hero complex or Stockholm syndrome or something?" he asked, even though he really, really didn't want to.

He wanted to wrap his arms around her. Wanted to whisper in her ear that he loved her too again and again.

"Time will have to tell," she said, and she was right. "But for now, let's just play it out."

"Play it out?"

"Yeah, let's play it out," she muttered. She grabbed the collar of his flannel, pulling him down to meet her lips and there was no stopping her this time. He pulled her waist closer, their bodies melting together as their lips finally met. Breathing her in, he tried to pull her closer. To deepen the kiss he'd waited for since he last kissed her in the hotel room. His forehead rested heavily on hers. Soaking in her breaths, he felt her body lock into place against his. This was *right*, even if only for the time being.

"Okay, horny teenagers, it's time to step into the room or break it up. There are kids around here," Eddie joked from down the hall. Separating from Flora, Dylan laid his head on her shoulder before responding.

"There are no kids around here, smartass."

"With the way y'all are going there will be soon."

Flora dragged his arms from around her waist and pulled him into her room. Laughing and flushed with heat and slight embarrassment, they dropped onto the bed, Dylan curling his body around hers. He peppered kisses down her neck and felt his lips curl into a smile he couldn't get rid of even if he tried.

"I need to do my hair tonight," Flora whined, tangling her fingers in his wavy, dark hair.

"Yeah?" Dylan asked, willing his confidence to make a move.

"Yeah, and Willow's not here to help me, again."

"I could help," Dylan rushed out, refusing to make eye contact.

"You know how?"

"I practiced."

"On who?" Flora gasped, surprise taking over her smile.

"On Eddie..."

"Well, let's get to work, then. Are you sure you want to help? It's a long process."

"Of course, I'm sure. Where's the extra hair?"

"Extra hair?"

"Yes, the extra hair. We are gonna braid till our fingers go numb and we have to shift so we can heal."

"I don't think our fingers are going to hurt that bad; our arms, maybe, but not our fingers," she giggled. Flora moved around the room to her hair bag, the one designed to carry any and all hair products she could possibly need. "Let's see what Eddie and Luxe taught you."

❧

SEVERAL HOURS AND A FULL HEAD OF BRAIDS LATER, a knock on the open door interrupted the pair. Felix entered without invitation, plopping down on the bed next to them.

"Are you here to help braid, Felix?" Dylan asked, adding a piece of thin hair to the medium-sized braid. Adding the hair extensions was harder than the videos made it out to seem, but he'd got the hang of it.

"No, but I got an update I thought you'd like to hear."

"What's the update, smart guy?" Flora asked.

"I've found a few areas owned by Cassandra and Romeo Bray, as well as some land that's under the name Klare Bray."

"Their daughter, Klare Bray, died a few years before they started their manufacturing company," Flora said, turning to face Felix.

"Yeah, well that property is a two-level family home just outside Moonlight City."

"So, what's our next move?"

"To finish braiding this lovely head of hair," Dylan cut in, planting a kiss on the top of her head. "We'll talk to Jackson tomorrow." He glanced at Felix.

"Don't leave me out, boys. I am a part of this," Flora warned, continuing to braid.

"Wouldn't dream of it, darlin'," Felix said. "Let's go meet your animal."

The surprise of the sudden realization that now was the time for the Pack to meet her panther settled in her bones, and Dylan could see the muscles in her body tense up as they stood.

"You'll be okay. I won't let anything happen to you," Dylan said, laying a hand on her lower back and guiding her down the hall to the backyard. The rest of the Pack would be waiting for them.

"I'm more worried about us than her."

"Shut up, Felix," Dylan snapped. "All will be okay."

"Put the knife away, Dylan," Flora said, barely glancing at him as he held the edge of his blade against Felix's throat, but he was only warning him. There was no need for him to make her even more nervous than she already was.

A giggle broke his focus. Glancing down at Flora, the small smile on her face lit a warm fire through his torso.

She was interacting with his Pack.

She was smiling.

It was so small, so gentle, he could barely see it, but he devoured it. He wanted to take it all for himself, keep her tucked in his arms and never let her go. He switched the pocketknife closed, sliding it back into his jeans.

"I could've maneuvered out of that hold, Dylan. You need some practice."

"Shut up," Dylan laughed, pushing Felix slightly.

"Hello, *ladies* and gentlemen," Jackson called from the forest line. The crew of three followed him into one of the many clearings on their plot of land.

"The trees do a great job of hiding this specific clearing so with that, know that your animal secret is safe here. I do ask that you keep your human consciousness aware just in case things go sideways so you can take control." Jackson explained to everyone.

"Today, we'll focus on meeting Luxe's wolf and Flora's panther. The rest of the Pack will stay human. Luxe, do you mind shifting first?" Jackson asked.

"I don't mind one bit," Luxe said, moving to stand in the middle of their little circle.

Kicking her sneakers off, she began to undress. Out of respect, the men didn't watch until they heard four paws hit the ground.

Luxe's wolf stood strong, shaking out its black fur and sticking out its tongue. She looked toward Jackson first. Holding his gaze before darting toward Flora. She curled her body around Flora's legs. Laughing, Flora reached down, her fingers curling into Luxe's fur.

"Hello, girly," Flora said, squatting down and giving the wolf a couple of pets.

"When did you meet Luxe's wolf?" River asked, standing in his usual graphic t-shirt and jeans. He watched Luxe's wolf as she made her way to each person sniffing their legs and hands. This was how Shifter's animals got to know each other. Scents were familiar, and once the animal knew your scent, they would be able to recognize friend from foe.

"It was a couple years ago and a complete accident," Flora said.

"Getting ready for your turn?"

Flora shrugged and looked at Dylan. He smiled down at her and intertwined their fingers.

"Don't piss yourselves," Dylan joked. "Her panther is pretty badass."

That earned a few chuckles, but Dylan knew they were just as nervous as Flora was.

"Alright, Luxe you ready to shift back?"

The wolf in the middle of their circle shifted back. Luxe dressed and stood next to Jackson.

It was Flora's turn.

Dylan gave her hand a squeeze before she let go and made her way to the middle of the Pack. She didn't bother undressing all the way before shifting into her panther. Her deep brown eyes quickly met his. She stalked toward Dylan, who squatted down to meet her. She nuzzled her head into his hand and cuddled into his neck just like human Flora did.

"Let's go, girl," Dylan said, standing beside her. They walked to each Pack member, repeating the same scent process Luxe did. Flora's panther got a good sniff of each member as they each got to pet the top of her head.

Dylan knew she'd be perfectly fine. Panthers weren't monsters; they behaved just like every other Shifter.

"You all lived," Dylan said as Flora shifted back into her human form and dressed.

"This time," Felix said, looking questionably at Dylan.

"Until you give her a reason to attack, she won't bite."

26

FLORA

Flora was back in Dylan's room now that they'd kissed and made up. She felt a lot better and more like herself. She wasn't sure where the hell her deep insecurities and depressed feelings rooted from, but she was glad they were pretty much gone. Now all she had to do was wait for Willow to come back.

"Panther!" Jackson appeared in the doorway. "Walk with me."

Matching his stride, Flora followed him down the hall and out the back door. Walking the Pack grounds in silence, she waited patiently for Jackson to say his piece. Nerves built in the pit of her stomach. The open yard closed off as they reached the tree line. The trees got denser with each step they took.

"What do you know about Packs?" he finally asked, his height towering over hers. She paused, trying to think before answering.

"I know they are typically a group of the same kind, who fit together like puzzle pieces, with a bond that goes deeper than blood families," she answered, tucking a long black braid behind her ear. "I also know there is a leader, an Alpha or

Luna, who everyone is supposed to follow and take orders from."

Crossing her arms, she looked anywhere but at Jackson. She wasn't sure where this conversation was headed. Was he going to tell her to leave Dylan? That they couldn't fit? That she could never be part of their puzzle board?

"Look, I respect you and your opinion, I do but —"

"But," Jackson stopped right in front of her. "But we're no normal Pack. Puzzle pieces can break, or have a wobbly fit, or go missing. Packs aren't perfect and each one is different. Most Packs don't fit the mold of a bossy, demanding Alpha with servant-like members. Take our family as an example. Each Enchanted Pack member is so different, yet we fit together so well. That's not always the case. Packs take time to build, heal, and grow. *And* not every Pack blindly follows an Alpha."

"That's amazing, Jackson, really. It's special what you've created here."

"It was all thanks to Dylan, he was an essential starting point to this Pack. We still catch heat for being a new Pack who's broken rule after rule, but it was all worth it."

"Rule breakers? I would've never guessed my good boy Dylan was part of a bad boys' club."

"Flora, our good boy Dylan was an assassin once upon a time," Jackson chuckled, rubbing his chin.

"How many rules did you really break? I mean how many are there?"

"For starters, I'm only 29. A Shifter shouldn't become a true Alpha until they are well into their 70s."

"Old wisdom. I could see that," Flora reasoned as they continued walking on.

"Also, for accepting people of different breeds." Jackson

glanced her way. She knew not everyone in the Pack was a wolf but to hear it proudly from the Alpha himself was telling.

"How did that happen? What made you accept outsiders?"

"We are more than our animals, but more importantly, we are more than our stereotypes. Each member brings something different to the Pack, whether it's Felix's tech skills or Eddie's lightheartedness. It was by chance we met each other and that they wanted to be part of the Pack."

"Not just a Pack, Jackson. *Your* Pack." River appeared before them.

"What are you doing all the way out here?" Jackson raised his eyebrows in question.

"Willow's here."

❧

"WILLOW, OH MY GOD. HOW LONG HAVE YOU BEEN back?" Flora asked, rushing her way through the living room to her friend. Soul-crushing relief flooded her system. Her best friend was back.

"Two minutes, Flora," Willow breathed, wrapping her arms just as tight around Flora.

"Are you...you okay?" Flora whispered, even though all the Shifters in the room would still hear them.

"No, but I will be. We have to focus on you now. Have we gotten anywhere with Cassandra and Romeo?"

"A few ideas, a few locations, nothing concrete," Dylan answered, leaning forward from his corner of the living room.

"What's the plan thus far?" Willow asked, keeping Flora wrapped in her arms, her protective vibe filled the room.

"We can't legally do anything yet. Nothing has happened on our land," Ryder said. Flora knew he was the legal representative and advisor of the Enchanted Pack. If anyone needed a sound mind, their go-to person was Ryder.

"What if we did things *illegally*?" Felix wondered.

"Honestly, it's a huge risk. If it goes to shit, there's a small possibility of us getting out of it."

"Even with your skills?" Jackson asked.

"Even with me," Ryder confirmed.

"Let's take your stuff back to our room," Luxe said, leading the way back to the girl's room.

⁂

A FEW HOURS LATER, FLORA SOFTLY STEPPED INTO the kitchen, weighing her options. She'd been at the Packhouse for a while now, but was she allowed to search the fridge? Eat their food in which she had no monetary involvement in? She was living here temporarily, so it should be fine. Right? Right. With a pull on the fridge door, the previous night's leftovers sat in a container practically screaming to be eaten. Grabbing the mac and cheese Jackson made, she put the whole thing in the microwave. Huffing, she leaned against the white counter. Pushing the anxiety of exploring her boundaries with the Pack around in her mind, she typed away on her phone, pulling up the latest episode of her current reality TV show. She removed the dish from the microwave, the cheese melting in her mouth. Homemade mac and cheese was the only kind she'd eat. The meal reminded her of home, how her father used to make it for her all the time, and she just never could replicate it correctly.

As a moan slipped through her lips, Jackson walked in.

"Hungry panther?" Jackson joked, pulling open the fridge door.

"I like how you constantly remind me of my animal." Her

sarcasm at its finest, she couldn't tell if he was trying to make her feel bad about her animal. Those days were over.

"I just can't believe I met a panther, and it didn't try to kill me."

"Why would I try to kill you?"

"Not you, the panther."

"Did she try to kill you when she met you? Cause I don't remember that."

Turning to face Flora, thoughts flew across his face as he walked closer, leaning on the counter.

"You know what, now that you mention it, no. She didn't try to kill me. In fact, she was a lot nicer than Eddie's bear was back when he first joined the Pack. There is no real reason to be so shell-shocked," he said, taking her empty bowl and washing it in the sink. "I'm sorry, Flora."

"I accept your apology, Jackson." She smiled, hoping she no longer scared him. She appreciated that he thought her panther was cool but calling her "panther" was taking it a bit far.

A knock on the front door pulled them away from their conversation. Dragging his body away from the spotless sink, Jackson strode to the door. Opening it with a smile; he welcomed in their guests.

"What are you doing here?" Flora asked, walking toward her parents.

"What are we doing here? My daughter is asking her parents what they are doing here after she was physically attacked — what, a few weeks ago — and forgot to mention it to her parents at any point in time." Lola Larkspur brought Flora into a hug that told her just how much she'd been worrying for her daughter.

"I'm sorry. I thought we'd handle it."

It was a lame excuse. Admittedly she didn't think to drag them into her problems. She was a grown adult, yet she'd got what seemed like the whole world dealing with her issues.

"We will always have your back, Flora," her father, Will Larkspur, said. He pulled her into a hug as desperately worried as her mother's.

Stepping back, she looked back at Jackson, confused. "How did you find my parents?" She guessed he had more tricks up his sleeve than he let on.

"I know people, Flora. Anyway, thank you for coming. Please, let's sit." He gestured to the living room. Following the crowd, Flora saw the rest of the Pack, plus Willow and Luxe, already arranged on the couches around the room.

"Surprise," Luxe weakly said, giving her best jazz hands as Flora gave her friends a joking glare. They probably knew this whole time that her parents were on their way, and not a peep came out of them. Not even Luxe, and she was horrible with secrets.

Off to the side was an empty two-seater for her parents. Jackson took his place, front and center of the room, while the rest of the Pack occupied the remaining chairs and couches.

Noticing there was no more room to sit, Flora walked to stand behind Dylan in his chair, but he was up faster than she could comprehend, guiding her to sit in his seat.

A blush covered her neck as she made eye contact with her parents who took notice of Dylan's actions. Clapping his hands to gather everyone's attention, Jackson began. "We pretty much know what's going on, but before I finalize a plan of action, I wanted to open the floor to suggestions."

Dylan reached down, lightly massaging Flora's shoulder; she guessed he could sense her discomfort. While this whole mess was because of her, she couldn't move her focus from the strong, calloused hand pressing into her shoulder. She didn't want to; she didn't want to think about what had happened up to this point. How her simply being there at the Packhouse instantly put everyone there, some she barely knew, in danger, and that didn't sit right with her.

What did she have that Cassandra and Romeo wanted? The only solution that she could come up with was that it wasn't really her that they wanted, but her animal. That was the only thing of value besides her business that someone would have an interest in. Enough interest in to try to steal.

Cage fighting was the reason panther Shifters kept their animal hidden, why others were so afraid of them. It shattered her heart to be in this mess when her parents fought tooth and nail to keep her out of it. They kept her hidden, yet things always seemed to come to light.

"I assume you know who's behind this?" her dad asked, running his hand down her mother's arm. The tension was apparent in both her parents' postures. Looking around the room, everyone was tense. Felix, more so than anyone else. His eyes were stuck on her dad. He looked about ready to dash from the room, and that didn't seem like Felix's style.

"We do," Dylan spoke up, letting his hand slide from her shoulder, the warmth going with him as he walked to stand next to Jackson. Why did he go over there? He was fine where he was. She wanted to demand he come stand by her again, put his hand back on her shoulder, and not to move away from her again. But she just kept her focus trained on the man holding her sanity together.

"We know the Brays, Cassandra and Romeo, are a part of it for sure and then there's Emery, Flora's ex-partner, who we're not sure about."

"Well, you can take Emery off that list. She's working with me," her dad said, leaning back on the couch.

"Dad, what?" Flora sputtered. Emery was working with him? Since when?

"Can I ask why?" Jackson took over, crossing his buff arms in front of his chest. Flora's gaze shot to Dylan, an "I told you so" glint lighting in her smile. But all he did was chuckle with a shrug.

Her dad made eye contact with Felix before he continued.

"I can tell some of you haven't heard the name WL, my cage fighting name." This Flora knew, but the Pack didn't. Their physical reactions were tame, but she knew inside they were reeling. When most people heard about his background, they became scared and would start to distance themselves from her and her family. Now that the information was out with the Enchanted Pack, she wasn't sure how to react to their response. Willow was making unbreaking, nerve-increasing eye contact that made Flora's feet want to take off running before anyone else did.

But she stayed planted in the chair. A deafening silence occupied the living room.

Willow cracked a smile. Flora knew she'd get through this.

"How'd you get out?" Dylan asked, his eyes moving from Felix to Will.

"I have the same question for the boy right there," he said, pointing to Felix.

Felix was a cage fighter? He looked 25, tops.

"That's not something he'd like to share," Jackson spat out, keeping his eyes trained on her dad.

"How could I forget WL?" Felix muttered to himself, running a hand through his hair and staring off into space.

"Okay," Flora's dad acknowledged before continuing. "I

escaped the ring by accident. The guards left a starving, angry panther in an unlocked cell. What I do now that I'm free is take down other rings and set other survivors free. Emery helps draw in the collectors who frequently try to kidnap strippers — people who typically have no one to miss them if they disappeared."

Flora knew this was what her dad did. Escaping a cage fighting ring was unheard of, and apparently, there were two people in the room who were successful at it.

Dylan, and his sock-covered feet had been making their way in her direction. One step after the other, she stared at his feet before he finally made it back to her. He stood behind her chair, tracing his hand up and over to land on her right shoulder. Taking the tense weight that was there, he replaced it with a warming, comforting feeling.

"So, Emery is officially off the suspect list?" Flora asked, hopeful.

"Yes, she is, kitten," Dylan assured with a deep laugh.

"Kitten?" Flora's mother teased, wrapping her own hand around Will's hand.

"Now you are welcome to stay here in the Packhouse so that you could be closer to your daughter if you'd like —" Jackson began to offer.

"We'd love that." Lola's heavenly voice cut through as she stood to meet Jackson's welcoming hand. Will chuckled and shrugged his shoulders, following Jackson to their guest room.

※ 27 ※

DYLAN

Somehow, in some way, Flora slunk past her parents' room and into Dylan's, much to his relief. A few nights apart didn't kill him, more like it prepared him for what was to come. They were on limited time. He knew he should be distancing himself, but he couldn't resist a morning cuddle.

Except this morning something quite different was next to him when he dragged his hand up to her side of the bed. Being met with rough animal fur, he nearly fell out of the bed, catching himself on the headboard. He awoke to the sight of a black panther in his bed. The following growl from his lack of contact made him quickly cuddle back, petting the animal's side.

"Flora," Dylan questioned, snuggling his dark head of waves against her panther's head. The purr that followed sat comfortably in his chest. He was growing to love her panther as much as he was growing to love her human. "Are you coming back to me? We're not allowed to shift in the house."

A growl met with another purr, a silent *no*. Knowing he had to get the panther out of the house before Jackson saw and lost his shit, Dylan dragged his body away from the panther and to the bathroom to get ready for the day.

"Your sharp eyes following my every move would be scaring the shit out of me if I didn't know you liked me." Dylan had no clue what to do with the 140-pound panther in his bed. Suddenly, she shot out of bed and darted toward the door.

Dylan followed after her, unsure of what the hell was happening. She pawed at the door, thankfully not using her claws in the process. He slid out the door keeping her inside. Something was riling her up. The scraping noise got louder and louder as he made his way out front. There Ryder, River, and Felix were trying to get a large bed frame through their front door.

"Damn," Dylan huffed, leaning against the staircase's banister.

"Yeah, tell me about it," River said. Even with super strength, getting that huge ass frame through the door had to be a feat. Dylan was thankful Jackson hadn't asked him to help.

"Need any help?" He didn't want to ask, but knew he'd have to offer. He hoped they'd say no, because he had a restless panther losing her damn mind upstairs, still pawing his door down.

"Nah, we got this," Ryder said, lifting the bed frame towards the stairs. "Get that panther outside before Jackson realizes."

"Already working on it," Dylan laughed, rushing up the stairs and sliding back into his room. The noise of furniture being moved was setting Flora off, so it was definitely time to figure out where to go for the day.

"Let's go for a walk." There were only so many places to go

as a Shifter. Even less if you were supposed to be in hiding. Cassandra and Romeo could be anywhere.

"Wanna go to the cabin?" he asked. Flora's head shot up in interest.

Bingo. That worked out perfectly for what he actually had planned for the day. Hopefully, at some point, Flora would shift back. In case of that, he packed a bag filled with clothes for both of them along with snacks.

"Alright, let's go, kitty cat."

THE HOUSE HE HAD BUILT ONCE UPON A TIME STOOD strong. The welcoming feeling of the house wasn't the same, though, he realized as he pulled up. That comforting sense of belonging was gone, and it scared him shitless.

He opened the car door, and the panther previously pacing his backseat took off. Her muscled legs powered her straight to the backyard, where the trees and bushes welcomed her full-speed run. Dylan grabbed their bags, setting them on the back porch. He slowly undressed, giving the panther more time alone. His wolf was clawing at the forefront of his mind, whimpering to be let out.

That impatient little shit. Laughing, Dylan ran forward before jumping off the porch and shifting into his gray wolf. He gave complete control to his animal as his paws hit the ground running. The wind whipped through his fur and past his ears as he searched for the panther. A playful game of tag began as the trees got denser.

Hours passed, and the chilling morning air turned into afternoon heat. Coming to a trot, the panther turned to face the wolf. Their animals rubbed their heads and licked each other behind the ears. They were worn out and ready to give back control to their human sides. Their animals came to a stop in a small opening in the forest.

Flora shifted first, slowly lifting a hand up to give Dylan a pet. He waited, patiently letting her get to know his wolf. His wolf was loving the attention from the pretty woman. Eventually, Dylan shifted back, her hand landing on the top of his human head.

"Good doggie," she said, patting his head and breaking out into a fit of laughter.

"Okay, kitty cat, let's get dressed."

Thank goodness his wolf went back to the porch and brought the duffle bag to a small opening of the dense forest. He opened the bag slipping on his own pants, before scooting the bag towards Flora. Pulling on a shirt, he looked over to see Flora's still naked body searching the bag.

"Dylan?"

"Yes?"

"Why are there no clothes for me?"

"Yes, there is I — it's right here," Dylan said, holding a t-shirt and sweatpants that belonged in his closet. He was playing dumb, of course. He knew what she was talking about.

"That looks like those will fit *you* perfectly, Dylan, but where are my size clothes?"

"I like you better in my clothes," he said, holding out the oversized clothes to her naked form. Unfortunately, there was no time for setbacks in what he had planned for the day.

"My panther acted all cute and cuddly and fluffy for you and you just ignored all that and packed whatever you wanted? No leggings, no nothing huh," she muttered, crossing her arms over her chest.

"Just put them on, kitty cat."

With a huff and a smile, she put on the clothes. "At least you packed my underwear."

"I almost didn't," Dylan chuckled as the perfectly timed *rustle* sounded from the forest.

"What was that?" Flora asked, her posture going straight as a board. Her human body was preparing her; that was good. But it was time to see how much she'd learned.

"Stay here, I'll check it out." He moved toward the sound, disappearing around the high bushes. It was time. He could perfectly see the opening Flora stood in. She was too cute standing there in his clothes. Thankfully she would be less mad about messing up his clothes instead of her own. Maybe the white shirt wasn't the best option for him to pick. But she shouldn't be focused on ruining clothes anyway.

"Dylan?"

No answer, he couldn't. It could mess everything he'd planned up. As soon as she took a step forward, a figure appeared from behind, grabbing her wrist firmly. They started off easy as instructed. Flora shouted before ripping her wrist away. She tried to take off running before the ski-masked man jumped on her, bringing them to the ground.

She then flipped, so she landed on her back instead of her front, once again remembering the many lessons Dylan had given her. The masked man's hands wrapped around her neck, squeezing almost enough to choke her. But the adrenaline wouldn't let her tell the difference between a strong grip and actual asphyxiation. She tried to pry his hands away, but missed a step, bringing her legs to his shoulders to try to bring him down.

"Fuck, I can't fucking remember." She tried to yell, tried to yank the masked man down with her legs. She soon gave up on that and clawed her way into his arms and sides, landing a nice scratch on his wrist. A sudden flash of realization crawled across her face, and she locked her hands around his elbows, bringing her legs back to his shoulders. Before the crack of arms breaking could occur, the man maneuvered out and away from her hold. Sitting back on his knees, the masked man looked toward the spot where Dylan disappeared to. Flora took the time to sit up and run in Dylan's direction. As he came out of his hiding spot, she crashed into him.

"Dylan!"

"It's okay," he said, wrapping his hands around her head. He was careful not to create too much friction on her freshly done braids.

"No, we have to go." She tried pulling him away. By the time she finally looked back, her masked attacker had pulled off the ski mask.

"Damn, wearing that shit gets hot fast."

"Leo!" Flora yelled, shocked.

"You're a fucking fast learner, Flora. You damn near broke my elbows for real."

"I thought it was real. I thought — Dylan, you planned this?" Hurt flashed across her face and landed heavy in his chest.

"You needed to know you could take care of your panther and yourself. Training and pretending to do the moves wasn't enough to prove that to yourself, so I took it further. I didn't mean to scare or hurt you, kitty cat. I promise."

"Told you she'd snap your neck bro," Leo chuckled.

"Look at you, baby. Almost whopped Leo's ass, nearly broke his damn arms. You are so much more than a panther; you're everything."

"I wouldn't say she nearly whooped my ass since I couldn't hurt her," Leo mumbled.

"I'm kind of hurt, Dylan," she finally said, looking at him. The fear that he constantly saw in her was back but heightened.

"I thought you'd be less scared...but I — it wasn't my intention to hurt you; I'm sorry." He wrapped her in a tight hug. "I'm so sorry. I fucked up."

"I get practicing but...but do it when it doesn't feel so real, maybe. No, it'll never feel less real."

And he knew she was right. Even if they were dead, Cassandra and Romeo would forever haunt her. He didn't take into account her emotions and applied his training on her without thinking.

"I should've thought this through. I'm sorry, Flora."

"How'd I do?" she asked, peering up between the two Pack members. The tense air was replaced with a playful wonder.

"Perfect, once you remembered the move."

"Yeah, you really had me scared for a moment there. I couldn't get away fast enough," Leo laughed, walking with them back to the cabin.

"Yeah, well, I am that bitch, so be careful. Tell your friends."

"I won't be doing that, sweet pea," Leo said.

Even though Dylan hurt her, he could see the chipped piece of her mountain of fear being left behind on the forest floor. So, in the end, a little pain would ease the waves of hurt and terror racking her soul.

28

FLORA

After dinner, Flora found herself pleasantly stuck in Dylan's room. He said he'd be right back, and so she waited. She played around with the TV remote, flipping between different reality shows, each entertaining only the subconscious part of her mind. The terrifying but seemingly harmless events of the day trampled around in her mind. She was truly scared and more so when she realized Dylan had planned it all. She now knew she needed the test; she just hated that she *needed* the test. Before this whole mess, she didn't have to worry about whether she could fight or not. If push came to shove, she could shift into her panther and kill whoever was the problem.

She prided herself on being a confident Black woman. She shoved the words down her own throat every day. She could do anything — be anything — if she worked for it, right? The truth was that confidence in oneself was a never-ending battle. Something she had to maintain, like a plant. She would always have to fight for that confidence and...and that was okay. The hold she had on her confidence would slip and slide in her grip but never fall. Her confidence in Dylan would never fall, so her own confidence damn sure shouldn't fall either.

It shouldn't have come to the faux attack in the woods for her to believe she could protect herself. The work and practice she put in should've spoken for her.

"Flora?" Dylan's voice sounded, breaking her train of thought.

"Hey, what's going on?"

"I got something for you," Dylan said, inching closer and closer with his hands behind his back. She crawled to the edge of the bed and kneeled up to meet his lips. He pressed closer, careful not to smush her, and she trailed her hands up into his soft, clean hair, gripping the waves and holding on tight.

"Wait, you're going to make me forget," he murmured, leaning back slightly. "You ready? I got you a gift."

"Yes."

"Now, I know this won't match all your outfits, you may not even like it —"

"Dylan, I'm sure I'm going to love it, now show me," Flora said, a big smile taking over her face. He took a deep breath before showing her the little box.

"You even wrapped it!" Even the quality of the polka-dotted wrapping paper was high, and she felt a moment of guilt for ripping it up. The velvet box within grabbed her full attention. She slowly opened the soft box.

"It's a risk to gift an accessory to an accessory designer."

"Dylan, I love it," she whispered, pulling the simple silver chain-link necklace, which matched his own, from the box. "How?"

"Well, I made this one, so it's a one-of-a-kind."

He smiled, clasping it around her neck. "I got mine as a way to remember home. I made one for you, to remember..."

"Remember what?" she asked, suspicion seeping into her tone.

"Remember the time we've spent together."

The silence was unbearable. The tension rose slightly before she smiled, wrapping him in a hug.

"Thank you. I love it." She inhaled his scent as if she would never get the chance to do so again. It almost felt like a good-bye, but she knew it wasn't. She couldn't let him go. Turning to face him again, she wanted to claim him. To bite him, sealing his fate with hers. To make him her soulmate. She could tell he wasn't ready yet. He wasn't sure of them, of her, and she couldn't decipher why.

With a smile, he kissed her forehead, down her nose to her lips.

"I love you, Flora," Dylan mumbled. "I love you, I love you, I love you."

"Dylan," Flora moaned as his hands started to travel from the dip in her waist further south, gripping her ass and hauling her closer.

"Yes?"

"I think I lied about not having a knife kink," she said. She could feel the rising heat around her eyes; her heightened emotions telling Dylan everything he needed to know.

Her hands followed the outline of one of his daggers in his belt. Chuckling, he reached back to grasp the one with the jade-colored handle, the one she liked the most.

"Are you sure 'bout that?" he asked lightly. Drawing the blade up her arm, he pressed down —not enough to cut her, but just enough to get her adrenaline going.

"Yes," she gasped. Her body went rigid with want.

Laying her back on the bed, her top rode up her stomach.

She felt her braids pressing into her back beneath her. And her chest *heaved*.

"You've been such a good girl, Flora," Dylan said, beginning to draw the blade a little harder against her. "You want to get dirty?"

"Yes!" she moaned, trying to gain friction between their clothed hips. "Please..."

That was all he needed. He dragged the blade up her arm and to her stomach, just above her pelvis.

"A little blood never hurt," he winked, finally drawing a light line of blood just above the edge of her pants. "Don't want to get these dirty." He proceeded to cut her pants off, starting with the side seam before ripping them straight off. With the pain of the cut matched with the anticipation of pleasure, Flora could hardly contain herself.

"I liked those pants," she said, biting her lip. Damn, that was hot. She was left panting and bleeding under him.

"I'll get you a new pair." He leaned forward, his lips dangerously close to the line of blood he drew. It started to drip around to the sides of her. He took his tongue and licked the little trail of blood clean.

"I'm no vamp, but you sure do taste good," he murmured.

Her hands found his head and gripped his hair tighter and tighter as each minute passed. Her body rocked when his tongue finally touched her skin, following each trail of dried blood back to its now closed source.

"It'll heal in a couple of days."

"I'm not worried about that, now *fuck* me."

"Your wish is my command, kitty cat." Dylan helped her shirt up and over her head, then completely undressed himself.

He feathered kisses over her as he crawled up her shining body. "God, you are beautiful."

"Oh, really?" she breathlessly said, smirking. She arched her back as he shifted to line their hips together.

"And intelligent, and strong, and confident, and caring." He took her nipple in his mouth. "I can't get enough of you."

Flora wrapped her legs around his waist and reached for his shoulders. Dylan eased himself into her. Her heels dug in his lower back as she moaned. Again and again, he drove into her. He pistoned faster and faster until her groans of pleasure filled the room, and her wetness covered her thighs.

She met every grind, pleasure singing over every inch of her skin. Staring up at the wolf, her eyes met his. His electric stare opened her soul. She loved him, and she could see in his deep, brown eyes he loved her too. He was her blanket, her protector, her world, and he was blind to it.

Dylan was so stuck in "what if's" he couldn't comprehend her emotions. She'd have to make him see, make him feel what she does. She didn't have any other choice.

Her orgasm shot from the base of her spine so hard she could've cried. Ecstasy filled her senses.

"My turn, baby girl." Dylan fucked harder, riding out her orgasm and chasing his own. His hips jerked and his pace became rapid. His thick, burning cum filled her, and the groan that slipped from his lips made her shiver.

Thank fuck she wasn't in heat. There would be no pregnancy scares today.

"God, Flora."

"Goddess, Dylan."

She laughed tiredly. Dylan pulled out and moved to lay next to her. His lean muscled arm wrapped around her, bringing her close. She felt her breathing come back down and her heartbeat slow.

"Flora?" Flora's mom's voice filtered through the room.

Lola waited patiently on the other side of the door while Flora shot out of the bed, untangling herself from Dylan's warmth.

"One moment," Flora yelled as Dylan's hands playfully tried to drag her back into his bed. "What the fuck? Was she standing out there the whole time?"

"Come on, stay."

"Dylan, my pants!" she gasped in disbelief. She ran to the closet and pulled a pair of leggings out.

"I said I'd buy you a new pair," he said, still chuckling at the situation.

"Flora, I'm not calling your name again," Lola said from the other side of the door.

"When did I become a teenager again?" she mumbled, putting her shoes on.

"Come back to bed, I'm not done cuddling." Dylan smirked and patted the empty spot next to him.

"I don't have time; she's about to burst through the door!"

"Then wear this," he said, getting up and grabbing a black teddy bear-type jacket and throwing it at Flora. "It's cold outside. I'll be waiting for my cuddle." Flora rushed out the room with a giggle, closing the door tightly behind her while putting the jacket on. She was instantly surrounded by Dylan's woodsy and mixed berry scent.

"He's got you giggling like a schoolgirl, huh," Lola said, walking off toward down the hall. "Walk with me."

"Of course."

"What is your interest in this Pack?" Lola came in hot with the questioning. Flora knew she would. Her mother was never a bullshitter.

"I'm not sure. It's not up to me," Flora answered. Regardless of whether Dylan became her mate or not, she couldn't force her way into the Enchanted Pack. She still wasn't sure how they felt after meeting her panther. They could say they were in awe or cool with it all they wanted, but she wouldn't be able to tell until shit hit the fan. Would they still think she was so cool? Would they trust her not to kill them?

"Do you remember my friend Vlad?" They stepped into the Enchanted Pack's backyard. The dense trees and bushes line an unmarked walkway, a pathway for privacy and protection. "He was a panther like us, more your dad's friend than mine, and he fell in love many years ago. Have you met his wife?"

"No, I've only met Vlad a few times." Flora shrugged, shoving her cold hands into Dylan's teddy bear jacket.

"His wife, Fern — don't get me started on the name — is a fairy."

Shock drenched Flora. A Shifter *and* a fairy? If she thought a wolf and a panther were societally mismatched, a fairy and a Shifter was even worse.

"How did that happen?"

"Fern's family are travelers, and local diners were *the* hangout spot for Shifters," she laughed, a glint of happiness in her eyes.

"We were on a date, Vlad and I, when a fairy with her wings out walked into Eleanor's Diner. I knew as soon as Vlad and Fern made eye contact that it was over between him and I. I could practically read the apology across his face.

"Their families were horrified, so they went off across the state. They live in a cute little cabin made perfectly for them. Enough space for her to fly around and enough woods for him to shift freely. They actually created a small community up North."

"That's...that's perfect," Flora muttered, her eyes wandering away from her mom. Is that what she wanted with

Dylan? To run off to a nice little cabin somewhere? No, their situation was different; that wasn't an option. Dylan had his Pack, and Flora had her business.

"The point of me telling you this is that anything can work out if it's meant to be."

"How do you know it's meant to be?"

"It hits you, suddenly, or gradually. There will be a moment when you just know. And when that moment happens, you'll wonder how you didn't know in the first place."

"Thanks, Mom."

"Hmmm, yeah, now who helped you with your hair? Some of this doesn't look like Willow's work."

"Ma — Dylan did," Flora giggled, guilt for laughing latching onto her soul, knowing he tried his best. "He just needs some practice. Don't laugh."

29

FLORA

Flora had never met anyone who brought forth the kinds of feelings Dylan had. Past boyfriends couldn't hold a candle to him. He made her feel wanted, appreciated, and beautiful. It was honestly hard to put into words. Waking the next morning, her eyes stayed glued to his sleeping form cuddled up to her.

He was perfect. He didn't care about being the big spoon or the little spoon. He didn't care that she was a panther Shifter. He looked at her, *always* looked at her. Not her animal, not her business, but her. She couldn't let that go.

She dragged her fingertips up his arm which was wrapped around her pulling her in even closer. She never wanted to think of a time without him. But how did she tell him that without him hightailing it out of there? Brushing his hair out of his face, she bit the inside of her cheek.

"You're my soulmate," she whispered, cuddling into his arms as tight as she could. "I know it."

She couldn't tell how he felt, not on something to this level. Soulmates in the supernatural world were your one-and-only. Flora wasn't sure which of the other species had an instant connection, but with Dylan, she had a connection. She fell for him fast and hard, and that should have made her nervous. It should have made her hesitate and question herself, but she was so sure that Dylan was her mate. She could bite him right now, leaving her permanent mark that would pair them together forever. He wasn't ready, though. She could read it in his eyes and his behavior; he still kept her at a distance. Still, she fell asleep, hoping he'd stay with her in the end.

She woke once more, the sound of the shower letting her know he was still around. Rolling out of bed, she decided she needed some air. Fresh air, with the wind whipping between her ears and her tail trailing behind her. Leaving a note on his nightstand, she rushed out to shift in the backyard.

Practically ripping her clothes off, she made it to the protected woods and shifted. Her panther was always ready to play. Staying in the Packhouse made Flora realize how cooped up she kept her animal. Her animal side needed to be let out way more than her human side did. Flora tried to be more in tune with her panther. To take care of her panther as her panther took care of her. Climbing trees and dodging bushes, she played for what felt like hours but must've been mere minutes.

Her instinct told her something was wrong. She couldn't pick up a specific scent but the air was...off. An unknown scent filled her nose but she couldn't place her finger on why it seemed familiar. Another Pack member maybe? Shit, there was a stranger on Enchanted Pack territory. Flora made the quick decision not to confront the stranger and to hightail it back to Jackson and have him handle it.

She was fast, but whoever was there was faster, more prepared than she was. A figure looped a leash and collar around her panther's neck. Her racing body was yanked back-wards. Landing on her back, she scrambled to get up. She tried to claw at anything: trees, bushes, rocks, to slow the pace of her capture. Her gut told her this wasn't a test but the real deal. She was failing to escape either way. The collar punctured her all around her neck, weakening her more.

Whipping her head back, she spotted Romeo. He had control of the leash as Cassandra walked forward. Flora's panther tried to scratch and bite her attackers, but Cassandra was smart and avoided getting close enough. Flora let out a deafening roar, her last attempt at escape, in hopes someone would hear her.

She wasn't alone anymore. She had people she could depend on. Unfortunately, none of them were fast enough to stop Cassandra's needle from piercing her body, quickly leaving her limp and unconscious.

DYLAN

A stark mixture of ice and dread covered Dylan's body the moment the first echo of Flora's roar met his sensitive ears. He couldn't move fast enough, stepping over his Packmates as every person in the house rushed outside to investigate.

"Flora!" he screamed, praying he wasn't too late. He had one damn job that he was fucking failing at again. He dashed through the same woods where she was supposed to be safe. On the same Pack land that was supposed to keep everyone safe. All under the rules of The Council, where they were to live peacefully and could be happy.

But he fucking knew — he knew the type of people Cassandra and Romeo were. He worked against those types of people for years. They didn't play by the rules; they never would. And neither would he.

"I can't pick up a fresh scent," Jackson confirmed as they met in the middle of the forest. Trees surrounded the empty walkway the Pack had been carving out for years.

"Oh my God," Luxe said, tracing her hand along a tree with deep scratches, likely made by Flora.

Fuck. He failed her again.

"They got her." River's voice was so low it was barely audible. Dylan looked at him, seeing the same hurt and pain he was feeling. In Felix, in Jackson, in everyone. It was surprising. This was his job; Flora was his responsibility, yet that didn't matter to his Pack. Someone was in trouble, and they'd save them together.

"What do we do?" Eddie questioned.

"Has anyone caught her scent? We could follow it?"

"I can't smell shit, it must be scent blockers. We'll have to come up with a strategy better than rushing in. Cassandra and Romeo obviously have planned this down to a T, so we need to come up with something fast. We have 48 hours to get Flora back. Meet in the meeting room in ten minutes," Jackson instructed, storming off with Luxe striding just as strongly beside him.

Dylan walked directly to the Pack meeting room. His weapons felt heavy on his body, he could feel them with every muscle he moved, and he itched to hurt someone. He needed time to think separately from the group. Flora was gone and he had to get her back. That was his mate in their hands.

His mate.

His *mate*.

He knew Flora was his fucking soulmate, and he still let her slip between his fingers.

"It's not your fault, hun." Lola's voice streamed into the room. Will followed close behind.

"It was my job to protect her, to keep her safe, and she's not only gotten hurt but now she's gone," Dylan complained, running his hands through his hair. Her parents were comforting him. Comforting him, how much of a joke was he?

"Do you think Will was able to keep me safe 24/7? All 30 years we've been together?" Lola asked, taking a seat beside Dylan and taking his hands in hers.

Will explained, "Cage fighting collectors got furious that a whole load of panthers escaped. They found out I did it and they came for my wife. This was before Flora was born, thankfully, and fairly early in the relationship." He rested his hands on his mate's shoulders. It looked as if the action was to comfort her, but Dylan could tell it was really for Will. "I lost her. I was crushed and could hardly breathe. I knew she was mine to hold, to keep, to love, and protect and I was already doing a shit job. But the important thing is that I got my shit together and found her then killed everyone involved."

"The most important bit being that he brought me home safe," Lola emphasized, a playful glare shooting at Will.

"You'll find her. Your Pack will find her." His daughter was in danger, there wasn't much he could say other than "find her".

"Damn right, Mr. Larkspur. Let's get this rescue mission started," Jackson announced, taking his seat at the head of the table. Lola and Will moved further down the table as the rest of the Pack filed in moments later.

Dylan sat stewing, already missing the heat of Flora's body next to him. He sat still, completely relaxed as the decision of his next assignment came to light. He'd been too lax and now he was paying the price for it. Protecting Flora was supposed to be just that. Protecting her. That job was over. It was time to save her and end this. Cassandra and Romeo should've never gotten a second chance and he'd make them regret taking that chance.

"Cassandra and Romeo Bray, I'm putting them on the List," Dylan said as the meeting came to an end.

"What about turning them into the Council? Are you sure, man?" Leo asked, sitting up straighter. They couldn't stop him, and they knew it; the ball was officially in Dylan's court. A court he knew like the back of his hand. where there was only one winner, and that winner was always him.

"Positive," Dylan confirmed.

He wasn't supposed to fall back into his assassin nature, but for Flora, he realized he'd do absolutely anything.

"What's the List?" Luxe asked slowly. Her eyes searched each of the Pack members. Most of them avoided eye contact, not wanting to lie to their future Luna.

"It means their asses are grass," Eddie snickered as Leo shoved him.

"More like their ass can be found several feet under the grass," River laughed and was met with an icy glare from Felix that shut him up immediately.

"Dylan?" Jackson asked, waiting for permission to share his life. Most were never ready to hear, let alone keep a secret, but he trusted Luxe with his life. He viewed her as his Luna already. They'd be together sooner or later.

"I was an assassin for six years. The List is where assassins pick up jobs. We can add or remove a target from the List with team approval. As long as we *add* someone to the List, the big guy will cover my ass if shit gets to the Council."

"Who's the big guy?" Luxe asked.

"My old boss," Dylan said.

Dylan turned his attention to the empty spot where Flora usually sat. Is this how it would feel after he eventually let her go? Empty, lost, heartbroken? Would the empty pain sit in his chest for the rest of time?

"Okay," Luxe said, staring straight into his eyes. "Dylan, if you don't think I wouldn't kill Cassandra and Romeo myself at this point, you'd be dead wrong. All things considered, good and bad aren't always black and white and if anyone knows that it's us."

"How are we getting Flora back?" Willow questioned, bringing her restless hands to the table.

"We have a location," Felix said, turning off the screen of his phone. "We actually have two. A house in Moonlight City and another in bum fuck nowhere under the name Klare Bray."

"Klare Bray?" Jackson muttered, running a hand over his face. "Who is Klare Bray?"

"Their dead daughter," Willow said, confusion written on her face.

"We need more of a plan than just showing up, a distraction maybe?" Luxe ran her hands through her hair.

"That could work, but we're not sure how many people are working with the Brays and why they're doing this."

"Isn't it obvious? Flora's a panther, why else would someone kidnap a panther? Cage fighting." Felix said, shrugging his shoulders.

"No, that can't be right. Cassandra is a panther herself; would she give up her own kind?" Ryder questioned.

"I wouldn't put it past her," Leo commented.

"If this involves cage fighting, we have less time than we originally thought," Felix sighed.

"Felix's right; collectors have gotten smarter. We have to move faster," Will said.

"Because of the lack of time, we gotta rush in. Ryder, River, Felix, and Will, you go to the home in Moonlight City and check if Flora's there. Eddie, Dylan, Leo, Willow, and I will go to their second location and check there. Amongst your-selves, pick who will distract and who will seek in. Let's move," Jackson said, already moving out the door.

"What about me?!" Luxe shouted in a rush, which stopped Jackson in his tracks.

"Can you and Lola hold the house down, in case Flora escapes and comes back here?"

"Of course," Luxe said, moving toward Lola. "Keep your phones on and brightness on low."

The air was filled with acrid dust and hints of nail polish remover. In her panther form, Flora pushed her human consciousness forward. Her eyes searched the light pink room she was in. A white twin bed frame with a horse painted on the headboard was situated across the room, next to a large bookshelf. She went to take a step closer, but a loud clunk and a tightening around her neck made her halt. Jerking her head back, she saw shiny silver chains reaching out from a matte black box stuck out of the wall. The chains appeared to be attached to a collar around her neck, a collar with inverse spikes poking into her neck.

Growling, the only thing she could really do was sit like a damn dog waiting for its owner. Every time she tried to move, the creaks in the wood floor blared to life, forcing her ears downward, as she tried to shy away from the noise, when a voice finally spoke.

"Hello, Flora." Cassandra appeared with an insulting kitty-sized water bowl in her hands. Her smile did nothing to comfort Flora, not like it used to. "There is much you don't understand."

Flora's panther was pushing for control, but this time, couldn't give it to her. Human Flora had to be in control this time. She tried to shift to human form, but the jarring pain in the back of her neck made it impossible. Another growl slipped past her lips.

"Your growls don't scare me darling," she said, her slick voice tensing Flora further. Cassandra took a gentle seat on the bed, smoothing out the blankets and taking the pillow and sniffing it. "The presence of a girl is gone. Nothing here smells alive anymore. It's all empty, dead."

Flora wished she could tell Cassandra to get on with her point. "You know, I had a daughter, Klare, she too was a beautiful black panther. She got it from her grandmother. My side, of course." Cassandra let out a small laugh, one filled with hopelessness and despair. "She died in a car crash." The woman sat the pillow back in its place; she then paced back and forth just close enough in front of Flora, so she wasn't in reach of an attack.

Flora knew their daughter had died, but nothing much beyond that. Hearing a Shifter was killed in a car crash was surprising. Normally, the Shifter would heal themselves by shifting back and forth from their animal state. The pain they'd be in would be hell on Earth but constant shifting would kick in the healing process. The problem probably lay in the fact Klare was young, she was only 17. Shifters under 20 couldn't shift as well as an adult could. Flora felt for Cassandra and Romeo, she really did, but the fear that terrorized her body now overpowered any sorrow.

"I couldn't go on without her, we tried to have another, but it never worked out. I couldn't get pregnant. You should know it's hard for mixed breed couples to become pregnant," she advised, finally looking down at Flora. "Well, I am not sure you'll actually need that information now. Most replacements don't live for very long. They get selfish and angry, and try to leave the comforting, loving home we've built just for them."

She sounded pissed as if the thought of her victims wanting to run was with utmost disrespect. "Here, darling." Cassandra placed the bowl down in front of her. "Drink up."

There was no way in hell Flora was willingly going to drink that water without the ability to heal. There was no telling what they could've put in it. She took her paw and swiped it back at Cassandra, spilling it over her ruby red shoes.

"You ungrateful little brat!" Cassandra exclaimed, proceeding to pick up the bowl and throw it at Flora. She could only sit there and take the hit because of her inability to move much.

Smoothing down her dress, she calmed down and smiled. "It seems you need more time alone." She strode out of the room, slamming the white wooden door shut.

Flora was alone, but she couldn't determine if that was a good or bad thing. All she could think about was how to get the collar off her damn neck.

❧

HOURS HAD PASSED, THE COLLAR FELT TIGHTER AND tighter, and the pricks of the spikes punching into her neck went deeper. Her panther had begun to fight Flora's persistence for control. Panther Flora believed she would get them out of there; the small problem was that Cassandra and Romeo were prepared for a panther's fight, a panther's stealth. What they weren't ready for was Flora's. Her newfound training with the Pack wasn't a lot to fall back on as she couldn't recall a lot, but her human mind was smarter than before. Flora could hear approaching footsteps.

Ding, ding, ding, round two began.

"I see you've already lost your water privileges," Romeo sighed, stepping into the room. He slid his tired body down the wall directly in front of her. He sat, one leg bent up toward his body and the other lying nearly too close to Flora's ready claws. He twirled a pen, acting entirely too nonchalantly, she thought. "Cassandra and I...we go back and forth between good cop and bad cop. When it comes to you, my sweet doll, she seems to have a soft spot for you. I sort of do too, to be honest," he said, rolling his head against the wall.

Flora's eyes followed Romeo's every movement. Every blink, every twitch of his fingers didn't go unnoticed. She needed to know everything she could about the way he moved if she was going to get past him.

"I'll tell you, the last girl that was here was over 10 years ago. She was a charming one. Charmed the trust right out of us. You know, she got to get her collar taken off. This dresser here," he said, pointing to the white dresser she'd memorized the tufts and scratches on, "is full of different collars. The one you have on is our beginner-level collar, so that you understand how things are going to be. The spikes remind you who's in charge. We are. Nothing too crazy. The next one, once you've earned it, will allow you to shift. It will also allow me to shock you. A simple press of a button will put you in an immense amount of pain."

"You should know not a whole lot of girls survive a shock like that in their human forms. Especially when I don't allow them to shift back and heal." Was that a warning? How long was this going to last? Flora tried to focus on survival, but the terror running laps in her mind was distracting as hell. But all you need to know is that if you mess up again, you'll have to deal with me and my toys."

His voice was so casual, so familiar, yet the threat was deafening. She thought that was it, that that would be all, and he would leave. That was until he stood up to the dresser in question. He wore a lazy smirk as he dug through a drawer.

Flora's panther was clawing at her mind, begging to take control. She knew what was coming and tried to protect Flora, but after 24 years, it was time for Flora to return the favor. She tried to remain confident, telling her panther she could take whatever Romeo was going to do to them. The real show was about to start.

"Only, that's not everything. I'll share one secret since you're my second favorite daughter. One that even Cassandra doesn't know." He took a moment to run his fingers over his weapon of choice. "Secrets must be kept at any cost. Are you willing to pay the price?" He squatted down in front of her, a black dagger shining between his hands.

"I guess you can't really answer, can you?" He smiled too big, too cruel to be the Romeo she once knew. The quiet, quirky, deeply-in-love man she thought she knew was a false perception of the monster in front of her. Terror ran up and down her spine as Romeo expertly twirled the dagger in his hands, blood trickling through the small cuts he made in his own hand.

"Most cut their pointer finger and mix their blood as an intense form of secret-keeping but you, little panther, don't really have fingers." He moved fast, the dagger piercing her paw. The searing pain shot around the area and deep within her. A growl slipped, but her panther consciousness stayed back. Flora took the brunt of the mental pain. She could cry, and it wasn't just for the pain Romeo was putting her in by jamming his bloody finger into her paw. Her panther trusted her fully. Her panther was depending on her to keep them protected.

"There, our secret will be kept between us, for as long as you live." He said, stepping back out of reach to sit on the bed, crossing his ankles and leaning back on his hands. He appeared completely relaxed and gazed at his dresser of weapons.

"There was a time when our baby, Klare, would go play out back in the woods. It started once a week; she'd go and play for a few hours every Wednesday. We asked to play with her sometimes, but she never wanted us to. We thought it was safe for her to play without us — there was no one around for miles," he started, blinking as if in a daydream.

"I should've known a vampire could've covered that distance in a matter of minutes," he muttered.

The shock of a vampire in the area chilled Flora.

"She was the same age as Klare. The vampire would meet her in the middle of the woods with a backpack of toys. They'd play every Wednesday for exactly three hours. She'd wait for little Klare to return to our backyard before she'd take off."

"She could sense me there from the start. One day the vampire waited and once Klare left she looked in my direction. I stepped away from the tree I was hiding behind and introduced myself and thanked her. Klare was shy, didn't have too many friends." He laughed as if being caught by a vampire, no matter their age, wasn't a death sentence.

"She asked if it was okay, playing with Klare. I made the deal that it was okay, as long as I could watch over them. So, it went on for years."

"The day Klare died, I had met the vampire, Remi, out in the woods and told her in the most humane way that her best friend had died. She cried, I cried. The problem was that I couldn't let go. I couldn't let go of Klare's best friend. I couldn't ignore the time Klare, Remi, and I spent together. So, I asked her to meet me at our regular time the next week."

"I had a week to prepare the shed and to learn how to trap a vampire. Once the time came, I was ready; I captured her," he laughed, his eyes staring out the window.

"Well, that's enough for the day. Behave, little panther." He took his leave, and Flora was left stewing, chained to the wall.

BASED ON THE PASSING OF DAYLIGHT FROM THE window, one day and night had passed since Flora woke up in the bedroom. After a night of figuring out how to save herself, Flora had come up with nothing. Cassandra and Romeo were too prepared. The only thing holding her captive was the leash and collar bolted to the wall. If she could figure out a way to get out of it without taking her head off, she was sure she could get back home.

"Good morning, darling. How have you been?" Cassandra walked in with another damn kitty bowl, this time full of meat. "You see, there is a system here. You have to earn things. Once you start behaving, you'll upgrade to cooked meat, from there you can shift, and get the collar off, and so on." There was no way Flora would force her panther to eat that. She could tell by the smell that it was expired. Her eyes peered up to Cassandra, who smiled down at her. She lightly kicked the bowl towards Flora.

Flora wanted to swipe her paw and throw the shit back at Cassandra, but that would backfire into a terrifying meeting with Romeo.

With a sigh, Cassandra left the room, leaving Flora to stare at the dish. She could go without eating for a while but not for much longer. Flora aimed her claws back at the chain that kept her hostage. She hated waiting for a savior. She knew the Pack was coming for her, but since she wasn't an official Pack member, she couldn't bet her life that *they* were coming. But Dylan, he was coming for sure. Something in her soul told her to wait it out and that he was coming. She just couldn't figure out if he'd get there in time. Cassandra was growing tired of her behavior, and Romeo was all too happy to inflict pain on her. Would he do this every day if she stayed? Her paw was still healing from the day before. Since she couldn't shift back and forth, she healed slower than the normal rate.

She really couldn't catch a break, and the heavy thudding of footfalls near her room told her it was Romeo. Did they really have to take turns coming to see her?

"Hello, darlin'." Romeo smiled, getting comfortable at the dresser. Digging through whatever weapons he had stockpiled in there, he carried on. "Not hungry? Maybe I'll have to convince you to eat. Starvation is not allowed here."

"No, not until tomorrow." Cassandra's voice dipped in. "Give her a few days to break. Let's go, Romeo, not today," Cassandra said, holding out her hand for Romeo's.

All Flora could do was stare, even when Cassandra uttered the words she'd been praying for. She'd get a few days. She'd have at least another day to figure out how the hell to get out of there.

They were husband and wife; that love was real. So real, in a way, Romeo listened and immediately moved like a magnet to her hand. The sound of the door shutting brought a level of peace to Flora — hopefully, they'd stay away for the rest of the day.

That hope was crushed only a few hours later when Romeo walked in once more, his grimy presence inching closer and closer. Cassandra's protection was as absent as it was limited. Romeo stabbed her paw, and for that, she'd defend her panther's honor by striking back. She'd have to wait him out. She had to appear weak and broken and wait for him to get cocky enough to come closer.

"So, what are we promising today, little panther?" he asked, crouching down beside her.

She was leaning against the wall, using the entire length of her chain. She glared at Romeo before turning her head away. She didn't necessarily need him in her direct line of vision; she just had to feel his presence. Feel the space he took up and pinpoint his location.

He got closer, stood closer and peered down at her as if he was the better, stronger animal. She had to give him some credit. He captured a panther, after all. But he was still weak. She was confident he'd mess up soon. His mistake was going to be an opening for her. She just had to be ready to take it.

"I know you're not ignoring me, little —"

His mistake was perfect. It was too fucking perfect. He took one step closer. That one step was all she needed to leap forward. Faster than he could see and swiped her large paw across his face. She might not have killed him with that blow, but he'd always remember it. Flora Larkspur had struck him deep enough to leave a scar if he didn't shift quickly enough.

"You fucking bit..."

He rushed out of the room. They both knew a panther was naturally stronger than a fox. If he shifted, he was as good as dead, and with that, Flora had won the battle. She could rest easy, if only for a few more hours until hell reared its ugly head in the form of a pissed Romeo. She had to get out now. But how the hell was she going to get this blood-pinching collar off?

As the blood seeped through her neck where the spikes dug in, she'd yank until she couldn't anymore. She would yank on that damn leash until the wall gave out, and she'd run like hell. She no longer had the time to wait for Dylan. She had to save herself.

32

DYLAN

Dylan had walked into scenes like these millions of times before. The houses were always dark, even in broad daylight. This was the same as all his missions before: save the victim and kill the capturers.

Except it wasn't. This was personal. He wanted to *kill* Cassandra and Romeo, but not more than he wanted to save Flora. The urge to save overruled his urge to kill and it threw him off balance. The weight of each step fell heavy but silent, dreading what he'd possibly see. From experience, he'd known there was no limit to the horror the state of the victim could be in.

Every single rug that lined this hall was crooked, except for the last one. Flora must be in the room at the end of the hall. A loud bang sounded from the room she must be in. His heart was beating too hard, and his urge to run was demanding. But he crept through the house as fast as he could, his hand heavy on the doorknob. He sent a silent prayer up to the goddess of the moon, hoping what he'd reveal on the other side of the door wasn't a sight from hell itself.

It was a kid's room. Pink walls with blood splatter painting the walls and the floor in front of a wardrobe. Quietly, he stepped forward, feeling the coldness of the room even through his long-sleeved shirt. Flora's panther was standing, ready to pounce. The only thing stopping this predator was a chain collar and leash connecting her to the wall. At least, that's what Dylan had assumed. There was a piece of drywall barely holding a black box to the wall; chains attached Flora's panther to the box. Sensing Dylan in the room, Flora's head snapped toward him. He couldn't move too fast or get too close in case her panther couldn't recognize him.

The possibility of her attacking him was very real, but he needed to know that she was okay. He carefully stepped closer when Flora's panther snarled in his direction. Dylan whipped his head behind him, making sure Cassandra or Romeo hadn't found him yet. He knew his Packmates could take care of themselves, but anything could happen. Dylan was with an angry panther so adding another possessive panther and sly fox to the mix was the last thing he wanted to do.

Edging closer, Dylan was just outside Flora's reach. She ran toward him, her heavy chain yanking her back. The black box must be heavy as hell. It had fallen off the wall with a loud clang. The box weighed her down to the floor now instead of the wall. Unsure if she had tried to attack him or had attempted to get his help, he reached his hand out slowly to see what she would do.

The panther slithered back up to him, sniffing his hand before pressing the top of her head into his hand. She let out a happy purr at recognizing Dylan. He yanked on the chain hooked on the black box, with no luck of getting it loose. He stuffed his hand in his pocket, taking out a bobby pin he kept on his missions, and tried to unlock the collar around her neck.

Flora's panther made his job difficult by trying to lick his face. The blood coating both the collar and her fur was no help either, but with a clang, the collar fell from her neck before Dylan could catch it. The sound was loud as hell.

"It's time to go, kitty cat." Dylan popped up, starting toward the door. Flora's panther rushed in front of him, standing protectively between him and the white panther that appeared at the door.

"Damnit."

Before Dylan could think of how to get them out of this situation without hurting his love, she wasted no time lunging for her captor, scratching across the panther's face. Flora launched with the right amount of strength and awareness to land an agonizing blow. She fought blow for blow and Dylan couldn't have been prouder and more terrified.

Being in the same situation again left Dylan with a sense of déjà vu. This time he was trained to fight a panther both in wolf form and human form. Except he didn't have time to pull his dagger, blade, or gun, because a big-ass fucking grizzly bear stood outside the door.

Who the *fuck* was that?

When the white panther swiped her paw at Flora, Dylan moved as fast as the human-enhanced body could. He wrapped his hands around Flora's panther, yanking her to him. The impact pushed them into the kid's bed behind them, just in time for the drooling grizzly to swipe its human head-sized paw at the white panther, slamming it into the wall next to them.

The incredibly pissed off white panther crawled out of the dented wall to face the bear, who left no room for her to recover before lunging at her with its teeth, holding it down by the neck and biting down hard.

Wasting no more time, he kneeled down to make eye

contact with his mate. "Please Flora, you're safe, please shift," he mumbled over and over as the bear continued to rip the dead white panther's limbs apart. A few pets and prayers later, Flora's human body curled into his. He quickly ripped off his own shirt to give to her.

"Flora? It's Dylan; we gotta go." He was met with silence as she focused on the mangled white panther across the room and the grizzly still going at it.

"Who is that?" Her voice was small, not finding the strength to stand.

"I don't know and that's why we have to go."

"Willow, you bitch. I fucking knew it," Flora mumbled, trying to grasp at Dylan's shoulders to stand. Blood still covered her neck and a spot on her hand where a hole gaped. While he wished he could get angry about the amount of blood coming from his mate, they didn't have time to waste.

"What? Flora, we have to go now," Dylan said, bringing her body up with his, trying to drag her to the window since the bear was blocking the only other way out.

"Willow!" Flora yelled, her complete focus on the bear.

The bear froze, its deep black eyes focused on Flora. It stared at them; the white panther's blood slowly dripped from the bear's body, sending chills down Dylan's arms. He wasn't sure who this bear was and didn't want to stick around to find out. As soon as he made a move to jump through the window with Flora in his arms, the bear shifted.

Shrinking down to the 5'7" foot woman they both knew, Willow's gaze focused on them. Flora rushed from Dylan's arms after giving his hand a squeeze.

"Oh my God, Willow," Flora said as she wrapped her friend into a death hug.

"You're okay? You're okay, Flora?" Willow's words rushed

out. Dylan removed himself from the window to close the door to the room. Romeo was still out there somewhere.

"Thank God it's you, Willow, but we still have to go," Dylan said, pulling Flora's hand in his. He didn't want to let go. She was his to protect, his to get to safety.

"No! We can't," Flora whimpered, flashing her eyes around the property.

"Why?"

"No, you don't understand."

"Then tell me, Flora, because we are running out of time." He was sweating and beginning to panic. He couldn't get them to move fast enough.

"There's one more," Flora rushed out, whipping her head around, looking for something.

"More what Flora?" Willow asked, tugging Flora out of Dylan's arm.

He could feel his anger rising. He respected Willow, liked her even, but taking Flora out of his arms was a dangerous move for anyone right now. He could feel his wolf edging for control, fought back the urge to reach for a blade, to yank Flora back firmly into his hold.

He wanted to hurt. Hurt others because he was hurt, more importantly, because Flora was hurt.

"A vampire."

Dylan could feel the returning rush of chills and terror consuming his body.

"Where?" he asked.

"In a shed, with a basement, in...in the backyard. A place Cassandra would never go. She been trapped here since Klare died." Flora wandered out into the hallway on a mission.

"How the hell did Romeo capture a vampire?" Willow asked.

"We'll have to ask her when we find her," Dylan murmured, racing through thoughts of past experiences with vampires. He'd worked with one before, but also fought one, and those suckers packed a bite. "What if she attacks us? Have you ever been on the opposing side of a vampire?"

Their rescue mission could turn sideways quickly. Flora could get hurt, and that wasn't a risk he was willing to take.

"Have you?" Willow asked, following Flora down the stairs to the backyard.

"Yes, and it isn't fucking pretty." He was trying his damndest to convince them to leave the vamp behind, but in reality, he wasn't sure if *he* could actually leave her behind. This was his job. This is what he did for a living. Saving those who were unlucky enough to fall victim to those who were stronger, smarter. Those with sick minds and too much cash.

"I'm not leaving without trying to save her, so let's go," Flora announced.

"Where are y'all going?" Eddie whispered, running toward the group. "And why don't you have any clothes on?" he questioned Willow. He proceeded to shove his own shirt at her, unnecessarily helping her arms through each of the oversized armholes and pulling it down her body.

"We have one more to save. Take Willow and Flora; have the car ready," Dylan said, guiding the two girls toward Eddie. He was going to save the vampire, but he wasn't going to put Flora or Willow at risk.

"But —" Flora said, trying to reach out back to Dylan.

"No, I will get the girl. You get to safety," Dylan was already taking off toward the wooded backyard. If Romeo was hiding a torture shed from Cassandra, it would be deep within the trees.

"Dylan!"

"Flora, if your ass isn't with Eddie, I'm not going to save her, so *go*. You'll meet me back here with the car. Promise," he yelled, running in the opposite direction.

"Promise." She dashed off with Willow and Eddie.

Running through the branches and leaves of the muddy forest, he knew there was no saving his clothes now. Going deeper into the brush, he found a small shed, maybe five-by-seven feet, and had a feeling Romeo was there, ready for a fight.

He silenced his steps so he could try to keep the element of surprise. Taking the handle of his jade blade, he broke the locked handle clean off the door. Edging it open, he stood behind the door, using it as a shield and listening carefully. He pulled out his gun, putting his Shifter pride away. He kept it trained in front of him, searching the small space and peering down the narrow staircase for any hiding spots Romeo could be in. That sly-ass fox could've hit the ground running the minute he realized he was outnumbered.

"Hello?" he called down the staircase. Slowing his steps, he flipped the light switch. Harsh lighting filled the basement. Directly in front of the staircase was a wall of bars, similar to a jail. Inside was a bed, a dresser, another door, and a desk. Standing in the middle of the room was who he assumed was the vampire.

"Who?" she asked, backing away from the bars. Her voice was small and broken. She pressed her back along the opposite wall. Her eyes followed every tick in Dylan's body. She was aware of him as much as he was of her. Dylan kept his gun trained on her. He couldn't risk an attack; those fuckers were strong. He had no clue how Romeo could trap a vamp without dying.

"This is a rescue mission. There was a panther Shifter trapped here and my Pack came to save her."

"Another one?" she questioned, moving a single step forward. She had long black hair, her taupe skin surprisingly smooth and clean for someone being held captive. She was young, just barely an adult.

"Cassandra is dead and the whereabouts of Romeo are unknown. You have a choice: you can come with me, or you can stay here."

"You have a gun pointed at me," she pointed out, nodding her head toward the gun. For someone who had been kidnapped, she stood strong, her stance wide. She was ready for a fight. Dylan figured she must have been constantly in fight mode with Romeo and Cassandra being part of the equation. "Why would I trust you? How do I know this isn't some test?"

"You don't have to trust me. You have a choice. I'll walk away right now; just say the word," Dylan told her. He didn't want to leave here knowing Romeo would be coming back for her, but he knew all too well you can't save someone who doesn't want to be saved.

"Okay, I'll go with you." Just as the words finished coming out of her mouth, Dylan shot at the lock twice, breaking it and sending it crashing to the floor. He waited for her to rush out, but she just looked at him.

"Let's go."

"I can't open the door. The bars are covered in something — a witch made it — it burns me."

Her eyes shined with pain. Those damn witches always made shit ten times harder.

"She must have also made these fuckers the scent blocker pills, too." He yanked open the door as wide as it would go, and the vampire shot from his line of vision. He probably wouldn't really care where she went if it wasn't for Flora. She'd want him to bring the vamp back to the Packhouse to ensure the vamp's safety.

Racing back outside, he found her standing in the grass, looking as if she had nowhere to go. "You can come with me," Dylan offered, grabbing her arm and dashing toward Eddie's oncoming car.

The door swung open, and Flora's relieved face eased the pressure of the mission from Dylan's heart. The vampire climbed into the car, and Dylan followed.

"Where are the others?" he asked, checking over Flora for the sake of his own mind. The wounds around her neck were closing up; little holes dotted evenly around her entire neck. The stab wound on her hand didn't slip past Dylan either. Romeo would pay the price for touching her.

"Chasing Romeo; he's a fast little fucker," Eddie said. Jackson, Leo, Ryder, and River would be able to handle that. If not, they'd come home, and Dylan would take it from there. Romeo probably avoided him knowing what it was like to fight him previously. "The guys raced here when they realized Flora wasn't at the Bray's other house."

"Next stop, home," Eddie murmured, pounding the gas and letting the car fill with the steady quiet they all needed.

33

DYLAN

The door of the Enchanted Packhouse busted open before the rescue crew could reach the front porch.

"Oh my goodness, my baby!" Lola gasped, yanking Flora from Dylan's arms. Lola ran her hand repeatedly over Flora's frizzed-up braids, pulling her in tight.

"I knew we could trust this Pack," Will murmured, looking over at Dylan. With a curt nod of his head, Dylan stepped back, giving the family some room. He had his time, and now it was their turn. He could share when he had to. This wasn't goodbye, he could give the woman time with her family.

Once Flora's parents released their daughter, Luxe wasted no time smashing Flora's body into hers. "Don't you ever do that again," Luxe said, half-joking, shedding a few silent tears.

"Who is this?" Lola asked, holding both her hands out to the vampire.

The girl had a childlike shyness about her, appearing unsure of whether to trust anyone yet. She stood awkwardly, her knees turned inward, and her hands shaking. For a moment, she froze. Her scared brown eyes pierced Lola's when she finally took one trusting step forward, which Lola met by pulling her inside the house to sit down.

"What's your name?" Lola asked, her voice smoothing, mothering.

"Remi," the vamp answered, her attention spreading across the room. Dylan knew the feeling and dealt with it often. She was watchful of everyone and the bigger the crowd got, the worse she'd feel about them. Rescued victims didn't quite understand when they were safe and wouldn't until something flipped their internal switch.

"Last name?"

"I can't remember."

"How old are you?" Luxe asked, squatting in front of her. Remi relaxed on the couch a bit, visibly calmed by being able to look down at Luxe.

"Seventeen, I think —"

"What the hell is a vampire doing on my land!" Jackson's voice rang out as the door burst open once more. Jackson stormed into the room, his broad shoulders and heaving chest taking up more space than normal.

"Jackson, it's okay," Luxe soothed.

His Alpha scent cracked the energy in the room. Dylan could tell Jackson wasn't aware of the power of his scent; his focus was completely on what he perceived was the threat.

The alpha was steaming, fresh from a fight, and his instincts were at the forefront of his mind. Meeting another paranormal, different from your species, was normally bad news. It meant war was either already here or coming.

"Jackson, Romeo had her locked up. There was no way we were leaving her," Flora said, her head turned down in respect. She stood next to Dylan, finally.

Dylan could hear his mate breathing in his scent. With each

inhale, her shoulders would release a little tension, and that in itself made Dylan feel on top of the world.

"She's just a kid," Luxe said, holding the teenager's hand. Dylan was sure that small physical connection was the only reason she hadn't taken off the moment Jackson entered the room. The Enchanted Alpha stared at Remi. She stared back and began to shake, probably itched to run, Dylan assumed. "She needs a shower and a change of clothes. She'll come home with me if you don't want her here."

"You'll take home a vamp you've just met?" Jackson asked, stress laced in his voice.

"That's what I just said."

"Romeo is still out there. You need to stay here," Jackson argued.

"Last time I checked, he wasn't after me, Jackson. On top of that, I am a Luna, I decide what I do, big man." They were toe to toe, the alpha energy ping-ponging between them. Luxe's eyes searched the room. She looked toward Dylan, then back at Jackson, and she sighed. She knew this technically wasn't her call to make. This wasn't her Pack.

"This is your Pack, your Packhouse, so you make the call. But I'll make sure she's safe and welcomed everywhere she is," Luxe muttered, dragging Remi upstairs.

"What happened to Romeo?" Dylan asked, looking over to Jackson, who took a seat on another couch. Leo, Felix, Ryder, and River sat as well, looking over to their alpha.

"He got away," Jackson said. "We're going to find him, don't worry, Flora."

"I'm not," she said, curling tighter into Dylan.

"Tonight, we rest. We got Flora back," Jackson announced, his eyes wandering toward the stairs Luxe and Remi disappeared too.

"What are you doing about the vamp?" Felix asked.

"Her name is Remi, not 'the vamp'," Willow said, sitting back in the recliner. She had been silent since they'd gotten in the car. Eddie's wrinkled shirt covered her thighs, but Dylan could tell she was still uncomfortable. Dylan guessed it was the lack of clothing plus her animal being exposed.

"Remi," Felix corrected. 'What do we do?"

"Let me think," Jackson answered, running his hands over his head. He calmed down now, "We are a Pack, we make decisions together. What do you all think?" he asked.

"Can she stay here?" River asked, playing with the curls that lay over his face.

"You need a haircut, my brother," Eddie commented, a playful smile on his face.

"That's up to us...and her," Jackson said.

"You mean up to Luxe? She was pretty clear."

"Pretty clear, and right. Remi is just a kid who's been stuck in a basement for who knows how long." Jackson shook his head.

"We need to call Madeline and Kingston," Leo commented.

"Who?" Flora asked, her head still tucked into Dylan's chest. He wouldn't let her go, wouldn't move until she did, that much he knew. He couldn't unwrap his arms from around her even if he wanted to.

"Madeline is the Vampire Council Member, and Kingston is the Shifter member," Ryder said. "Can she hear us? Remi?"

"Yes," Dylan answered. Vampire hearing far surpassed Shifters'. If she was paying attention and Luxe wasn't talking her ear off, she could hear every twitch any one of them made.

"They won't hurt her, will they?" Willow asked, worry etched on her face.

"No, Kingston won't. Madeline...we won't let her."

"We starting a fight with the vamp of all vamps?"

"Not if we don't have to, but you know how this Pack rolls. We protect those who can't protect themselves," Jackson said, his decision final. "I'll call in the morning. For now, everyone goes to bed. Thankfully another bed for one of the guest rooms just came in."

Everyone said their good nights. Flora gripped Dylan's hand. A sign of forgiveness for failing to keep her safe from Cassandra and Romeo. "Let's go," he whispered, guiding her to his room.

The door shutting was the beginning tick on the timer on his apology and the limited time they had left.

"Flora, I'm so sorry," he started, turning to face her and grabbing both her hands. She just stared at him, breaking when a single tear slid down her face, and yanked him into an undeserving hug.

"Babe, you don't have anything to be sorry about —"

"No, I do. You hired me to protect you, and I failed. They were never even supposed to touch you, yet they got past me. I'm so sorry."

"Dylan, that was bound to happen. Were you supposed to be my bodyguard for the rest of my life? Do you think they would've stopped? Found another panther, kidnapped her, no — it's not just about me anymore," she ranted, her brown hopeful eyes peering into his.

"My job was you."

"This wasn't even a job, Dylan. You wouldn't even let me pay you."

"I need it to be. I need to have just failed my job because it breaks me to think that I failed you."

"You saved me, Dylan." Her voice was desperate. Her eyes bled with worry as she gripped his shirt.

"No, you saved you. Willow saved you. Not me."

"You saved me, Dylan. You came for me. *You* protected me before I knew how to protect myself. You taught me how to fight for my panther. You've done your job and more." Her hands ran up and down his arms, comforting him for what he hoped wouldn't be the last time.

❧

FLORA WAS SAFE. IN THE COMFORT OF HIS HOME, IN HIS arms. She laid her head on his chest, watching mindless TV while he watched her. She didn't say anything about his racing heart or his clammy skin. Maybe she was afraid of ruining the moment just as much as he was. Maybe she knew what was coming and was uncomfortable bringing it up. It was time. Time to let go.

He knew this wouldn't last. It was time to let the bird free of its protective cage. Let her fly free and find where home is. He hoped she'd come back to him, but why would she? He didn't know if this was the last time she'd ever cuddle with him, the last time she'd kiss him, the last time he'd see her. Turning his head away, the heartache in his chest brought a single tear down his face, which landed in Flora's hair.

"What's wrong?" she asked, turning her body to face him, still sitting between his legs. To finally say the words out loud solidified the fact she had to leave him. She was going to leave him, and there was no guarantee she'd ever come back. He traced his pale palm across her cheek. The smoothing action helped him and hurt him all the same.

"Flora, I think..." He could hardly breathe, tears he wished he could hold back fell down his face more freely. "I think you should leave with your parents today."

"Like I should spend some time with them? I mean that's fine, they must be tense with their daughter being kidnapped... so a few days here and there —" she paused, her eyes searching his. "You...you're breaking up with me?"

"We've spent so much time together, time spent in dangerous, emotional-heightening experiences, and I loved playing hero but —"

"But what, Dylan? You think I can't decipher my own emotions?" She pulled away, her voice turning tense and her eyes glared up at his.

"Yes...no, wait. I need to know, you need to know, if what we're feeling is real. I've saved you, helped you, and you can't tell me that that doesn't impact the way you feel for me. You don't need me anymore. You never really needed me in the first place. Feelings change now that you don't need me anymore." Dylan tried to explain, but nothing came out right, leaving his fingertips resting above hers. He still couldn't let her go all the way. If only things were different. If only he wasn't her bodyguard.

"It won't." Her confidence almost made him completely change his mind and take back everything he'd said.

"You don't know that. You could have, like, Stockholm syndrome or something. I've seen it happen."

"Seen what happen, Dylan?"

"The people we save...fall in love with us and," Dylan said, clenching his jaw, "it's not love. It was never love."

"Dylan, don't ruin this." She was begging now, and that broke the last string that connected his heart together.

"I'm not. If it's meant to be, it will be. You've had doubts and concerns about me working for you and if that's impacted my emotions towards you...if we separate, leave it to fate, then we will both know if what we have isn't —"

"Dylan, I may not need you anymore. But I want you. Don't you know that?" she tried persuading him. She ran her hands over his shoulders, trying to calm him down, but it wouldn't work. He had to let her live. To have the chance to choose.

"Okay," Flora whispered. "I can't convince you. Your mind's made up."

She yanked her clothes out of the closet without any care she'd shown her clothes before.

She turned on him, "Who put you up to this? Jackson? Felix? Wouldn't want a big, bad scary panther in your ranks anyways, right?" Her fake smile was punishing. The hurt glazed across her face was another blow to his already torn heart.

"You know that's not what this is about. No, this was my decision. You know I'm right. We need time."

"Yeah, okay. I'm gone, outta your hair."

He had weeks to accept this outcome, but he still hadn't truly. To expect her to within minutes wasn't realistic. "I thought we —we'd survive. I was wrong."

She stormed out, the door slamming behind her. Leaving him in his room filled with her scent. He couldn't help the tears that streamed freely down his face. He gripped his chest where his heart was and let out a silent scream. Fuck, that hurt. That hurt so damn bad. What if's played hopscotch in his mind as he got up to lock his bedroom door. He didn't want to see anyone. He couldn't stop the hurt spewing from his heart.

"Dylan?" Felix called out on the opposite side of the door. Dylan wanted to be mean, nasty, and tell him to fuck off for his terrible advice on letting Flora go and having true love bring her back. But Felix was right, and Felix didn't deserve to feel the pain he was feeling.

"I can't."

"Okay," Felix replied, walking away from the door. Hopefully, the rest of his Pack would let him wallow in his sadness for as long as he needed.

DYLAN

Dylan hadn't felt this kind of heartbreak before. The soul-wrenching-deteriorating-from-the-inside-out type. He could hardly breathe through the pain at this point. It'd only been three days since Flora left. He cried like a damn baby. His heart was truly broken.

"Dylan!" A voice came from the other side of the door, which was swiftly opened by River. "What the hell, Dylan?" he asked, shutting the door behind him. A door he might have well kept open because his ass was leaving.

"No, River."

"No, Dylan, it's been three days and you actually smell like pure ass," he said, taking a step back from the stench.

"It doesn't matter," Dylan mumbled, turning his back. The anger and confusion steaming off the younger wolf was a mix Dylan couldn't quite figure out.

"Why did she leave?"

"I asked her to."

"You love her, though. Why would you let someone go when you love them, and they love you?" River asked.

"It's not that simple."

Of course, it wasn't. If it were, he wouldn't be on the verge of a depressive episode, would he?

"Then explain."

"No."

"Well, I'm the first of six, so get ready to talk and for the love of everything nice, take a damn shower," River said, taking his leave.

He could be upset if he wanted to be. It wasn't like Dylan was missing out on work. He didn't have a job anymore. Lust Lane had their problem resolved with Will and Emery on the case, and Flora...Flora didn't need him anymore. Even if she did, she probably didn't want him.

"How did you like working again?"

"How did you get in here without me noticing?" Dylan said.

"You're so wrapped up in pity and hurt, a gorilla could sneak by you," Leo said, sitting on the end of his bed.

"Not now, Leo."

"Answer the damn question."

"Yes," Dylan answered, still turned away from the door where everyone kept appearing from. The growing silence was almost peaceful before the strain of Leo's unbreaking presence sucked the life out of it. "I miss it."

"Miss her or the work?" Leo asked.

"Both."

"So, what are you going to do about it?"

"Nothing, she —"

"Not her, the work. You need something for yourself. You do everything for others and absolutely nothing for yourself. You've become unhappy."

"No, I..."

"Dylan, that can't continue. Not when life isn't just about you anymore."

"It's not about me, it was never about me."

"Exactly, when it's just you, you don't have to think about you. About what makes you happy or fulfilled. Your life impacts more than just you Dylan. It hurts us, it hurts her when you're not thinking about yourself. When your partner enters the picture, you'll bring her down into the selfless pit of unhappiness whether you know it or not."

Dylan couldn't look at him. He was making sense, but Dylan wasn't ready. He only felt hurt, a hurt so deep he couldn't sleep the pain away. Something needed to change, he wouldn't live much longer down this road. He sighed as he finally looked toward Leo. Flora wouldn't choose to be with him as the broken man he was now. He had to become the man she would choose. The man he would choose. Someone who was dependable, happy, and healthy. "Okay."

"Okay?"

"Yeah, okay, I'll think about it." Saying he would make a change was easy, but actually doing it was worlds harder to do.

"Dylan, you can be so hard-headed sometimes," Leo breathed out before closing the door on his way out.

He knew what he had to do. He knew what he wanted to do. He wanted to get his job and the girl back. He wanted to have everything, except it wasn't up to him now. Flora coming back could not —would not — be up to him.

Dylan needed her to choose him to be her mate. Choose him because she loved him. He couldn't live knowing she didn't choose him, but fell into him, confusing love for gratitude. She said she loved him, but when the heat died down and people returned to their normal lives, would she still feel that same love?

That was what scared him. He was down bad, no question. But he wanted her to have the chance to explore what she truly wanted and if she wanted him as a mate or not. Dylan couldn't be just her boyfriend or friend; she was his mate. He couldn't accept anything less. With Flora, it was all or nothing.

He dragged his body out of his bed, untangling his Flora-scented sheets from his body. Leo was right. Before Flora could love him, he had to love himself. He had to get his life back; he had to be happy. He couldn't give her a happy, loving life if he couldn't even give that to himself.

He went to his desk in the corner of his room and opened the little drawer. A business card he'd kept neatly on the top of his desk. All it held was a phone number. One that was written in handwriting he was all too familiar with.

"I guess I have a call to make," he murmured, dialing the number.

Someone was waiting for his call. Each ring brought another hit of anxiety to his already frazzled state, but he was doing this for him. He'd found something for him. He started out a desperate poor second-in-command wolf and turned into a killer, rich, second-in-command wolf. In a world of good and bad people, he had to be okay with falling into the bad category. He saved the good ones and gave people a second chance at life while hunting their enemies and providing for his Pack. His pride didn't only stem from being a working part of his Pack but from helping the Shifters, vampires, witches, and fairies from fates too close to hellish.

This was a part of who he was. Part of what made him Dylan Enchanted, and there should be no shame attached to his name. He knew this was the move to bring forth the Dylan he so desperately wanted to be.

"Hello, Dylan."

He took a deep breath, a chilling happiness nestled in his chest. "I'm ready."

"It's about damn time." The deep voice on the other line laughed, a second family waiting for him to come back home. The Boss man who knew everything and everyone. The guy who put the team together and handed out assignments to save people around the world, delivering cruel justice on a silver platter.

"I've got something though, one thing to take care of before I take on another assignment. I need your help."

Too much was still at stake, and he needed to take care of the Flora situation the way he was trained to, not the safe, legal way he thought he should have followed as her bodyguard.

"Whatever you need."

"So, here's the deal — there's a fox Shifter, I need him located."

"Does his name happen to be Romeo Bray?" the Boss said with a chuckle. Keystrokes sounded through the phone.

"Of course, you already know," Dylan said.

"Can you make sure you find out how he trapped a vamp in his shed?" Boss asked. It came as a surprise to Dylan the Boss didn't already know, which meant Romeo was in deeper shit than he originally thought.

"It was a witch," Dylan answered.

"I'm on the witch; you deal with Romeo." A ding from Dylan's phone indicated he was sent a location.

"Thanks."

"No problem, your first assignment after this will start on Monday next week. You'll have the details by then."

"So fast?"

"The world doesn't seem to run out of evil audacity, my friend."

❧ 35 ❧

FLORA

"He fucking left me," Flora said. "That asshole let me go."

"Men are stupid, honey," Luxe chimed in, continuing to eat her lunch. Now that Cassandra was taken care of, Flora went back to her regularly scheduled life. No one would tell her about Romeo's whereabouts, but it was time to get back to work. That extended trip turned "vacation" put her next collection behind by three weeks. Silk-lined hats were hot, and Dainty Rebel needed to get on the train.

"You don't want to hear this, but he was right," Willow said, giving her a pointed look.

"Too soon," Luxe whispered as if Flora couldn't hear her. "He's still an ass."

Flora suddenly turned from anger to hurt; she could still feel his knife pierce her heart as she had stormed out the door. Embarrassment pressed hot against her cheeks as tears pricked her eyes for the hundredth time since she left.

"Yeah, there was some truth to his words, but if we were meant to be together? Now what?" Flora asked.

"I don't know, babe," Willow answered, sadness covering her face as well.

Damn, that's not what Flora wanted. She was spreading around her heartbreak, and it wasn't fair.

"I'm sorry guys, let's focus on the collection."

⚜

It had been 168 hours and counting since Dylan kicked her out.

Dumped her, left her, whatever. Flora stood outside of her old apartment. She hadn't stepped foot inside since she left to stay at the Enchanted Packhouse. Her apartment wasn't the same; her life wasn't the same, she wasn't the same. The memories lived on, and she wasn't escaping them anytime soon.

Unlocking the door, she stood stock still on the welcoming rug outside. Staring down at her pumps, with a metal chain hanging from across the heel, she eventually took a step inside. She was sure her neighbors wondered what the hell was going on, but this wasn't about them.

Everything looked the same. The same entryway with perfectly cared-for shoes lined up by the door. The open concept black-themed kitchen and living room. It was once a dream she let be destroyed. But she simply didn't have the energy to fix what was broken. Turning on her heel, she shut the front door behind her and walked back down to her car. She'd been staying at Luxe's apartment since leaving the Enchanted Packhouse. It was nice, she was entirely grateful, but Luxe had a smaller place, and Flora could tell she had overstayed her welcome, even if Luxe wouldn't admit it.

Sitting in her car, she dialed a number she knew by heart and let the phone ring on speaker.

"Dad?"

"Hey, sweet pea. What's going on?"

"Can I come home?"

Her parent's driveway felt unfamiliar. She knew she didn't truly belong here anymore; this was her childhood home. Yet her parents stood welcoming with open arms.

"Come here, baby," Lola demanded in her sweet, loving voice, dragging Flora into a much-needed hug. Flora ugly sobbed into her mother's arms, a safe place to finally cry. No pressure, no expectations, no need to appear like the heartbreak wasn't literally breaking her.

"I need a place to stay for a while."

"I thought we got rid of ya," Will joked as they crowded the couches inside.

"Nah, I just —"

"You don't have to explain; we will always have room for you," Lola said.

"Until we move out for a smaller place."

"Stop messin' with my baby." Lola slapped his chest playfully.

"So, what are we doing tonight to welcome you home?" Will relaxed on the couch and picked up the remote.

"Movie night?" Flora suggested twiddling with the hem of her blazer.

"Perfect."

❧

"How long are you going to let that sweet pumpkin pie go on by?" Emery asked, twirling her blush brush along her cheeks. Flora sat backstage at Lust Lane on the uncomfortable stool next to Emery's mini booth. Lola told Flora it was time to get her big girl panties on and hang out outside of the house. But Flora knew she'd be kicked out for good soon.

"Of whom do you mean?" Flora asked, a small sliver of a smile gracing her lips.

"Wolf boy, Flora. You weren't this heartbroken when *we* broke up."

"We didn't actually break up, so to speak. We just ended up good friends."

"Flora, cut the shit."

"He doesn't want me," Flora let out a huff, leaning back on her stool.

"Did he say that?"

"No."

"Girl, I'm pulling teeth here." Emery rolled her eyes, her auburn hair and green fairy make-up glittering as much as the glint of humor in her eyes.

"What's so funny?" Flora asked, starting to get pissed.

"I've never seen two people fight so hard to be away from each other on the basis of 'what if,'" Emery laughed, pulling on the new and hopefully last prototype of Flora's largest platform heel. Flora was doing one last test before the collection was put through production at Heartful Production, another production company she had Felix do a background check on before reaching out to work with them.

"He hasn't reached out to me," Flora said, the tear in her heart beating and pulsing faster. "No calls, no texts, nothing. He must not want to see me."

"Have you, oh I don't know, called him, texted him, went and seen him?"

"He kicked me to the curb, remember?"

"Okay, okay. Unfortunately, I have to go on stage now, we'll finish this later. Enjoy my set."

"Good luck," Flora said, stepping out to the main floor. Taking a seat in a random chair, the dark room hid her perfectly. She could completely let go, and at that time, she needed it.

Staying with her parents was a blessing, truly, but this wasn't a permanent solution, and they agreed with Emery that she should go fight for Dylan. But they weren't there. They weren't there when he...broke up with her. She couldn't beg a man to take her back. Isn't that the opposite of being a girl boss?

"Hey." A voice startled her, causing her to jump. Ryder Enchanted grabbed a chair next to her and whipped it around before taking a seat.

"The stage is the other way, and I don't do lap dances," Flora said, her dry humor shining through her sadness. A deep chuckle poured from his lips as he smiled.

"Dylan would chop me into pieces, honeypot," Ryder said, staring off into the distance.

"Honeypot?"

"Is Dylan your mate?" he asked, aiming right for her torn heart.

"You know I can't answer that." The welcoming energy changed as immediately as his questioning did. She could see why he was the business personnel of the Pack.

"You can't?"

"The rejection would set in and kill me."

Everyone knew that. Rejection from your soulmate would cause the Shifter body to slowly self-destruct, starting with months of immense pain before the body decided the pain was enough. Once a Shifter's mind, body, and soul accepted another as a mate, no one else could compare.

"You're right. You shouldn't tell me. You should tell him."

"After he already asked me to leave?"

"Did he ask you to leave forever? Did the words 'You're not my mate' come out of his mouth?"

"Why would I go back if he's the one that told me — not asked — *told* me to leave? If he wanted me back, he would come get me." Flora was heated; how dare Ryder come in there and tell her what to do?

"What would you do for your mate?"

"Anything," Flora spat out without hesitation.

"Then act like it." With those final words, Ryder left with a goodbye nod and left a hefty tip on the stage for Emery as he walked out the door.

Ryder was like the annoying smartass older brother she never had, and that was something she seemingly wasn't missing out on. The problem was that he was right. Dylan wasn't the type to fight for himself. To do things for himself. He needed someone to put him first and to fight for him, and Flora wanted to be that person. She could admit this area of dating wasn't one she was an expert in but if she wanted Dylan back, she'd have to learn.

With two lectures back-to-back, she needed a damn drink.

"Flora, come with me," a familiar voice spoke.

"What are you doing here, Willow?"

"Come home with me," Willow said, taking Flora's hand in hers. "Come spend some time with me. Outside of work."

Without another pointed glare, Flora took Willow's hand, grateful to be comforted instead of hounded.

36

DYLAN

Dylan stood outside the basement door at his cabin.

His lovely home away from home, held a secret. It was a guilty pleasure of sorts: the final straw that confirmed Dylan wasn't normal and would never truly be. Taking one last relaxing breath, he slowly opened the heavy door.

Strapped to a chair with all too familiar chains was Romeo Bray. The one who *thought* he got away. Blindfolded, Romeo's senses were heightened. Exactly how Dylan wanted him: aware and terrified. A collar similar to the one placed on Flora was tight around Romeo's neck to prevent him from shifting. Romeo started to shake as fear and dread filled his body. Dylan's heavy black boots thudded on the floor as he slowly locked the door behind him, causing Romeo to shiver and Dylan to smile. Twisting around a butterfly knife, Dylan remained quiet as he walked up to his captive.

"It's too bad Cassandra died before I could do what I do best." Dylan frowned, even though Romeo couldn't see him. Dylan wasn't too upset, though. Besides Flora, Willow was the next best person to deliver the final blow that would take out the enemy. Willow was one badass grizzly, and obviously, messing with someone she saw as her own was a deadly mistake. Dylan was happy the bear didn't give Cassandra a quick death. Death was entirely too easy for the kidnappers. But Dylan couldn't be too picky deciding their fate.

Dylan wasted no time, cutting the blindfold off, slicing the side of Romeo's face in the process and drawing blood. Just enough to let him know the show was only beginning.

"I'm not one for many words. We both know what you did, why you're here. But what you don't know is that you got lucky. Flora didn't want anything to do with you," Dylan began, pulling his jade knife out. Stalking around the chair, he reached up, knife in hand, and swung his arm down, piercing the knife through Romeo's thigh. A scream full of pain and spit was Dylan's reward.

Smiling, he looked directly at Romeo, who had been silent since Dylan walked in. "See Flora has a heart; it shines and it's warm. Her panther, not so much. Getting mauled by a panther you betrayed would've been worse than death itself."

"Unfortunately for you, your luck ran dry soon after and now you're stuck with me, and I don't fight fair." Laughing, Dylan pulled the knife out and stabbed Romeo's other thigh. "Not when it comes to men like you, and especially not when it comes to my woman."

"A round of questions seems due. For each one you get wrong, a finger comes off. Once all ten are off, your time is up, and the game is over."

"Games can be won right?" Romeo trembled, tears falling from each eye. He thrashed, trying to break the chains around him until he finally figured out it was no use. Bargaining was his next attempt at being freed.

"Yes." No, but Dylan decided to keep that little bit of information to himself.

"First question, what is my woman's name?" Dylan asked, a smirk covering his face.

"Flora Larkspur," Romeo answered, hope filling his eyes.

Just as Dylan planned. For a man who was used to everything going his way, Romeo was predictable.

Dylan moved to stand right behind him, tilting his head as if to give the man's answer a thought. Taking out another pocketknife, he sliced off a pinky.

"What the hell, I was right." Romeo screamed, pain and suffering evident in his composure.

"Wrong, it's Flora Enchanted now," Dylan shrugged. It wasn't, not yet, but Romeo didn't need to know that. "Next, when was the first time you put fear into Flora's brilliant mind?"

"In the parking lot of that clothing store," Romeo sobbed. Just what Dylan wanted to hear. This time he wasted no time cutting another pinky off.

"Damn, wrong again. It was the first night you followed her home, a few weeks before she met me. How the hell did you not know that?"

Dylan reminisced about that meeting that changed his life. Flora complained about walking in the gravel in her high heels, all sexy and beautiful as hell. Little did he know he would fall in love with the way she talked to him, took care of him, loved him.

"That was Cassandra! *Fuck*, just kill me already," Romeo pleaded, straining in his chains.

"You don't mean that, we'll keep going till you do. Don't worry," Dylan confirmed.

Five hours, four fingers and three toes later, Dylan began to get bored. His version of justice only lasted so long before the treatment just became cruel. He put his bloody knives down on the floor. Out of reach of Romeo, of course, who only had at most three fingers to grip something.

"I would say now you know better than to frighten and kidnap someone again, but there won't be a next time," Dylan said, sitting crisscross on the floor. Romeo's head lolled to the side, tear-stained cheeks shining in the dim light, an overall bloody mess.

Dylan got up, loosening Romeo's chains till they dropped to the ground. Circling around in front of him, he smiled. "On second thought, I guess you can go. I don't really feel like cleaning up a dead body on top of all this blood." To further add evidence to his words, he walked to the back of the room giving Romeo the space to run. Leaning against the wall, Dylan crossed his arms, waiting for the trembling man to make his move.

"Why?" A shaky voice finally asked after five minutes had passed. Romeo still sat in his chair even though he was no longer chained to it.

"Flora will look over her shoulder for the rest of her life, whether you are dead or not. The damage is done. Just like the damage I've done to you," Dylan explained with a shrug of his shoulders.

Romeo didn't move. True to his word, Dylan didn't stop his torture taking fingers and slabs of skin until the light died out in his captive's eyes. The lack of effort to escape the room spoke for itself. He was done.

Dylan waited. Because of the blood loss from the stab

wounds, it wasn't long before the last breath left Romeo's body. Taking out a cloth, Dylan wiped his blade. The jade-colored handle reminded him of the moment he shared with Flora when he tried to make her breakfast in the hotel.

He really needed to learn how to cook.

The Brays weren't a threat anymore; nothing would be a threat to Flora while he was alive. Even then, he knew if he wasn't there for her, his Pack would be. They would always be in her corner.

"She may not know it yet, but she's my soulmate," he whispered, staring off at the wall.

He'd let her go and prayed she'd choose him.

37

FLORA

The hot chips weren't enough. Since when were chips not enough? They didn't fill the gap in Flora's heart. Why didn't she storm to the Enchanted Packhouse and demand Dylan take his head out of his ass and be her mate? Why was she still sitting in Willow's apartment when she could have everything she wanted a few neighborhoods over? Her tear-stained cheeks were proof that Dylan was worth the fight.

So why was she still sitting there?

She missed the man who had been breathing down her back for the last few months. She missed the man who saved her countless times. She missed the man who taught her to fight for herself. She missed the man who couldn't warm up a toaster pastry to save his life. So why was she still there? Ass parked on the couch, called out of work, and a mountain of empty chip bags lying on the hardwood floor of Willow's otherwise pristine apartment.

Did being part of a Pack scare the hell out of her? Yes. Did being in love with a wolf terrify her? Yes. But continuing without Dylan was a disaster she didn't want to be a part of anymore. She couldn't believe what she was thinking.

Rushing off the couch, she grabbed her keys to her car and prayed that it had enough gas. When it started up, she finally got a whiff of herself. Good lord, she wouldn't win Dylan back smelling like she'd been sitting in a pile of dog shit. Yanking the door back open and racing up the stairs, she headed straight to the shower and then pulled on a random suit set with a plain white long-sleeve shirt. Pulling her curled braids up into a high pony, she headed back out the door. She was going to win back the man who never should've gotten away.

Nerves covered Flora's body. Pulling into the Packhouse driveway unannounced, shaky hands were the least of her problems. She prayed Jackson wouldn't take offense to the intrusion.

She took a deep breath. This was for Dylan; she needed to do this for him. Choose him, for him, nothing more, nothing less. He was hers. This was her soulmate; she needed to fight for him, give this life a fighting chance. Slamming the car door shut, she leaned back against it, trying to find some stability before walking to the white wood porch.

Would they even want her to be a part of the Pack? Trying to put the questions to rest, she pushed off the car. Everyone in the house would know she was there; there was no backing out now.

Dylan stepped outside alone in the same outfit he wore the first time they met. She grew to love that hoodie and flannel combo on him.

"Flora?" His deep voice broke their staring contest. Seeing him confirmed everything she was feeling. As much as he was hers, she was his.

"Hi." Flora knew she should spit out what she'd come here

to say, but the adrenaline choked her; she could hardly breathe standing in front of him. He was handsome and incredibly tall. Strong, kind, an ass at times, funny, loving, *hers*. Hers, if he'd want to be. Inhaling as much air as she could, she let it all back out. Tears escaped, trailing down her face as she smiled.

It was now or never.

Inhale. "You're my mate." She knew it would hurt and be absolutely soul-crushing if he rejected her as his mate, but he was worth the risk. "Dylan Enchanted, Second-in-Command, wolf Shifter, member of the Enchanted Pack, you are my soul-mate. If you'd have me, I want you. In my life, as my lover, forever." Exhale. All the cards were on the table, and it was his turn to play.

Nothing, he was giving her nothing. The silence screamed in her ears. She had no idea what was going through this man's mind, and she desperately wished she did. Biting the inside of her cheek, she picked at her manicured nails, trying to give him the chance to say anything. Whether it was 'I hope I never see you again' or 'I love you, too.' She'd take either at that point.

"Bye, Dylan Enchanted." Flora broke the growing silence between them. She turned, defeated, her heels kicking up the gravel driveway. Her braids hung heavy in her ponytail as she walked away. It was too good to be true; who would mate with a panther and let her join their Pack?

What in the world was she expecting? He didn't feel the same. Dylan's Pack was everything to him, and the possibility of giving that up for her must have been too much. Tears started to drop one after the other the minute she turned her back, heartbroken. Reaching for her car door, her arm was suddenly yanked back, and her body was spun around to crash into a warm chest.

"You'd seriously leave your soulmate if he asked?" he asked, an eyebrow raised. He fucking *smirked*.

He was toying with her! Her conversation with Ryder played on a loop in her head. A man wouldn't let his mate walk away, so neither would she.

"No, I wouldn't," she glared. "Not forever. What you fail to realize is that you're mine now. I'd give you time and space, but eventually, you'd miss me. See, Dylan, I get what I want. I wanted to start a business, so I did. I wanted to live on my own, so I did. I wanted a fucking jungle gym in my office, and so I got one. And now, I want you."

"You really think I'd let you go a second time, Flora?" Dylan asked, wrapping his arms around her waist, his heat and woodsy smell encompassing her senses. A short intake of breath and a sob was all Flora could manage. She pressed her face into his chest, soaking his flannel with her tears. She lightly slapped his arm before rubbing the spot she slapped, pissed that he would let her think he didn't want her.

"Ow, Flora."

"Don't ever do shit like that again," Flora mumbled, pulling him impossibly closer. Hearing applause, they turned, still wrapped in each other's arms.

"You know what this means, right?" Eddie asked, looking over to Jackson. The whole Pack was standing on the porch. Felix, Leo, Ryder, and River were crowding the porch.

"Flora, can you come forward?" Jackson asked.

Looking up at Dylan, her nerves began to build. The Alpha got the final word on who joined the Pack. What if he changes his mind and doesn't want another Shifter type to catch heat for? What if he didn't like panthers anyways?

"Before you say anything," Dylan began, holding eye contact with Jackson. Giving her hand a squeeze, he continued.

"Look, you guys are my family, my brothers. I love you guys and would do anything for you, you know that." Taking a deep breath, he pulled Flora closer.

"This is my woman. My lover, my life." Not standing down, he wrapped an arm around Flora. "Flora is staying with me."

"And what if I say she can't join the Pack?" Jackson asked, crossing his arms. Flora couldn't breathe, she could only imagine how Dylan was feeling. Smiling down at her, his deep brown eyes stared into hers, a look that spoke volumes.

"Then we go."

"Dylan, no, he won't be going," Flora rushed out, barely knowing what to say, trying to pull herself away. The last thing she wanted was to break apart the Pack. "Dylan, you can't do that. I love you. I do, so much. But because I love you, I can't let you walk away from something you love so much. We can work this out a different way —"

"Well, then it's a good thing I was going to ask Flora to join the Enchanted Pack," Jackson cut her off, turning his full attention to her. "Flora Larkspur, will you join the Enchanted Pack?"

The spotlight was all on her. Hardly breathing, she couldn't believe what he was asking her.

"Why would you want a panther in your Pack?" Now she couldn't believe she'd given him a chance to take the invitation back. What the hell was going on today?

"Though you have one badass animal, you're more than your animal, you're Flora. If Dylan's willing to leave his Pack for you, a Pack he's sacrificed so much for, then you're special to him. If you're special to him, you belong with him," Jackson explained. "Plus, we already have a bear and a crow among this

Pack of wolves what's adding another breed? I don't care about that kind of thing."

Looking up at Dylan, she nodded. She knew what she wanted to do.

"Jackson, I would be honored to join the Enchanted Pack," Flora said, turning to look at her new Alpha. Shock filled her; she, a black panther, joined a Pack. A Pack wanted her, a wolf Pack, of all things. She could hardly believe it.

"Okay, now that you're part of my Pack, my own question can't wait any longer," Dylan said, taking both of Flora's hands into his. "Flora Larkspur, will you be my soulmate?"

Flora pulled her hand from his to caress the side of his face, warm love and admiration filling her gaze. Her heart pounded at the rush of being in love. Of being in love with a wolf. In being a panther who was part of a Pack. All of it felt like a fantasyland dream she'd never want to wake up from. Dismissing all her fears, doubts, and worries about being a mixed-breed couple, she leaned into Dylan, her eyes meeting his.

"Yes." Her breathless answer left her lips as she landed a kiss on Dylan. The kiss of a lifetime, his warm lips covering her tear-stained ones. Their combined heat exploded between them.

"Of course, I'll be your soulmate."

EPILOGUE PART 1
DYLAN

He was officially obsessed with the sly panther lying under him. From day one, he should've known that Flora Enchanted would have him wrapped around her finger. That he'd proudly follow her around like a lost puppy. Only being truly lost when he wasn't with her. He never thought he'd have it all. His mate and his Pack both chose him. He couldn't ask life for more.

He dragged his kisses lower and lower down her panting body. The curves and waves of her brown skin glistened with sweet sweat. Her little groans urged him to do more. To take a bite of her large hips and mark her over and over again until he'd completely covered her mind, body, and soul. The mating marks they'd left on each other's shoulders shone proudly. He mindlessly ran his hand over the mark, a reminder to both him and her, that they belonged together.

"Love," Flora moaned, her fingers gripping the sensitive strands of his outgrown hair. "Don't cut this." Her leg hooked over his shoulder, the newfound strength in her consistently trained muscles squeezing his head closer to her center.

"So, you have something to reign with when I do this," he said, taking a precise lick up her cunt, paying special attention to her pretty clit. He was sure he wouldn't need a haircut the way Flora pulled. The pain mixed with the rapture he found while pleasing Flora.

"So fucking wet."

He couldn't get enough. Simply sucking on her clit would never be enough for his wanting lover. She'd want more, crave more, just as he did. Her body thrashed under him, and her thighs held on tight as he slipped two fingers inside her. Edging her closer and closer to her peak with each circling motion. He kept at it until the rush of his reward graced his lips, and even then, he worked his fingers until she was finished.

He'd do this every day if she'd let him. Getting her off was a hobby he'd quickly become advanced in, practicing for hours on end. Shared pleasure was usually a vamp thing, but damn, was their connection just as close.

"I need you," she gasped, pulling his head tight against her.

"Whatever you desire, kitty cat," Dylan murmured.

"Dylan."

He was slow, dragging out the pleasure with the pain of waiting. The strain of wanting and not receiving that he knew she secretly loved. Someone telling her no. Something having full control over her. He lunged for a kiss. A kiss so desperate, so wild. A smile from both parties brought a sense of peace. His hands wrapped around her neck, bringing her closer to him. The kiss she returned told Dylan everything he needed to know.

This was his soul mate. He had been blessed enough to meet such a beautiful soul.

"Flora, I love you."

"Fuck, Dylan, I love *you*."

He stuck his thigh between her legs to check if she was still ready. The wetness he found was more than a sign, and he lined up with her.

"Yes?" he asked.

"Yes!" She clawed at anything she could. The sheets, his arms, his chest, she couldn't stop. He sure as hell didn't want her to. He wanted to be marked as much as he wanted to mark her.

"Flora."

"Yes," she whimpered, "Yes, yes, yes."

She knew him; she knew him too damn well. He could feel her walls squeeze him. It made him rampant. He withdrew just so he could thrust right back in with the strength from his wolf side.

Her breathing became staggered, and her grip on his body more intense. He got her to come again. Her legs and arms fell back to the bed, and he finally let himself come. But he didn't withdraw. Didn't want to be done, didn't want to let go of their connection. He'd stay like that forever if he could.

"Baby?"

"Yes?" Dylan answered. His heart was wrapped in chains she had full control over. Anything she wanted; he'd do.

"What do you think about having a baby?"

"I think you know," he said as he pulled out, pushing a drop of cum back inside her swollen pussy.

"What are we going to do with a hybrid baby?"

"We'll find out in due time," Dylan said, his heart swelling.

Who knew he'd find someone who actually chose him? He wasn't in second place with her. He wasn't the next best alternative. She fought for him, and he'd spend the rest of his life loving her as she deserved.

EPILOGUE PART 2
FLORA

"We're investing in soundproof walls in every single room in this damn house," Felix said, plopping down on a layout chair in the backyard.

It was the monthly Pack barbeque. Every month while the weather permitted, the Pack hosted a barbecue. Another family quality of a Pack Flora wasn't expecting. The party was for Pack members only, so sadly, Luxe and Willow weren't there.

She was now Flora Enchanted. Since she and Dylan mated and had their mating marks, they were official under the eyes of the council, and since she took the Pack's last name, she was now a Pack member. She was truly happy. She had everything she could ever want: a career she loved, friends she could trust, a mate who was as obsessed with her as she was with him, and a Pack who treated her like family.

"Yeah, because these two can't stop. Damn, are you sure your animals aren't bunnies?" Eddie said, laughing his ass off a little too hard.

"Bunny Shifters are shaking in anger over your stereotype," Felix said, laughing just as hard.

"We'd have to break down the walls again," Leo mentioned, flipping burgers on the grill.

"Worth it, starting with their room first. Ryder, can you figure out our finances?" Jackson asked.

"So, Jackson," Flora said, turning her attention toward him. "When am I going to stop being the only girl in this Pack?" It'd been a week of living with roommates. A week of sharing a home with seven Shifter men and a vamp teen who wasn't technically Pack. While she was incredibly grateful for her Pack, they were still men with men-like tendencies of leaving the bathroom smelling like a bomb site, and clothes lying on the living room floor.

"Flora, you've been the only girl for a week. Plus, there's Remi."

"Yeah, but Remi's not here right now. Plus, you've been in love with our female Alpha for how long now?" River slyly asked.

"I'm not ready; this Pack is not ready," Jackson slowly commented. Turning his gaze to the hole in the ground that was slowly turning into a pool. "Plus, Remi is coming back. Luxe doesn't have enough room for her in her one-bedroom apartment."

"Where's your mate, Eddie?"

"Don't start with me, wild cat."

"Any of you? There's no way all of you attractive Shifters are single," Flora questioned, earning a chuckle from the group.

"Talking about Willow, what was that whole thing about her leaving?" River asked, kicking around a soccer ball.

"She hasn't told me," Flora said. Even if she did know, it wasn't her business to share. Pack or not, Willow was her girl.

"It must have been serious," Felix said as the final comment on the subject, practicing a twirly knife trick Dylan had taught him.

"Yeah, something about her past catching up to her. That's all she would tell me," Eddie murmured, looking over to Flora. She could tell he knew more but wasn't saying it.

"We shouldn't gossip," Flora muttered. It seemed as if she didn't know her friend as much as she thought. She played with the chain around her neck that Dylan had given her. Admittedly it didn't go with every outfit, but she wore it almost every day anyway, just as she'd spend every day with him.

"You okay?" Dylan whispered, playing with a braid of hers. His warm, comforting body wrapped around hers.

"With you? Always."

ALSO BY JORJOR BATTLE

Short Story

A Rose to Remember

Upcoming

Stained Memories

ACKNOWLEDGMENTS

Holy molly my first novel is complete. The last two years has been amazing, and I can't believe I can say I've written an entire book. Between being in school and working part time, the finish line felt as a goal I would never reach but here she is. I'm not one for many words outside the creative writing field, so I'd be honored to give thanks to everyone involved in the process.

Writing a book is one step and publishing it is a entirely different step. I wouldn't have been able to do either without the help of my parents, who will be receiving a special edition copy with all the spice scenes blacked out. Without them, I this book would have taken years longer to produced and for their love and support I am forever grateful!

Shoutout to my sisters, who also showered me with love and support. Without my twin telling me to take my hand at writing a book, I would have never taken the leap and found purpose to my life.

Thank you to my beta reader, Allyreads on Fiverr, I have no idea how I was blessed to find someone on that site who put so much love and care (and use detailed feedback) is truly a blessing.

Also to my discord author group Eclectic Pages and all the amazing friends on there, thank you guys so much for sprinting with me and creating a wonderful place for our author community to communicate and grow.

My cover designer over at AS Book Designs was a dream to work with. You really captured the image I wanted for Stained Perception, and I can't wait to see what we come up with for book 2!

Thank you to my editor Kaitlyn at Beausoleil Editorial, for editing this book. You've put as much work into making this book the best it can be as I have, and I'm so appreciative of the work we were able to do together.

Last but certainly not least, my readers! MY lovely readers, thank you from the bottom of my heart for giving this book a chance! Thank you for all the love I've received on my social media too. In times I fell, you helped pick me back up, and I'm so happy to be able to share the work we've been waiting so long for. I hope to see you guys again in book 2!

ABOUT THE AUTHOR

Jorjor Battle is a college student pursuing her bachelor's degree in English while pursuing her dreams of becoming a romance author. She'd prefer to fall in love in real life but, for the time being, accepts her unhealthy obsession with love in the forms of books, tv shows, and movies.

Follow her on social media to hear about upcoming projects and all things about being a writer and book lover!
Instagram: readingjorjor
YouTube: JorjorB
TikTok: jorjorbattle_